TEST DRIVE

ROAD TRIPPING SERIES

SAMANTHA CHASE

TEST
Drive

PRAISE FOR SAMANTHA CHASE

"If you can't get enough of stories that get inside your heart and soul and stay there long after you've read the last page, then Samantha Chase is for you!"

-*NY Times & USA Today Bestselling Author* **Melanie Shawn**

"A fun, flirty, sweet romance filled with romance and character growth and a perfect happily ever after."

-*NY Times & USA Today Bestselling Author* **Carly Phillips**

"Samantha Chase writes my kind of happily ever after!"

-*NY Times & USA Today Bestselling Author* **Erin Nicholas**

"The openness between the lovers is refreshing, and their interactions are a balanced blend of sweet and spice. The planets may not have aligned, but the elements of this winning romance are definitely in sync."

- *Publishers Weekly, STARRED review*

"A true romantic delight, *A Sky Full of Stars* is one of the top gems of romance this year."

- *Night Owl Reviews, TOP PICK*

"Great writing, a winsome ensemble, and the perfect blend of heart and sass."

"Damn. That's a good word."

Staring down at her phone, Willow Andrews sighed. It looked like her grandmother was going to win yet another game of *Words With Friends,* and she wasn't sure which was sadder–the fact that she was going to lose again or the fact that this was what she was doing on a Friday night.

"I clearly have a problem." She was about to put her phone down when it rang. Looking at her grandmother's sweet and smiling face, she knew it would be rude–and pointless–to ignore the call. Swiping the screen, she said, "So now you're calling to brag?"

The soft chuckle greeted her first. "Oh, now don't be like that, my little Willow bell. I can't help it if I'm good with words. I did spend forty years as an English teacher, you know."

"You could let me win once in a while," she said miserably. "You know, something to boost my confidence a little."

"Still no luck with the job search, hmm?"

"Nope. I swear, it's like there must be some sort of poster with my face on it with a big circle with a slash going through it. No one will hire me, and if I don't find something soon, I don't know what I'll do. I'm babysitting my neighbor's little boy in the morning and then take care of the dogs in the afternoon."

"How many are there now?"

"Um...I'm up to twelve. I added a French Bulldog last week."

"Gracious! Twelve dogs? You're not taking them all out at the same time, are you?"

"I tried that once. It didn't go well, as you can probably imagine. The leashes all got tangled, I nearly had an asthma attack because they pulled me along, so I had to run instead of walk, I skinned my knee and twisted my ankle so...lesson learned."

"Well, it sounds like you're not doing too bad, Willow. You have two jobs, and obviously, you're getting out and meeting people."

"Yeah, not so much. These are all people in my apartment complex that I knew already. However, the dog-walking gig gets me out of the house. Getting my Vitamin D and all that." She sighed. "But...I'm never going to get ahead at this rate and my savings isn't going to take me much further. I need something with more stability and that pays better."

"Sweetie, you know you really should talk to your parents. I'm sure they would help you out..."

"Gammy, we've been over this," she explained. "I got my degree in psychology because that's what *they* wanted. It was never something I was interested in and I graduated by the skin of my teeth. And look where it got me? If I ask them for help, they'll lecture me on all the ways I'm self-sabotaging and how if I would just focus, I'd be able to find a real job." Groaning, her head fell back against the cushions.

"You know they'd love for you to join their practice, right?"

It was a topic that came up often, but it was never going to happen. "I know, but that would mean re-locating to Seattle, and that isn't something I'm willing to do. I'm a New York girl. All my friends are here."

"But not your family."

Unable to help herself, she chuckled. "All the more reason to stay here."

Luckily, Gammy laughed too. "Okay, sassy pants, let's get serious. If you could do whatever you wanted to do for a career, what would you do?"

"Gam..."

"No, I'm serious, Willow. This is a judgment-free zone. You know you can tell me anything."

"Well...I always wanted to be a Rockette..."

There was a soft tsking sound before her grandmother said, "Willow, I'm being serious. And remember your ballet recital?"

"I was seven!" she cried. "I'm sure, given enough time, I would have learned to balance better."

"And gotten over your stage fright?"

"Not sure I want to risk throwing up in front of a crowd again."

"I know, dear. So let's cross Rockette–or dancer of any kind–off the list. Okay?"

"Fine."

"What about a chef? You're very good in the kitchen!"

"I hate the feel of raw chicken. It freaks me out."

"What about a baker? You always make the most decadent desserts!"

"You have to get up at like...three a.m. to go to work, and you know I'm not a morning person."

"Hmm...okay, what about a nurse? You could go back to school. I'm sure your parents couldn't possibly find fault with you wanting a career in the medical field."

"Gammy, I pass out at the sight of blood. I fainted the last time I got my flu shot."

"Oh my goodness! How much were you bleeding?" she asked, sounding horrified.

"I wasn't. I was just afraid that I might and..." Willow paused and put a hand to her forehead. "Can we change the subject? I'm feeling woozy."

"From just talking about blood?"

"Gammy!"

"Okay, okay, okay...what if you found a full-time job to tide you over? There's waitressing?" But before Willow could answer, her grandmother said, "No. You're a bit acci-dent-prone."

"Gee, thanks."

"Need I remind you about the Japanese tea set incident?"

Groaning, Willow closed her eyes. "No. But in my defense, your cat tripped me."

"Mr. Marshmallow would never do such a thing, and he doesn't appreciate you pointing the finger at him."

"He's a cat, Gammy. He has no idea about any of this."

Gasping dramatically, she replied. "Nonsense. Mr. Marshmallow understands everything I say to him!"

"Right."

"He's also an excellent judge of character. Why, just the other day, we were talking about the Romeos and..."

"The what?"

"Not what, who."

"What?"

"Willow, focus!"

"On what?"

"The Romeos aren't a what, they're a who. Actually, they're a group of whos."

"You're literally making no sense right now."

"Romeos – retired old men who eat out," Gammy explained.

"That doesn't spell Romeo, that spells Rom-we-o. You'd think for an English teacher…"

"And you'd think at your age you'd learn not to sass your grandmother," she huffed.

"Sorry."

"It's all right, dear. I know you're stressed."

"You have no idea."

"Well, when you come to visit at the end of the month, we'll carve out some time just for the two of us. You know I prefer talking about things like this in person. Oh, and are you bringing that boyfriend of yours with you?"

Oh. Crap.

"Um…"

"I'm very excited to meet him, Willow. He sounds wonderful. Plus, I'd love to get his input on what career path you should be taking. You're far too smart to be wandering like this, and I hate hearing you sound so sad." She paused. "Why isn't this young man perking you up more?"

"Perking me…?"

"Back in my day, a man knew how to keep a smile on a girl's face." Then she giggled.

Seriously. Giggled.

"Then again, the Romeos are pretty good at that too."

Oh, dear Lord…

"Now I'm not going to be a prude while you're here and insist that the two of you sleep in separate rooms or anything," she went on. "Your folks are staying at that little boutique hotel down by the town square that they love so much because I told them I promised you the room here."

"Gammy, you didn't need to do that."

"Well, you know how they prefer their privacy and how much I enjoy sitting and talking with you. I'm getting up there in years and there's only so much time left for me to impart my wisdom onto you."

Here it comes...

"I see so much of myself in you, and talking on the phone is all fine and well for casual stuff–you know, basic blah-blah stuff–but I want to see the look on your face when we talk and laugh. I hope your young man won't mind giving us some girl time."

"Yeah, about that..."

"Oh! We can send him out with the Romeos! I bet he'd have a fabulous time!"

"No, Gammy, you don't understand..."

Off in the distance, she heard a doorbell ring and knew their conversation was about to end.

"Willow dear, I need to go. That will be Donald. He's a Romeo. Sweet man, really. He has the eyes of a wolf and the hair of a silver fox!"

"There's an image for you," she muttered.

"What?"

"Nothing! Go and enjoy your date! We'll talk soon!"

"Yes, we will! Now don't quit our game! Let's finish it up! And who knows, maybe you *will* beat me! Love you!"

"Love you, too!"

This time she did toss the phone aside with a groan of disgust. Willow knew she was many things, but she wasn't normally a liar. Unfortunately, sometimes desperate times called for desperate measures.

And listening to her grandmother go on and on about her romantic social life definitely qualified.

It had seemed like a harmless thing to do—make up a boyfriend! And with Willow living eleven-hundred miles away, she really didn't think it would ever be an issue.

Like now.

Gammy was turning 75 and wanted her whole family to come down to celebrate with her. That meant her fake boyfriend was either going to have to break up with her or become miraculously real.

Well, crap.

Her phone chimed with a reminder that she was due to meet up with the girls at McGee's Pub for their end of the workweek roundup.

Seriously, she felt like a fraud going since she was the only one not really working. Well, she babysat and walked the dogs, but that really didn't count. The babysitting was so much fun—Josh was the cutest little boy, and they shared a love of trains and Mickey Mouse. And the dogs were...well, that was fun too. While her friends were out working real jobs, Willow felt like she was just sort of hanging out and doing enjoyable tasks that she happened to get paid for. There was no workweek to end, so why go out to celebrate it?

The other thing that made her hesitant about going?

Her fake boyfriend was based on a real guy.

The bartender at McGee's—Levi.

Unable to help herself, she sighed dreamily.

"I am so screwed."

Of course, Levi had no idea she was using him in her

make-believe relationship, and if he ever found out, she'd be mortified.

And that was saying something since the only reason they ever met was because she had fallen flat on her face on the sidewalk right outside McGee's and he had witnessed the whole thing. He had run out of the pub and helped her up and then carried her inside.

Was it any wonder she was crushing on him? He was practically a knight in shining armor, for crying out loud!

He'd cleaned her up and made her call her friends to come and hang out with her at the pub until she felt better. After that, it had become a weekly thing for them.

Not her falling on her face, but the hanging out part.

Although she had been known to trip a time or two...

Her phone chimed again, and she picked it up and swiped the screen to shut it up. Sighing, Willow considered her options. She could bail and text the girls that she wasn't feeling well, but, like she said, she hated lying. Another option was she could go for just a little while and then fake a headache...

"Pretty soon I'm going to be smelling smoke because my pants will be on fire! Why is this so difficult?"

Knowing she'd feel too guilty with either of those choices, she got up and went to freshen up her makeup and put on something other than yoga pants.

"Why haven't yoga pants become acceptable sociable attire yet?" she wondered. But once she walked by the full-length mirror in her bedroom, she knew it wouldn't matter even if they were. There was no way she was going to parade around the pub in front of Levi—or any male for that matter—looking like this. Willow knew and accepted the fact that she wasn't one of those girls who looked super-cute in yoga pants.

She just looked schleppy.

"So not the look I want to be remembered for."

Fifteen minutes later, she grabbed her purse and headed out the door like she was heading to her own execution.

And secretly hoped she could get from her car to the pub without hurting herself.

"Hey, Boss, can you add a case of beer glasses to the next order?"

"Why?"

"Because Dex just dropped a rack of them when he was unloading the dishwasher."

Groaning, Levi walked into his office and turned on his computer. With a frown, he pulled up the program he used for orders and quickly made the notation. "That's the third rack this month. From now on, he mops floors and takes out the trash. That's it."

"You got it."

He waited until the office door closed before relaxing in his chair. It was a Friday night, and McGee's was busy as usual, and yet not so busy that he didn't notice that Willow and her friends hadn't shown up yet. Besides the fact that he'd just walked around the pub looking for her, no one had mentioned it to him either.

Friday nights had become fun again since meeting Willow and he couldn't help that he looked forward to seeing her and hanging out with her. Ever since the day he saw her face-plant on the sidewalk and ran out to help her, they'd bonded. Granted, he was friendly with everyone who came into McGee's, but...some more than others.

Willow was sweet and shy and funny, and he found himself stepping away from the bar more and more on Friday nights so he could hang out with her.

And her friends.

Okay, he seriously wouldn't mind if her friends opted to skip a Friday or two—or seven—but they were a package deal and it was fine.

Sort of.

Mildly annoying, but...whatever.

Normally he would have considered flirting with Willow, or simply asking her out, but she was different. Not only because she seemed incredibly shy, but he was enjoying getting to know her without the pressure of it turning into something more. And again, she was never alone—seriously, her friends were *always* with her—no matter how many times he casually dropped hints that she should come in any other night. Alone.

And he'd dropped a lot of them.

He thought he saw a hint of interest on Willow's part, but it had been so long since he'd gone out on a date he might have been imagining it.

The real problem was that McGee's was his life. Two years ago, he had officially taken over the pub and ever since, he'd been consumed with making it a success.

Okay, the pub had been his grandfather's on his mother's side, and Levi had been working here since he was sixteen.

Well, *formally* working there. He'd been going there for years and hanging out with his grandfather and learning all about the business.

When his grandfather passed away two years ago, Levi had been shocked to find out he had willed the pub to him. There was a stipulation that if he didn't want the responsibility of taking on the business that he could sell it and split the profits with his sisters. But it had been a no-brainer. McGee's had always been a part of his life, and he loved it, and everyone in the family knew it. His sisters had been adamant that he take it on—even if it meant less of an inheritance for them.

Not that it was the only thing their grandfather willed to them. They also received some money and some sentimental items he knew they would love. But ever since the papers were signed and the pub officially became his, Levi had spent all his time making sure he was doing everything to make his grandfather proud and for the pub to be even more successful than it had ever been.

It was, but that didn't mean he should slack off and get too comfortable. There were always improvements he could make, new things he wanted to try, and even though he had a great staff—with the exception of the accident-prone Dex—he never felt right about taking any time off for himself.

But if he ever got up the nerve to point-blank ask Willow—or anyone—out, he'd take the night off.

Probably one of the slower nights, but...still. He'd do it.

Maybe tonight he should test the waters. Maybe he could flirt a little bit and see how she responded, or maybe he should just ask her outright and see what she said. Or... maybe he was just crazy and shouldn't rock the boat. He would hate losing her as a friend because...well...he genuinely liked her.

Raking a hand through his closely cropped hair, he let out a long breath as he started to think about some possible ways to broach the subject.

And his mind went completely blank.

"How is that possible?" he muttered. "I've dated dozens of women over the years. How the hell can I have no idea how to do this?" It was a bit mind-boggling how nervous he was and how badly he wanted her to say yes.

But seriously, what was he going to do if she said no?

How would he face her? Would she even want to talk to him afterward or would she even come back to McGee's ever again? Would her friends all glare at him or mock him?

"Great, that's just perfect. Psych yourself out with every worst-case scenario. Awesome."

And yet...that's exactly what happened. It seemed his brain was in rejection mode and all Levi could envision was getting his face slapped, Willow running from the pub, her friends kicking him in the nuts, and everyone in the pub looking at him with a mixture of pity and disgust.

"Okay, so maybe tonight isn't the night..."

There was a knock on his office door and his assistant Anthony came in. "Hey, I just wanted to let you know your girlfriend just came in," he said with a knowing smirk.

Closing his eyes, he grimaced. Had he been that obvious all this time?

Opening his eyes, he forced a smile. "Thanks. I'll be out in a minute."

"Want me to tell her that?"

"What? No!" he cried. "I mean, not unless she asks for me. Which, let's be real, she won't. She doesn't, right? She never asks for me when she gets here with her friends. Are her friends with her? Is she alone?" With a snort of derision, he went on, "Of course her friends are with her. Why would she come here by herself?" Slapping himself in the head, Levi let out a string of curses. When he noticed Anthony's wide-eyed stare, he snapped, "What?!"

Hands up defensively, Anthony said, "Nothing. Nothing at all. I'll just leave you and your multiple personalities to work it all out."

"Shut up." Standing, he kicked the chair away from him. "And I don't have multiple personalities."

"That dialogue you just had would say differently."

"You're crazy. I was talking to you."

"Were you? Because you asked questions and then answered them yourself. I had very little to do with any of it."

Walking around his desk and toward the door, Levi muttered, "You're a dick."

Chuckling, Anthony replied, "Tell me something I don't know." Together they walked down the hall that led out to the pub. "You ever going to ask this girl out or what?"

"None of your damn business."

Another low chuckle was Anthony's response before adding, "You really should make your move or someone else will."

Levi immediately glanced around the pub to see if anyone was looking in Willow's direction–other patrons or anyone on his staff–but luckily, they weren't. Obviously they were all blind because his eyes were always immediately drawn to her.

Because we're friends and I'm just looking out for her.

No big deal.

"If you're looking to worry about something, go make sure Dex isn't breaking anything. At the rate he's going, we're going to have to restock all of our glass inventory." Luckily, Anthony took the hint and walked away. Meanwhile, Levi felt like his feet were glued to the floor. Willow and her friends were sitting at one of the high tables near the front corner of the room. In a minute, one of them–whoever drew the short straw–would go up to the bar and buy the first round of drinks.

And that meant he needed to get behind the bar pronto and play bartender.

Okay, he wasn't really *playing*. He *was* the bartender.

Groaning, he walked over to the bar and nodded to Maxi and Eric, the other bartenders. Friday nights were always busy, and it wasn't unusual for him to step up and make drinks, but he'd taken a renewed interest in it lately.

No sooner was he in place and wiping down the bar than Willow was approaching.

Perfect. Timing.

He looked up and smiled at her and noticed the slight flush in her cheeks. Her lips were pink and glossy, her dark hair fell past her shoulders, and her curvy body was wrapped in faded blue jeans and pastel pink top. She looked way too soft and feminine to be hanging out in a pub and she wasn't a big drinker—neither were her friends—so he had to wonder why they kept coming back.

Part of him was hopeful that maybe *he* was the reason, but...he was also a realist. Willow didn't flirt with him or show any interest beyond their friendly conversations over the bar. That couldn't possibly be enough to keep her coming back week after week, could it? Did she feel obligated because he had helped her up when she had fallen?

God, I hope that's not the reason...

She smiled at him as she stepped up to the bar. She had a fantastic smile.

"Hey, Levi," she said. He could barely hear her over the noise and wanted to shout out for everyone to shut up.

That wasn't an option, so he just made sure he leaned in close to hear her when she spoke again. "Hey, Willow. Did you have a good week?"

Resting her arms on the bar top, she shrugged. "It was okay, I guess."

"Uh-oh. That doesn't sound good. The big dogs giving you trouble again?"

"Scout had a bit of a run-in with a squirrel that I got dragged into–literally–and Matthias ate one of my hats, but other than that..." She shrugged again.

"That sounds like a bit of a nightmare for his owners."

"Nah, he didn't eat it whole. Definitely got some big pieces of it, though. But they're used to it. Apparently he's famous for eating socks."

"Those poor people."

"Yeah, but they love him." She let out a soft sigh as she looked down at her hands.

"You sure that's it? You look like you've got something on your mind." To busy himself, he began making her drinks. Their order was always the same: draft beer for friend number one, a Cosmopolitan for friend number two, and a Malibu and pineapple for Willow.

I should probably learn her friend's names...

Whoever was the designated driver only had one drink, and they tended to stay for several hours so they were clear to drive. Plus, they normally ordered food. So he had to wonder...

"Who's the DD tonight?"

She slowly raised her hand. "I drew the short straw again."

He put the beer on the bar. "That's three weeks in a row, isn't it?"

Nodding, she sighed. "It's okay. I'm not much of a drinker anyway. Besides, Donna and Jen both had rough weeks so they deserve to kick back and unwind."

"A minute ago it sounded like *your* week wasn't so hot either. Don't you deserve to kick back and unwind?" He placed the Cosmo on the bar.

"Well, my week wasn't really bad, just today."

"How come?"

"Just family stuff."

Bracing his hands on the bar, he stared at her until she explained further.

"I lied to my grandmother and now I can't go and see her for her birthday," she said sadly. "This will be the first one I'm missing in like...ever."

"Damn, Willow. Whatever you lied about, I'm sure she'd forgive you."

But she shook her head. "It's complicated. And on top of that, I can't afford to fly down and see her. I'm still not working steadily so..."

"No leads on anything, huh?"

"Nothing I'm good at."

"Any chance you're good at waitressing?" For the life of him, he had no idea why he was offering. It wasn't like they were hiring.

With a small laugh, she shook her head again. "I can barely walk and chew gum at the same time without hurting myself. I have a feeling I'd end up owing you money at the end of my shift."

"Good to know," he replied with a wink. "What kind of job are you looking for?"

"That's the problem, I don't know." She groaned. "I graduated back in the spring with a degree in psychology, but it's not what I want to do."

"Then why get your degree in it?"

"It wasn't my idea, trust me."

"Ah. Gotcha. Parental pressure, huh?"

"Bingo."

Placing her drink on the bar, he offered a small smile. "Want me to help you carry these over?"

"That would be great. Thanks."

He used to think she accepted so they could keep talking, but now he realized it was because she was afraid of dropping the beverages.

Well, damn.

Stepping around the bar, he picked up the beer and Cosmo and followed her over to her table.

While admiring the soft sway of her hips, and how perfect her ass looked in her jeans.

"Good evening, ladies," he said smoothly, placing their drinks down. "Having a good night?"

"Absolutely," Jen said.

At least, he thought that was Jen.

"We're just trying to cheer Willow up," Donna chimed in.

"Oh, uh...really?" he asked, unsure of how interested he should sound.

Jen nodded. "We're trying to convince her to go and see her grandmother and to stand up to her parents."

"Jen!" Willow cried, her cheeks turning a furious shade of red.

"It's true," Donna stated. "We just need to find a way for her to get down to Florida and get everyone off her back."

"Um..."

"You guys know why I can't do that!" Willow argued, although really, there wasn't a lot of heat behind her words. "I'm not going to argue with my parents and ruin Gammy's birthday. That wouldn't be fair."

Gammy?

"Oh, please! You know they're not going to care about making a scene. They're totally okay with poking at you and picking at you in front of everyone, so why do you care about doing it to them?" Donna asked before taking a sip of her beer.

Willow glanced nervously in his direction and Levi thought maybe that was his cue to leave.

"Um...you ladies have a good night," he said, taking a step back. "If you need anything, you know where I'll be."

"Levi, wait!" Jen cried, reaching out a hand toward him. "Can we ask you something?"

"Jen..." Willow warned.

"Oh, shush." She grinned at Levi. "Let me ask you a question–do you think it's wrong to lie about being in a relationship?"

"Uh...what?"

This time Donna spoke. "Yeah, like if it meant getting your family off your back, would you be opposed to making up a fake girlfriend–or boyfriend–just so they'd stop worrying about you?"

He glanced at Willow as some of this was starting to make sense.

"You told your grandmother that you had a boyfriend and that's why you can't go visit her," he stated, waiting for her to make eye contact with him.

All she did was nod.

"It's not a terrible lie, right?" Jen asked.

Shrugging, Levi said, "No, it's not terrible. And it's not hurting anyone either. If you go down and visit her, all you have to do is say your boyfriend couldn't get the time off or say the two of you broke up. I don't see it as a big deal."

"That's what we said," Donna commented. "Hell, we even suggested she ask a friend–a guy friend–to go with her to play the part if she didn't want to go with the breakup thing."

Suddenly, Levi felt like he had the perfect solution.

For both of them.

And he was either completely crazy or absolutely brilliant.

"I'll go with you," he said matter-of-factly.

"What?!" All three women cried.

Nodding, his eyes never left Willow. "If you don't want to go alone and you don't want to admit there never was a boyfriend, I'll go with you. I'll be your boyfriend."

2

As soon as Levi's words registered, Willow wasn't sure if she wanted to throw herself at him or throw up.

Definitely not both.

Her eyes went wide, and she couldn't seem to make her mouth form any words, but her two BFF's didn't seem to share her problem. They were both positively chattering with glee.

"Oh, you are amazing, Levi!"

"That is super sweet of you, Levi!"

"Why aren't all guys like you, Levi?"

"You are so lucky, Willow! Levi's going to make the best fake boyfriend ever!"

Ugh, she wanted to yell at them both to shut up, but... her voice still wasn't cooperating.

Levi stepped in close–really close–and put his large, wonderful hands on her shoulders. It was hard to focus on anything except how amazing they felt, but he tilted his head toward her and then she felt the heat of his body wrapping around her.

"You don't have to say yes, Willow," he said gruffly, his

words soft against her ear. She knew he did that because the music was getting a little louder and it was harder to hear each other, but she kind of liked it. He straightened, and slowly her gaze traveled up to meet his eyes, and holy crap. They were so incredibly dark that she couldn't tell if they were blue or brown or what. "If you're not comfortable with this..."

It was her turn to lean in. And get on tiptoes so she could reach his ear. "What color are your eyes?"

"Excuse me?"

"Your eyes," she repeated. "Like I'm looking right at them but the lighting isn't the greatest in here and I can't tell. You should tell your boss the lighting needs to be better."

He pulled back and looked at her like she was crazy. "You want brighter lights?"

She nodded.

"In a pub."

Another nod.

"And you want me to tell...my boss."

"Yes, exactly." This wasn't the first time she thought about the interior of McGee's, and as she looked around, more ideas came to her. "And while you're at it, you should mention that he really should get some new signage in the windows and change out these tables and stools. They're very worn and your crowd here is a little more mature. Not quite the wine bar crowd, but not college kids either. Something a little more sophisticated."

"Sophisticated?"

"But seriously, what color are your eyes because right now they look almost completely black."

He laughed, and it was deep and rich and yummy, and

Willow knew it wouldn't be a hardship to have Levi as her pretend boyfriend.

"They're blue," he replied, leaning in again to talk closer to her ear.

A girl could get used to this...

"Wow," she whispered breathlessly and instantly pulled back, horrified.

Bad, Willow!

His smile was slow and sexy as hell, and suddenly she began to wonder if maybe this wasn't the best idea. If she was ready to rub up against him over a few whispered words, what in the world would she be like after a week of playing boyfriend and girlfriend?

Someone would probably have to turn the hose on me...

Unable to help herself, she giggled. Levi's expression went from sexy to confused. Willow immediately cleared her throat and glanced at her friends, who were watching all of this with pure amusement.

Damn them.

"Um, I really appreciate the offer, Levi, but..."

"Don't listen to her!" Donna cried out, jumping off her chair and crowding in with them. She gave Willow a stern look. "You know this is the perfect solution! It's killing you to miss out on going to Florida, and the biggest obstacle was the whole boyfriend thing! This is a total answer to a prayer!"

"I wouldn't exactly say a *prayer*, but..."

Jen flanked her on the other side. "You know it was breaking your grandmother's heart. If you didn't show up, her whole birthday was going to be ruined. Do you really want to be responsible for doing that to her? I mean, she's not getting any younger. Why devastate her and risk giving her a heart attack or something?"

"*A heart attack?*" she said, gasping. Eyes wide, she stared back and forth between her friends. "Do you really think that could happen?"

"Do you really want to take that chance?" Donna asked, solemnly. "Take Levi up on his very generous offer, Willow. Trust me."

Now she had no choice but to look at Levi, and she couldn't quite read his expression. "You know this won't be a quick trip, right?"

"Right now, I don't know anything about it," he said lightly. "But maybe we can get together tomorrow for lunch and talk about it?"

She practically sagged with relief. A night to think about it would really help, and to be able to sit with him without her friends hovering would be even better.

Smiling, she nodded. "Sounds good! Where should I meet you?"

"Why don't you meet me here tomorrow around noon and we can pick a place to go then," he suggested.

"It's a date!" she said and then realized she was already *way* too into this fake relationship than she should be. "I mean...it's not really...it's..."

He squeezed her shoulder. "Willow, I know what you meant, and yeah, it's a date." Smiling, Levi winked and took a step back. "You ladies have a good night. I'll be at the bar if you need anything." And then he turned and walked away, the crowd swallowing him up.

But that didn't stop her from trying to watch.

"Oh. My. God!" Jen said excitedly, slapping Willow on the back. "This is amazing! Not only do you get to see your grandmother like you wanted, but you get to do it with a hot boyfriend! Yay, you!"

"I don't know..."

"One week of having that sexy man all to yourself!" Donna chimed in. "How awesome is that?"

Sighing loudly, Willow faced both her friends. "I never said I was going to do this."

They both looked at her like she'd lost her mind. "Why wouldn't you?" Donna asked. "What's the matter? Is he not hot enough? Nice enough? Sexy enough?" She huffed with annoyance. "When a hot guy offers to help you out, you say yes!"

"What if he's crazy, huh? What if he's like some sort of deranged murderer and this is his MO? We don't even know him!" Willow countered. "It's not right to just go on a trip with a stranger! I may never come back!"

"Okay, no more late-night serial killer documentaries for you," Jen murmured as they all sat down around the table.

"I do *not* watch serial killer documentaries," she murmured.

"Oh, please! You are such a liar!" Donna cried. "We've binge-watched several of them together!"

"Maybe a few..."

"Last month, we spent an entire Saturday watching them!" Jen added. "Remember? You brought your famous death by chocolate brownies, and we all thought it was the perfect dessert for a serial killer marathon?"

"Okay, I think we're getting off-topic here. The fact is that we know nothing about Levi!"

"We know..."

"And saying he's good looking doesn't count!" she quickly interjected before either friend could bring that up again.

Like she needed the reminder of how attractive he is–

tall, muscular, sandy brown hair, dark blue eyes, and a dimple.

Yeah, she was *very* familiar with Levi's looks.

"It's obvious that you're attracted to him," Donna said. "And now you get to like...practice date him."

"Practice date? What does that even mean?"

"It means you get to sample the goods before committing," Jen said, laughing. "Like...you know...a test drive! You get to date him for a week, and if there's a spark there, you can explore it afterward. But you'll have the week you're away with him to see if you might be a good fit."

"It's perfect, Willow. The two of you could fall madly in love and..."

"We don't even know his last name for crying out loud!"

"So you'll find it out tomorrow on your date. What's the big deal?" Jen asked. "You spend a couple of hours with him and...you know...interview him."

"Interview him? What does that even..." She paused. "Okay, how do I do that without being obvious or sounding like a complete dork?"

"Well, you're going to be obvious, Willow," Donna said. "You're going to have to have a list of questions that you need him to answer so you'll be believable in front of your family."

"Yeah, and as for the dorky part...um...just...don't," Jen reasoned.

Opting to ignore that comment, she looked at Donna. "Like what kind of questions?" Groaning, she added, "This already is beginning to feel like way too much work."

"Oooh! I know!" Jen said excitedly. "Let's finish our drinks and go back to your place! We'll pick up some ice cream or something on the way, and when we get to your apartment, we'll help you think of all the things you'll need to ask him."

"You're going to have to come up with a story about how you met..."

"Why can't we just use how we really met?" Willow asked, feeling more confused and overwhelmed by the moment.

"Okay," Donna said, patting her on the arm. "That will work, but you may have to adjust your timeline based on when you first told your grandmother you were dating."

"Oh! And his name! You may have to ask Levi to change his name based on whatever name you gave your grandmother." Jen looked at her expectantly. "Well? What name did you give?"

Oh, God...this is embarrassing.

"I..." Willow paused and wrapped her hands around her drink as she stared down at it. "I *may* have said his name was Levi."

"Oh, my God!" both friends cried in unison.

"I just..."

"Are you not getting how perfect this is yet?" Jen asked, bouncing in her seat. "We couldn't have planned this better ourselves!"

"We have a *lot* of prepping to do," Donna said, pulling the drink from Willow's hand. "Sorry, no drink for you. You need to drive. Sooner rather than later."

"But..."

"No. No buts. We have work to do, and I know I've already got a running tally of things you're going to need for tomorrow," Donna explained. "You can drink when we get to your place."

"I don't think they offer to-go cups here..."

Her friends laughed and finished their drinks. "You are

so funny, Willow! Levi is going to *love* you!" Jen said as she climbed off her seat.

Glancing over her shoulder, Willow caught of glimpse of him and sighed.

If only...

"So, um...how old are you?"

Levi did his best to not laugh. Willow was sitting across from him at his favorite sushi place and reading from a small notebook. From what he could see, she had a lot of notes written down.

Like seriously, a lot.

"I'm thirty," he answered, knowing they were just getting started.

"Have you ever been married before?"

"No."

"Are you currently dating anyone?"

"You mean other than you?" he teased.

Looking up, Willow's hazel eyes were wide. "We're not...I mean...not really. I meant..."

Reaching across the table, Levi placed his hand over hers. "Relax, Willow. Please. I know what you meant, and I was trying to lighten the mood. But just to be clear, no. I'm not dating anyone. I never would have volunteered to be your fake boyfriend if I already had a girlfriend. That wouldn't have been cool."

"Oh," she said softly, seeming to relax. "Okay."

"Okay, then." He smiled but didn't remove his hand. "Next question."

Their waitress approached before Willow could respond. "Are you ready to order?" she asked.

Levi looked across the table. "I know what I'm having, what about you?"

"Um...can I please get the salmon bento box with the California rolls?"

Nodding, the waitress wrote down Willow's order before looking at him.

"Can I please get the spicy tuna roll and the dragon roll?"

She nodded again. "Would you like soup with that?"

"No, thanks."

"Thank you," she said with a smile before walking away.

"So..." Levi said, getting them back on track. "What's the next question?"

Willow studied the page in front of her and frowned before she closed the notebook, placing it on the table. "Can I ask you something?"

"I thought that's what we were already doing."

Her laugh was soft–like the way she was currently blushing. "Why did you volunteer to do this?"

How the hell was he going to explain that? There was no way he could come out and say it was the only way to guarantee that she'd go out with him, so where did that leave him?

"Levi?"

Slowly, he pulled his hand back. "Honestly? I saw how upset you were and...I don't know...this seemed important to you." He shrugged. "I figured I'd try to help."

"But you have no idea what all this is going to entail, and you don't even know me!"

"Well, I was hoping you'd tell me what it was going to entail over lunch. As for not knowing you, I disagree," he stated. "We've hung out together every Friday night for the last two months, so you're obviously not a stranger."

"You know what I mean," she said wearily. "And we don't really hang out together. I just happen to go to McGee's while you're working once a week. It's not the same as you sitting at the table with me and us spending the night together." Then she gasped and blushed even more. "Oh, my gosh, that is not what I meant! I swear!"

Reaching out, he touched her hand again. "I know what you meant and I guess I don't see much of a difference." He paused for a moment and studied her. "Do you remember the night we met?"

"Ugh...I wish I didn't..."

"Why?"

"Why? Levi, I was a total klutz who face-planted on the sidewalk!" She groaned. "I had a giant bump on my head, everything fell out of my bag, my phone screen cracked, one of my shoes came off, and I cried! I'm a grown woman who cried because she fell! It was mortifying!"

He thought she was cute as hell, but he had a feeling she wouldn't appreciate that observation right now.

"You tripped on an uneven sidewalk, Willow. It wasn't like there wasn't a good reason for it."

"I wasn't paying attention to where I was going. I was staring up at the clouds because they were incredibly fluffy that day."

He wasn't going to touch that comment with a ten-foot pole.

"Anyway..." He carefully began. "We sat and talked for almost two hours straight that day. We talked until your friends were able to get there, and then I kept coming over and checking on you. We may not be lifelong buddies, but I'd like to think we're friends."

"I know we're friends, Levi..."

"Just a minute ago you said we barely know each other." And yeah, he knew he was acting just a wee-bit babyish about the whole thing, but it kind of bothered him that Willow didn't see him the way he saw her.

Hopefully, by the end of this trip–if she agreed to it–she would.

Her expression turned a little sad, and he knew he needed to get them to move on. "So, where does your grandmother live?"

"Um...Florida. She lives in a retirement community called The Villages."

"I've heard of it," he said and watched as she relaxed a bit. "Central Florida, right?"

"Yes. She's lived there for around fifteen years now, and we always go down to visit for her birthday. This year she'll be 75 so it's kind of a big deal."

"My grandmother just turned 80, and we threw her a big party at her favorite restaurant. She loved how so many people came out to celebrate with her. We have a very large family and pretty much took over the whole restaurant that day."

"Well, our family isn't all that large. This is my grandmother on my father's side and he's her only child."

"What about you? Do you have any siblings?"

She nodded. "A brother and a sister. Both married with children. I'm the youngest, so now everyone's wondering when I'm going to follow suit and settle down."

"Settle down?" he repeated, laughing softly. "I didn't think people said things like that anymore."

"They do in my family," she muttered before opening her little notebook again. "So, um..."

"What do your siblings do?"

"Do?"

"Yeah, you know...for a living?"

Willow let out a small groan and leaned back in her seat. "Other than being the perfect children, you mean?"

He had a feeling he'd just opened a can of worms.

"They're your stereotypical over-achievers. My brother Miles is a doctor, and my sister Audrey is a lawyer. And then there's me, the unemployed sibling with no high aspirations. Much to my parents' chagrin."

"Chagrin?"

"Yeah, you know...they're embarrassed by the fact that their youngest child won't fall in line and do what they want her to do."

"Which is...?"

"Psychology. I hate it. I have a degree in it, but...it's just not for me."

"So, what *is* for you?"

"I wish I knew. I mean, I know I'm going to have to decide on something sooner rather than later, but for right now, I have no idea what that is. I keep thinking it's going to just come to me in a dream or something, but so far, no luck."

"Wow."

"Did you always want to be a bartender?"

"Not exactly."

"What does that mean?"

It wasn't something he wanted to get into right now. It was a bit of a long story and he felt like they had more important things to discuss.

"When is this visit supposed to happen?" he asked instead of answering her.

"You're avoiding the question, Levi."

"Not really. Just postponing it for now because we

have more pressing matters to cover. If we're going to do this–and I really hope you'll accept my offer–then I'm going to need to know specifics. If I'm going to take off of work..."

"Oh, my goodness...you're right! That really should have been the first thing we talked about. Gammy's birthday is at the end of the month, and it's a two-day drive from here to Florida, so..."

"Wait, we're driving?"

She nodded.

"But...why? Flying would give you more time to visit."

"Like I said, I'm not really working right now."

"Willow, you're practically a nanny to Josh, and then there are the dogs..."

"Um, yeah. They cover the bills but...it doesn't leave a lot for extras. Like travel," she murmured and sighed. "If it's okay with you, we'll drive. It'll cost less."

"O-kay...and how long will we be gone for?"

"Two days driving there, two days to get home, and four days there, so...a little over a week. Will that be okay for you? Will your boss be okay with you taking that much time off?"

He waved her off. "Yeah, it won't be a problem."

"Are you sure?"

"Absolutely." He smiled. "Okay, so driving down. Where will we be stopping and staying along the way?"

"Someplace budget-friendly since I'll be paying all the expenses," she said, blushing again while not looking at him.

"Wait...why? I don't have a problem helping to pay for stuff. There's no reason you have to do it all."

Now she did look at him. "Levi, you're helping me out! You're doing me a favor! You're missing work to help me! Covering your expenses is the *least* I can do, and you're not going to change my mind. I can be very stubborn, and on this, you're not going to get your way!"

Willow had a feisty side that was kind of adorable.

"What if I knew of a place we could stay along the way that wouldn't cost anything?"

She frowned. "Like where?"

"My sister lives in Richmond. We could stay there for the night. What do you say?"

"I don't know...won't that be weird?"

"Nah, I'll explain to Nat what's going on. It won't be deluxe accommodations or anything–probably the couch and the floor–but it will be free, and we'll get dinner and breakfast out of it."

"I'd feel like I'm taking advantage..."

It would be wrong to blurt out just how badly he wanted her to take advantage of him. So instead, he said...

"Are you kidding? Nat's always saying I don't come and visit enough. So really, you'd be doing me a favor."

"If you're sure..."

"I'm positive. Trust me."

Sitting up a little straighter, she smiled at him. "Okay then. Richmond's not quite halfway, but it still should work."

"I have another sister in Savannah. Maybe we stop a second night and hit the road early the next morning, so we get to your grandmother's by lunchtime. What do you think?"

"Hmm...three days of driving is kind of long..."

"Depends on how you look at it. If we did the drive in two days, we'd arrive at your grandmother's kind of late at night. You won't get any real time to visit her that day. But if we stop in Savannah and leave early the next morning, you'll get almost a full day with her when we arrive."

"I didn't think of that," she said thoughtfully. "That probably would be a lot better for everyone. Especially since we'll be staying with her."

"We are?" Okay, that was brand-new information.

Although...most of this was brand-new information. He just hadn't thought about the logistics of their arrangements once they arrived in Florida.

Nodding, Willow explained, "My folks stay at this boutique hotel near one of the town squares. Neither of my siblings can go this year, but honestly, I'm the only one who stays with her. She lives in a two-bedroom bungalow. It's super cute and cozy, but definitely not a lot of room for everyone to come and stay."

"So who else is going to be there? You know, other than your parents."

"We're the only family that will be there, but she has a ton of friends. My parents are hosting a party at the local country club for her. She loves that place."

"So we'll need to dress up at least one night," he commented.

"Yeah, the other nights will be way more casual." She paused and looked down at her notebook. "We really do need to work out some stuff about our relationship before we get there. We can use our real how we met story if you'll agree to leaving out what a klutz I am." A small nervous laugh followed that request, and Levi was beginning to see just how little confidence she had in herself.

And that bothered him a lot.

How could she not realize how special she was? Granted, they didn't know each other that well—yet—but he could already tell that there was so much more to her than she let on.

"We can totally leave that part out, but if you ask me,

it's part of what makes the story so sweet." When she went to argue, he held up a hand to stop her. "Think about it. We can say you fell on some uneven pavement–which isn't a lie–but we don't give all the details you described earlier because that's not what I saw. I saw a beautiful girl fall, and I ran out to help her by scooping her up in my arms and carrying her inside to tend to her injuries. Your grand-mother will practically swoon from that!"

"Oh, she totally will! She loves romantic-sounding stuff like that."

"Then there you go. That's how we met and it wouldn't be a lie." He smiled proudly. "Okay, what's next?"

"Now is the getting-to-know-you stuff–favorite foods, favorite color...all the little things we should know about each other."

Just then, their waitress appeared with their meals. Once all the food was served, and she was gone, he knew how he wanted the rest of their "date" to go.

"Tell you what, we have about two weeks before we leave, right?"

Willow nodded as she opened her chopsticks.

"Why don't we just let the rest of our time today go naturally, and we can pick up the getting to know you stuff while we're driving. What do you say?"

She looked at him oddly. "We're not going to get together again like this before we go?"

Could he really be this lucky?

"Willow, we can get together as often as you'd like before we go. You tell me when you want to go out, and I'll be there."

Her eyes went wide. "Really?"

Levi couldn't help but smile. "Yeah," he said gruffly. "Really."

3

"What's in the cooler?"

"Um...drinks?"

"Why?"

Levi looked at her like she was crazy. "Um...because I thought we might get thirsty?"

It took a minute for Willow to realize she was sounding a little accusatory rather than curious. "Oh, uh...sorry. I just thought we agreed that I would handle the road snacks and all." They were standing in the parking lot in front of her apartment building and loading her luggage into his car. It was another thing he had offered, and she had no choice but to accept. Levi's car was much newer and nicer than hers, so it was basically a no-brainer.

Actually, it was one of the coolest, sportiest cars she'd ever seen. The cherry red color looked amazing on the Camaro, and the fact that it was a convertible made it just a little irresistible to her. Part of her couldn't wait to drive with the top down at some point.

"What's in your cooler?" he asked.

Looking down at her own small cooler, she wondered if

she should just run back inside and put it away. "Some brownies, fruit, and a couple of bottles of water." She shrugged. "You know, nothing much."

He picked it up and placed it in the back seat next to his newer, larger cooler before turning and grinning at her. "Are the brownies homemade?"

And she couldn't help but smile back. "Maybe."

Over the last two weeks of them getting to know each other, Willow had shared her love of baking with him. In return, Levi had shared his love of enjoying freshly baked goods.

And maybe, just maybe, she opted to make brownies because he said they were his favorite.

"Any chance they have chocolate chunks in them?"

Her cheeks heated. "Maybe."

"Willow..."

"And lots of icing."

The next thing she knew, she was in his arms and going totally stiff. This was...new. They'd done nothing more than touch hands briefly when they got together, so this was...unexpected.

"Okay, you're going to have to relax," he said, keeping his voice soft and without letting her go.

"How come?" Forcing herself to unclench a bit, Willow stood with her arms still at her side.

"Well, if we're going to tell people that we've been dating for three months, then they're going to expect us to be comfortable around each other. So if I hug you or hold your hand, you can't freeze up like this."

"I...I'm not...I mean...I didn't freeze up." And then she over-compensated and practically went limp in his arms.

His laugh was low and husky. "We probably should have thought about this sooner."

"Why?"

Pulling back, Levi looked at her with amusement. "Seriously?"

"Oh, right," she said, trying to look like this was all no big deal. "I get it." He released her, and she looked in the car to make sure she had everything.

"Do you?"

"Huh?"

"Do you get why we should have thought about this sooner?"

Why did he want to keep talking about this?

"Because it's the one thing we didn't prepare for," she replied. "Right?"

"Well, there's that. But it's going to be hard to practice it while we're driving."

That did make sense, but Willow simply figured it was something they'd deal with when they had to. All she had to do was pretend that it was completely natural for Levi to touch her like he wanted to and like he had to.

Or that he wasn't acting and doing her a favor.

That she was practically paying him to do.

Which left her bank account close to empty.

"You okay?" he asked, concerned. Stepping in close, he gently grasped her shoulders. "You went a little pale."

"What? Oh, it's nothing. Really." She turned and looked at the car again. "So? Are we ready to go?"

Luckily he didn't push her for an answer. "Yup! Let's do this!"

Relief washed over her as she climbed into the passenger seat. Once she was settled, she looked at the dashboard and gasped, her hands immediately flying over her mouth.

"Problem?"

Oh, God...

"This looks like the dashboard of an airplane or something," she said after a minute. "I don't think I've ever seen anything like this." Every time they had gotten together over the last two weeks, she either met him there or they'd meet at McGee's and walk to whatever restaurant they were going to–mainly because the pub was right in the heart of downtown and near everything. Honestly, either his boss was the biggest jerk and didn't like Levi being gone for long, or he was totally trying to bank as many hours as he could since he was taking a week off to help her. This was the first time Willow was actually sitting in his car.

He laughed softly. "It is a little overwhelming. I went with all the tech upgrades because I couldn't resist. It took me about three months to figure out how everything worked. But I think I've finally got it all figured out."

"I hate to say it, but you're going to probably end up doing all the driving."

"How come?"

"Because just looking at this dashboard has my head spinning." She let out a nervous laugh. "Plus, in case you haven't noticed, I'm kind of on the short side. I don't think I could even see over the steering wheel!"

Levi laughed with her even as he did his best to assure her. "The seats are adjustable and you can definitely get them to a position that has you sitting higher. But if you're not comfortable driving, that's more than okay with me. It's not often that I take any road trips or even long drives, so this is going to be a real treat for me."

During some of their conversations, Levi had mentioned how he works a lot of hours at the pub, so it totally made sense that he wouldn't have time to really go out and drive anywhere. "How about we take it all as it comes," she suggested.

"Sounds like a plan."

And as he pulled out of the parking spot, Willow had to wonder if this was really the smart thing to do. Getting to see her grandmother was a definite perk, and Gammy was beyond excited to get to meet Levi, but just being in the cozy confines of his sports car had Willow feeling just a wee bit overwhelmed.

The car smelled like Levi's cologne, and the seats we buttery soft and warm. It was like she was surrounded by him and she was already on sensory overload. If this was how she was feeling after three minutes in the car with him, what the heck would she be like after three hours? Or three days?

Groaning, she tried to think of something else.

"You don't get carsick, do you?" he asked, somewhat nervously.

"No, why?"

"You just groaned, and it made me wonder."

"Oh, uh...no. I wasn't groaning because I wasn't feeling well."

"Then, why?"

"Why what?"

He chuckled. "Why did you groan?"

Think, Willow! Think!

"Um...just thinking about all that can go wrong," she blurted out and immediately regretted it.

He laughed again. "Okay, so you're an alarmist."

"What? No, I'm not!"

"Willow, we've barely pulled off your block and you're already worrying," he reasoned. "Is it because of the hug?"

"Hug?"

"Yeah, are you still freaked out about that?"

"I wouldn't say *freaked*..."

Reaching over, Levi took one of her hands in his and held onto it, resting them on the center console. "How's this? Freaking you out?"

"Levi, I already said I wasn't freaked out."

But she was and wasn't sure how to pull her hand away without being too obvious.

He was onto her and every time she tried to slide her fingers from his, he held on a little tighter.

Turning his head slightly toward her, he grinned. "Tell you what, how about you just let me hold your hand until we get to the Verrazano Bridge, okay?"

"Um..."

"After that, I swear I won't try to hold your hand again until we're halfway through New Jersey. What do you say?"

"I think you're making fun of me," she said, but she wasn't really upset.

"Maybe just a little."

"This just feels...I don't know...a little weird."

"Is there something wrong with my hand?"

"No! There's nothing wrong with your hand at all!"

"Not a big fan of intimacy?"

A million thoughts raced through her head, but all she could say was, "I never really thought of hand-holding as being intimate."

"Well, for two people who are newly dating, it's a step in that direction. So what do you say? You up for holding my hand for the next thirty minutes or so? I promise it won't get too sweaty."

Now he was really teasing her.

She sighed dramatically. "I guess I can tolerate it."

"That's my girl."

And it was silly how much that little phrase made her feel better.

———————

It was crazy how nervous he felt, but...he was.

And for some reason, holding Willow's hand only seemed to amp up those feelings.

For two weeks, they had seen each other almost every day. She would come to the pub for lunch, or sometimes they'd go out for sushi or pizza, but every time they got together, Levi could tell she was relaxing more and more around him.

And maybe if you hadn't been so worried about her relaxing, you could have gotten a grip on yourself.

Yeah, it was weird for sure. For a guy who was usually all about confidence and paying close attention to details, somehow he had forgotten to get his own feelings in check.

"How long do you think it will take to get to your sister's?"

Okay, conversation...that he could do.

"About seven hours," he said. "A little less if traffic cooperates." It was a Wednesday morning, and they had already missed the morning rush hour, so he was hopeful things would go smoothly for them. "I figured we'd stop for lunch once we cross into Maryland if that's okay with you."

"Absolutely! That's what I usually do too."

"Really? I thought you normally flew down to Florida."

"Most of the time, yes. But when we were kids, my father used to like to drive rather than fly."

"Well, with three kids it was probably expensive."

"Yeah, no," she said with a soft laugh. "It was more like he wanted us to have time in the car–uninterrupted–

so he could talk to us about the importance of education and then challenge us to all kinds of IQ and personality tests."

"Sounds...fun?" he asked lamely.

"It was exhausting. I swear, I think the reason I hated college so much was because of him. He put so much pressure on us, but I'm the only one it caused a negative reaction."

"You said your brother and sister were..."

"Miles is a doctor and Audrey is a lawyer." She looked over at him, her hand still in his. "Prepare yourself to have to listen to all the bragging my parents are going to do. No doubt you'll hear about some crazy, life-saving medical procedure Miles performed and how Audrey won some major legal victory." Groaning, she shook her head. "Then they'll both look at me expectantly and want to know why I still haven't found a practice to join before reminding me I can move to Seattle and join theirs." Another groan. "No, thank you."

"So that's what they're really after–having a big family psychology practice?"

"Something like that," she murmured.

"And other than not wanting to be a psychologist, how do you feel about moving to Seattle?"

He knew how he felt about it.

Miserable.

They were just getting to know each other and even though this was a fake relationship, Levi had a feeling a real one would be pretty amazing.

"There's no way I'd move to Washington. I'm a New York girl through and through. Even if I didn't join their practice, it's not someplace I want to live." She paused before explaining further. "Don't get me wrong, it's really nice there and I love all the food and the city of Seattle, but...I don't know...this is home."

"I get that."

"Plus, I've lived on Long Island my whole life and I still get lost pretty much everywhere I go. And don't even get me started on how many times I've gotten lost when I go into the city. Everyone tells me it's so easy to find my way around, and yet no matter what, I end up getting turned around and completely overwhelmed."

"Maybe you just need someone who's good with directions to go with you," he suggested, hoping she'd take the hint that *he* was good with directions.

"Donna can get us anywhere with her eyes closed, and I even manage to get her lost."

Okay, hint *not* taken...

"Anyway," she went on, "the reason I'm bringing this up is that I want you not only to be prepared to hear about my siblings, but for them to be a little...snarky toward you."

"Me? What did I do?"

"They're going to grill you on why you're a bartender and how you should be aspiring to do more with your life."

"Um..." At that moment, he realized he probably should have corrected her on all her earlier assumptions that he was just the bartender. He owned the pub and had worked really hard to make that happen! Why didn't he open with that when he first met her?

"Personally, I don't think there's anything wrong with it. I think it's great that you're doing something you love." Then she paused and turned her head toward him. "You do love it, don't you?"

"Well...yeah. But that's not..."

"I envy you, Levi," she went on, ignoring how he was trying to explain his response. "I don't even really know what I'm passionate about. I mean, I love walking the dogs, but...that's not something I can make a career out of. Or at least, that I *shouldn't* make a career out of. Ugh...can you imagine how that would look. I can hear my parents now. *Our son Miles is a doctor, our daughter Audrey is a lawyer, and Willow picks up dog poop.*"

Don't laugh...don't laugh...

"They sound like the kind of people who are too uptight to say poop..."

"Seriously?" she cried, pulling her hand away. "That's all you can say?"

Levi didn't release her hand and knew he needed to think fast. "I was trying to lighten the mood, Willow. And for the record, the issue is with them, not you."

"Yeah, that's what Gammy says too."

"So then why don't you believe it?"

"Because everyone wants their parent's approval. Don't you want yours?"

He shrugged. "I have it. They're very proud of me. I make a very good living and I'm happy. That's all they've ever wanted."

"They never pushed you to do something different? Something other than making drinks?"

"You seem fixated on that one fact," he said thoughtfully. "Bartenders happen to make very good money."

"Apparently."

Narrowing his gaze, he asked, "What does that mean?"

"It means you must! You were able to take a week off without even giving it a second thought and look at this car! I don't pay a lot of attention to the price of sports cars, but even I know this is brand new and expensive."

"Well, I saved up for a long time for this. Up until six

months ago, I was driving the car I bought in high school. A pickup truck, actually."

"Really?"

"Yeah. Don't get me wrong, I loved that truck and probably would have kept driving it, but I decided it was time to grow up a little and get a real car."

"A real car with as many tech options as a jet plane..."

"It's really not so bad, Willow. At some point over the course of the week, you'll have to give it a shot."

"I don't know...if anything happened and I did something to the car, there would be no way I could pay for it. I'd feel terrible."

"I'm sure you're not going to damage the car."

"Oh, please, I'm a walking accident," she said with a small pout. "That day outside the pub? That's practically an everyday occurrence for me."

"Seriously?"

Nodding, she twisted slightly in her seat to face him a bit. "I broke my wrist when I was five."

"Willow, most people break a bone in their life."

"That was the first time. I broke it three more times after that."

"Oh."

"I broke my ankle once at a skating rink."

"Ice skating is kind of dangerous if you don't have good balance."

"Well, it was a roller rink, and I hadn't even gotten to the skates. I tripped over one of the benches that blended with the carpet."

"O-kay..." He was starting to see what she was getting at.

"I never played any sports," she went on. "Even my PE

teachers used to suggest I sit out on certain activities because they knew I'd hurt myself."

"Wow."

"I know. I both appreciated it and was offended."

There really wasn't anything he could say to that.

"I haven't broken anything in a while–which is amazing considering how often I fall."

"Like in front of the pub?"

"Yeah," she replied wearily. "You should really tell your boss to see about getting that sidewalk fixed. I purposely park on the next block so I can approach the pub from the opposite direction."

"Oh, Lord..."

"It's okay. I don't mind, really. It gives me a chance to window shop every time I go to McGee's. Plus, I discovered there's a daycare near where I park. They're open until eight to accommodate working parents, and sometimes I stop and chat with them and the kids–especially when the little ones have artwork that they're waving around to show anyone who walks by."

"I had no idea that place was open so late."

"They are, and I think that's awesome. I had asked about any open positions, but it turns out I don't have the right degree," she admitted sadly. "I could probably take some classes at the community college to get the credits I need but...I don't know. It was just an option."

There was more to this story, he thought, but he'd bide his time before delving any deeper.

"Any other places you like to check out on your way to the pub?"

"Oh, yeah. There's the little bakery on the corner–you know, the one that only does cupcakes–and they always have the cutest displays, and the smells are amazing! And the pottery place always has some fun pieces in the window. I've often thought about going and doing one of their girl's night events, but I have a feeling I'd break more than I'd make and paint."

"You don't know that."

She gave him a look that pretty much screamed, "Really?"

"Okay, it could be risky, but you won't know until you try!" And he hoped he sounded encouraging.

"You know what I've noticed when I'm walking up your block?"

"No, what?"

"The front of the pub could use a little facelift."

All he could do was stare.

"You know, maybe a new awning, some window boxes, and...if your boss fixes the sidewalk, some bistro tables for out front. You know, something to draw in the lunch crowd."

"We have been talking about expanding the menu..."

"I'm telling you, just perk up the exterior and you'll draw even more people in!"

It was definitely something to consider. Actually, every time he and Willow got together, she always had some helpful tips for him to give to his "boss". He was starting to feel guilty about not explaining how *he* was the boss, but there never seemed to be the right time.

Now. Now would be a good time!

"So, let me ask you something."

Or not. Whatever.

"Sure!"

"We covered a lot of stuff over the last few weeks— favorite foods, favorite movies, music, and TV shows..."

"Right..."

"But I feel like there's still a lot of stuff we didn't cover."

"Really? Like what? We've talked so much that I feel like I know everything about you!" She smiled at him like she was impressed with herself. Should he really crush that feeling?

"Let's be real, Willow, there's no way to know everything about someone in only an hour a day for two weeks."

She straightened a bit in her seat and seemed to consider what he said. "Maybe. But I think we learned a lot."

"Oh, we definitely did! But you never told me what hobbies you have or anything particularly silly about yourself. Little things that I might know if we were dating for real. And definitely nothing that someone who's in love with you would know."

"Whoa...we're just dating. Well...not really dating, but you know...in the fake way. And even if it was real, would we really be in love so soon?"

"You don't believe in love at first sight?"

She snorted and then laughed nervously. "Are you serious?"

"Yeah. Why wouldn't I be?"

"Oh, well...I don't know. No one I know has ever had it happen, and I know it's never happened to me, so..."

"That doesn't mean it's not possible."

"I guess." She chewed on her bottom lip and went quiet.

They drove in companionable silence for several minutes and Levi took the exit to get onto the Belt Parkway. It was a stretch of road he wasn't particularly fond of, and every pothole and bump had him cringing and worrying about his car.

It was a stupid thing to worry about, but it was a good

distraction from the conversation he and Willow had left hanging.

So she didn't believe in love at first sight. Did he? It wasn't something he'd ever really thought about, but he certainly believed in attraction at first sight. The moment he picked Willow up in his arms that fateful day, he was drawn to her. While their relationship had been along the lines of friendship, it didn't stop Levi from acknowledging that he thought she was beautiful and that his feelings weren't all based on them being friends.

Not that he'd admit that to Willow.

Not yet, anyway.

But fake-relationship Levi might...

They drove on for several more minutes until they approached the Verrazano Bridge, and he released her hand–not because he wanted to, but because there was more traffic at the bridge entrance and he needed both hands on the wheel to maneuver his way through it.

Out of the corner of his eye, he saw Willow bend forward and start looking for something in her purse. It didn't take long for her to pull out her phone and sit back up. He figured she was looking for a way to pass the time– maybe check her emails or text someone–so he focused on driving and left her to it.

They crossed the bridge, and within minutes, they were in New Jersey.

One state down.

They had at least two hours before they crossed into Maryland and could stop for lunch, but he had no idea how to kill time between now and then. Obviously they were going to talk, but...about what? Willow had gone quiet on him and now was studying her phone.

How long was he supposed to wait before he tried to get

her to talk to him again? And should he even push or just wait her out?

Or maybe...

"Yay! I found it!" she said excitedly.

"Found what?"

"The perfect way for us to learn more about each other and sound like we're more in love."

"Um...and how is that?"

"There's this set of questions you and your significant other can ask each other and it's supposed to make you fall in love."

Levi swallowed hard. "Um...what?"

Beside him, Willow was looking down at her phone, nodding. "Yup. The article says there are 36 questions you can ask someone if you want to fall in love, or make your love even stronger if you're already in love." She looked over at him and smiled. "What do you say? Ready to fall in love with me?"

4

OH, God...why would I ask that?

"I mean...fake fall in love," Willow quickly amended. "This is all for the sake of us sounding more realistic, right?"

Levi had both hands on the steering wheel in a white-knuckled grip, and she didn't take it as a good sign.

Way to go, Willow. He's probably trying to come up with an excuse to turn the car around and bow out of this trip.

"So you just ask me questions and that's it?" he asked.

"Well, they recommend taking turns asking the questions, but since you're driving–and this isn't really real–I figured I'll ask the questions. But we both have to answer them."

"And...how personal are they? Like is this going to be embarrassing stuff about sex and all that?"

She gasped. "Oh, my goodness! I hope not! I don't think so. It didn't say anything about sex, so..."

"Okay, how about this–you start asking the questions, and if any of them make us feel uncomfortable, we skip them. How does that sound?"

"Hmm...that seems fair." Swiping the screen, she

scanned the instructions and cleared her throat. "You ready for this? It says it should take about an hour."

He laughed softly.

"What's so funny?"

"I was just thinking about what we were going to talk about for the next two hours, and now I know."

"Oh, well...that's convenient." She did her best to get comfortable and felt a little giddy. "Here we go. Question number one. If you could invite anyone in the world to dinner, who would it be?"

"Easy. Wayne Gretzky."

"The hockey player?"

Nodding, Levi replied, "Yup. The Great One. I'm a huge hockey fan."

"See? This is extremely helpful information!" Willow exclaimed, hopeful the rest of the questions would go as easily.

"What about you? Who would you invite?"

"Hmm...Anna Kendrick."

"Who?"

"Anna Kendrick. The actress."

"Really?"

"Yeah, why?"

"I don't know. I just didn't think you'd pick a celebrity."

"Oh, um...I guess then I would pick..."

"No, no, no...," he said, quickly interrupting her. "That's not how this works. And I wasn't judging you, Willow. We're supposed to be learning about one another. That was me learning something about you."

She nodded and quietly cleared her throat. "Okay, question number two. What would constitute a perfect day for you?"

"First you have to tell me why you want to have dinner with this Anna person."

"Kendrick."

"Whatever," he said with a low laugh. "Why her?"

After letting out a long and drawn-out sigh, she said, "I really like her as an actress. She just seems very relatable and like she'd be someone you can sit and talk with, and she wouldn't be stuck up." She shrugged. "I love all her *Pitch Perfect* movies."

He nodded again. "There, that makes total sense. Thank you." He glanced at her and smiled. "Okay, perfect day, right?"

"Yup."

"Hmm...I would have to say I'd love for it to be on vacation. Someplace warm, but not tropical. I'd get up and go for a run on the beach, have a big breakfast–bacon, eggs, home fries, the works. Then I'd love to go out on a boat and do some deep-sea fishing, drink some beers, catch some sun... then come in and have someone clean and cook the fish for me." He paused. "No, yeah...no need to do any work on my perfect day." Another pause. "Then I'd enjoy this spectacular meal that I caught myself while sitting around the fire and relaxing."

"All by yourself?"

"What? No. I guess I'd have my friends with me. Or...someone."

"Someone?"

"Depends on when this perfect day is. Maybe I'd be dating someone, and they'd be with me." He shrugged. "But other than the company, all those things would constitute a perfect day."

"Okay then."

"What about you?"

"Oooh...it would be all about getting pampered," she replied dreamily. "Like you, I'd love to be someplace warm–maybe one of those deluxe spas in Arizona or something. I'd get to sleep late in one of those super-comfy beds, and I'd get served breakfast there."

"Breakfast in bed is definitely a good one."

"And as much as I hate to admit it, I'd love one of those big breakfasts too. Only I'd go for the bacon and eggs and some waffles. Preferably Belgian ones," she added with a grin. "Then I'd go for a manicure, a pedicure, and a massage. I'd take a nice nap out in the cabana and then go for a swim before getting ready for a gourmet dinner. Surf and turf is a favorite. Then I'd sit out and stare up at the stars while enjoying some sort of decadent dessert that was covered in chocolate." Humming, Willow closed her eyes. "Yeah. Perfect day."

"Again, you totally surprised me."

"How?"

"I don't know. I didn't peg you for a spa girl."

"I think everyone can be convinced to try a day of getting pampered, Levi."

"Not me."

"What? Why?"

"Some strange dude oiling me up and rubbing his hands all over my body? That's a hard pass."

Unable to help herself, Willow laughed. "There are female massage therapists, Levi."

But he shook his head. "I don't know. It just seems weird to me." Looking over at her, he smiled. "And that's why it's a good thing our perfect day preferences don't have to match, right?"

"I guess." And suddenly she wasn't so sure they were going to pull this off. They were much more different than she let herself imagine. He liked sports, and she didn't. She liked massages, and he didn't. And the thought of fishing made her cringe. Sighing, she shared her thought with him.

"Willow, this is really just for information purposes. Maybe if this was a true compatibility test we should reconsider, but...this is for fun, right?"

It took her a minute to think about it, but...yeah. He was right. "I'm being ridiculous. Sorry."

Waving her off, he said, "Nothing to apologize. Really. So what's next?"

"When did you last sing to yourself and to somebody else?"

His bark of laughter filled the space and had her jumping slighting in her seat. "Trust me, I am no singer. Not for myself and not for anyone else."

"Oh, come on! Everyone sings! Even if it's just the happy birthday song!"

He shook his head. "Not me. I make sure I stay silent when that goes on."

"What about when you're alone in the car and your favorite song comes on?"

"Nope."

"How is that possible?" she cried. "How can you go through a day without singing to the radio or humming or... or...singing in the shower?"

"I don't know," Levi replied. "I'm just not really someone who's into singing." Glancing at her, he added, "And I'm guessing by your reaction that you sing a lot."

"Oh, my goodness, yes! Like all the time! Even though I probably shouldn't."

"Why not?"

"I have a decent voice, but not the kind of voice that makes people ask me to sing. Except for Josh. He loves it when I sing." Laughing, she went on, "I was always in the chorus in school and I've been singing around the house practically since I started talking. It makes my family crazy."

"Why?"

"Because they're all so serious and level-headed and think my singing is just...pointless."

"I know I keep saying this, but...wow."

"I guess I can get annoying with it."

"How? Do you sing at inappropriate times?"

Do I?

"I sing with my nieces and nephews," she answered after a moment. "I know the words to every Disney song and enjoy getting into character while singing them too."

"What the heck does that mean?"

"You know...all the hand gestures and dance moves...all of it. And the kids love it. Like seriously love it. I get to be fun Aunt Willow–which I love." She let out a soft sigh. "As for inappropriate times...no. It's not like I break out into show tunes at funerals or anything, but if there's music play- ing, chances are I'll be singing along."

"Nothing wrong with that, I guess."

This was turning into a great, big disappointment, and they were only in New Jersey. She was afraid to think about how much less they were going to have in common by lunchtime.

"Okay then. Next question." And she read it and shook her head. "We should probably just skip this one."

"Why?"

"Because if you don't sing, I'm pretty sure you're going to say you don't cry either."

"That's the next question? If I cry?"

"No, it's when did you last cry in front of someone and by yourself?"

"Well, then prepare to be shocked but...I cried a few months ago at my grandfather's funeral."

"Oh, Levi, I'm so sorry." Without thinking, Willow reached over and placed her hand over his. Levi immediately linked his fingers with hers.

"He passed away a month before my grandmother's 80th birthday. I think everyone in the family cried. So...I cried in front of and with them and...I even cried alone when I got the call."

"As you can probably imagine, I cry around once a week. I cry over commercials or out of frustration. The last time I cried in front of anyone was..." She had to stop and think about it. "Oh, last week in front of the dogs."

"The dogs? Really?"

She nodded. "I had taken the smaller dogs out for their walk and Gia stepped on something and let out the most pitiful little sound. I scooped her up in my arms and cried because I felt so bad for her!"

"O-kay then..."

"You think I'm weird, right?"

"I wouldn't say that..."

"You're definitely regretting being on this trip with me. I can tell."

"I never said that, Willow."

"You don't have to. I can tell. You have a very expressive face." When he turned to look at her like she was crazy, she waggled her finger at him. "There! Right there! You think I'm crazy!" Sighing, she went on, "It's okay. I get that a lot. I guess it's why I don't date a lot. Most guys don't want someone who's as...emotional as me."

"There's nothing wrong with being emotional," he countered. "And honestly, I don't think you're weird."

"Really?"

"Yeah, really. I'm not used to someone being so honest about themselves. I think this test or quiz or whatever it is you want to call what we're doing really is kind of fascinating. I don't think I've ever had a conversation like this with anyone I've ever dated."

"Me either."

"Can I ask a question?"

"You should probably stay focused on the road."

He laughed, and it was low and gruff and so masculine that Willow almost hummed dreamily.

"I meant can I ask a question that's not part of the quiz."

"Oh, um...sure! Why not?"

"Actually, I have two questions."

It was hard not to tense up. It was one thing to be the one in control of the questions and to wrap her head around them before she had to answer, it was quite another to have no idea what was coming her way. So instead of internalizing and freaking herself out, she said, "Lay them on me."

"How did you get the name Willow?"

"Gammy named me."

"And she's the one we're going to see, right?"

"Yup."

"How come she named you?"

"Because she told my parents they were picking uptight names, and she thought my siblings were a little on the serious side. So she challenged them to let her pick my name and they would see if the name really affects our personalities."

"So you were like...an experiment?"

"I never thought of it like that, but...I guess."

"And that doesn't offend you?"

She shrugged. "Like I said, I never really thought about it." They drove in silence for several minutes. "What was your other question?"

Levi seemed to consider his words carefully before asking, "What's the most embarrassing thing you've ever done?"

Okay, clearly he hadn't thought this through because once Willow shared her most embarrassing thing, he was going to have to do the same.

"Falling in front of you kind of tops the current list," she said with a hint of humor.

"You didn't really fall in *front* of me..."

"It was right in front of the window at McGee's and you saw it because you ran right out to help me. So, yeah. That's a biggie."

"But is it *the* most embarrassing?"

"I believe I've shared enough of my embarrassing moments earlier. Let's put Levi under the microscope, shall we?"

"Well...I guess that's fair. After all, you did tell me a lot about you."

"Levi?"

"Hmm?"

"Quit stalling."

Her bluntness was kind of cute in this instance and he knew she had him pegged. "Fine. The most embarrassing thing I ever did was...back in high school, my buddies and I streaked across the football field during the halftime show."

"No!" she cried, her hands going over her mouth as she started to laugh. "You did not!"

"Unfortunately, I did."

Lowering her hands, she giggled a little more. "Did you get caught?"

"Nope," he said proudly. "We had a plan and knew exactly where to run to. Plus...we had football helmets on so no one could see our faces."

"Oh, my gosh! Why would you do that?" And yet, she was still laughing.

"Because we were stupid and thought it would be funny," he replied, shrugging. "You know how immature guys are at 18. Looking back, I'm shocked we didn't get caught even as much as I'm shocked we did it at all. Still...it makes for an interesting story."

"Do you share it a lot?"

He grinned at her and saw she was blushing slightly. "Not in a long time."

They drove in silence for several miles and he wondered if he'd thrown them so far off track with the test that Willow didn't want to continue. And for the life of him, he had no idea why he felt the need to ask his own questions.

No, that wasn't true. He was genuinely curious about her name. Her siblings had fairly normal–almost boring– names. Willow was the name you would think of two free-spirited parents would choose for their child. Certainly not the one two seemingly uptight psychologists would pick.

Curiosity and all...

The other question? Yeah, he had no clue. It was something that just came to mind. The silver lining to it was that she could see how he had a way more embarrassing story than she did. She was a klutz, that was a given, and unfortunately that meant things were going to happen that were out of her control. His story proved that he opted to embarrass himself. Maybe it would make her feel a little better about herself.

Or maybe he was just an idiot.

Either was an option at this point.

"So, what's the next question on the list?" he prompted, needing to break up the silence and hoped she still wanted to play at getting to know you.

"Oh, um...let me pull the quiz back up," she said, staring down at her phone. "Oooh...this one's interesting. Do you believe success comes in the form of money or happiness?"

"Wow, that is a good one." And one he was all-too-familiar with. "Happiness. Definitely happiness."

"Tell me why."

"Well, there's the old adage how money can't buy you love or happiness, so..."

"Okay, but what about personal experience?" she challenged.

"Well, take my job. You mentioned earlier how your parents wouldn't approve of my being a bartender, but...I'm very happy at my job. And I'm making good money."

"But that sort of disproves what you're saying. Maybe you're happy at your job because you're making good money."

Wait...was he?

Well, shit.

Levi let that settle in for a minute and then shook his head. "Nope. I was happy with the pub before I was making good money, so I stand by my original answer. I felt successful because I had a job I loved." And with a big smile, he glanced at her. "Your turn."

"Hmm...if I listen to my parents, then I would have to say money equals success."

"But that's not what the question asks," he reminded her. "It asks what *you* believe."

"Oh. Right," she mumbled before letting out a long sigh and continuing. "I think being happy makes you successful and it shouldn't matter what it is that you do for a living or where you live or who you're with. I mean, some of the wealthiest people in the world are miserable while some of the poorest are happy."

"Exactly." Reaching for her hand again, he gave it a gentle squeeze. "Remember that when you're around your parents."

"Ugh...you'll have to remind me." She stared down at her phone and laughed.

"What? What's so funny?"

"The next question."

"Uh-oh..."

"How do you feel about your relationship with your mother?" Looking at him, she said, "You better go first."

It was on the tip of his tongue to tell her she didn't need to answer at all, but...maybe there was more to the story than he realized. Instead, he was more than happy to talk about his own relationship with his mother. "I know it sounds corny but...my mom is literally one of my best friends."

"Really?" she asked, her voice laced with awe.

"Yeah. She's been my biggest fan and champion my whole life. She's been to every event, every game, every... everything for me. I can tell her anything, and she's perfectly happy to call me out when I'm doing something stupid or when she thinks I need to work on something."

"Wow."

"I know. But you have to understand, I've got three older sisters–two that you're going to meet in the next two days–and I was a little outnumbered growing up."

"And what about your relationship with your dad? Is he...you know...are you close to him too?"

"We are. I think my dad was psyched to finally get a son, and we do a lot of stuff together, but he's just a big softie with my sister's too."

"That sounds...weird." Then she let out a laugh that was a little more of a snort. "Sorry. That was mean of me to say."

"It's okay, Willow. It's obvious we grew up with very different family dynamics. Most of the time when you mention your parents, I feel like you just did; it seems weird to me. I can't imagine not laughing and having fun with my folks." He was still holding her hand and squeezed it again. "Maybe when we get back home after this trip, I'll introduce you to them."

"After...after the trip? Why?"

He shrugged. "Um...because I thought you might like them?"

"But...we won't be fake dating anymore."

Damn. He hadn't thought of that.

"Yeah, but...we'll still be friends, and all my friends have met my parents." Then he held his breath and waited to see how she responded.

"Oh," she said, smiling. "Then that sounds wonderful. I can't wait!"

At some point, Levi knew he was going to have to come to grips with his feelings for Willow. When he first offered to be her fake boyfriend, it seemed like a nice thing to do. A way to help a friend out. But deep down, he knew he was lying. He had feelings for Willow. Real feelings that had nothing to do with being her friend and everything to do with her meaning much more.

Unfortunately, this trip was not the time to be introducing that topic. It seemed she was already tense enough about being around her parents and pulling off this whole fake relationship thing and he didn't want to add any more pressure to her.

But once the trip was over...all bets were off.

"So...do you want to answer the question?" he asked cautiously.

"Believe it or not, I have a good relationship with my mother. It's not perfect, but...it's good. She genuinely wants me to be happy, but she doesn't always agree with what exactly that means."

"Huh?"

"To her, I should be happy going into a field where I can make a good living. Her theory is that I went to school for it, I'm educated in it, so, therefore, I will succeed and then be happy. She can't grasp the flaw in that logic."

"I'm guessing you've discussed this with her."

"Too many times to count."

"How does she feel about you walking the dogs?"

"She doesn't quite...understand it," she said slowly. "My father is not a dog person, so we were never allowed to have one when I was growing up. So she doesn't quite get why I'd choose to do this or why that was the job I chose instead of something more stable."

"And what do you tell her when she asks?"

"I change the subject," she said, laughing. "There's no way to explain to her that I love the feeling of these dogs just loving me for me. The unconditionalness just...it's awesome! They're always happy to see me, always excited to go out with me, and their owners appreciate me." She groaned. "Oh, boy. That made me sound totally pathetic. Forget I said it. All of it."

"Willow..."

"No, I'm serious! Um...next question! What do you value most in a friendship?"

If they weren't in the middle of the New Jersey Turnpike, Levi would be tempted to pull over and hug her. Because if anyone needed a hug, it was Willow. Since he couldn't, he squeezed her hand again and said, "Honesty. I think honesty is the most important aspect of a friendship. Or any relationship, really."

"Oh." When she went to gently pull her hand away, he didn't stop her.

But he hated to think that he'd hurt her feelings, so...

"And the ability to pack the perfect snacks for trips," he added. "Especially if there's chocolate involved."

That did the trick.

"Then this is your lucky day," she said cheerily. "Because I just happen to have my famous death by chocolate brownies. I've been told they are literally to die for." Twisting in her seat, she turned to grab her cooler from the backseat.

"Well, I'd hate to die and miss out on the rest of this little adventure of ours, so...feed them to me with care."

And when Willow held a piece of the brownie up to his lips, he knew death was definitely on the menu.

The death of him thinking that he was going to be able to pretend this wasn't real.

5

"Oh! And if you ever need someone to do a quick alteration on your dress or anything, Levi is definitely your guy!"

Beside her, Willow heard Levi groan even as his sister laughed.

So this is what a normal family is like...

"I'm telling you, Willow, my brother is an absolute whiz with a needle and thread! Our nana taught him how to crochet too! Want to see the afghan he made for me last Christmas?"

"Nat! Geez!" Levi cried with exasperation. "What the hell?"

With a mischievous grin, Natalie stood. "I just think this is information your girlfriend should know."

"Oh, uh...we're not really boyfriend and girlfriend," Willow explained for at least the tenth time in the last two hours. For the life of her, she couldn't understand why Natalie wasn't getting the fact that this wasn't real.

Natalie–who looked a lot like Levi–waved her off and walked back to the kitchen. "Can I get you guys something more to drink? Soda? Water? Dinner will be ready in an hour or so."

"I'm good, Nat!" Levi called out before he leaned forward and hung his head. "Why did I think this was a good idea?"

Scooting closer, Willow studied him. "Your sister is very nice, Levi. Very friendly."

"And she's got a big mouth."

They sat in silence for several minutes before she blurted out, "So you can really sew?"

"Oh, God..."

"Why does that freak you out? It's a great skill to have! I can do the basics like fixing a small hole in a shirt–and I usually stab myself in the finger several times until I bleed and then practically pass out–but I certainly can't do any kind of alterations."

"You should see what he was able to do with my old prom dress!" Natalie said when she breezed back into the living room. "It was like he deconstructed it and made me something I'd actually wear again! And I did!"

Levi muttered a curse while continuing to stare at the floor. Reaching over, Willow gave him a gentle pat on the knee before smiling up at Natalie. "I'm not good with things like that. I'm a bit of a klutz, so..."

Again, Natalie waved her off. "Well, as long as you're dating my brother, you won't have to worry!" She sat down in the large, oversized chair opposite the sofa where Willow and Levi were sitting. "And believe me, you have my sympathy on the klutzy thing. My younger daughter, Olivia, is the same way. I swear, my poor girl trips over her own shadow."

Willow nodded sympathetically. "Yeah, me too."

"And she struggles so much because her sister, Penny, is a dancer. I swear she came out of the womb dancing."

Willow couldn't help but smile. "She's lucky. I took ballet when I was little, but...as you can imagine, it was a bit of a nightmare."

"Olivia tried too, but...even she knew when to throw in the towel." She shook her head. "Levi, remember when the girls were both in that Christmas recital two years ago? I sent you the video?"

"And Olivia knocked down half the set?" he said, shaking his head. "I still say you should take her for martial arts classes. I think she'd be awesome at that."

"Oh, no! She knocked down the set?" Willow asked, shocked that they were making light of it. "Was she hurt?"

"Oh, no," Natalie replied. "She did it on purpose because the teacher made her be a tree. One of her branches was particularly long, and she thought it would be funny to use it when the narrator mentioned a storm was brewing." She laughed. "You've got to hand it to her, she's clever!"

"I don't doubt that," Willow said. "But maybe she was sad because she was given a menial part. Was Penny in more of a lead role?"

Natalie nodded.

"It was her way of getting the attention on her," Willow reasoned. "It's got to be hard on her to have a sister who can do all the things that she can't. And even if she doesn't say it bothers her, her actions say otherwise."

"Willow...," Levi said quietly.

"No, no, no," Natalie interrupted, holding a hand up to her brother. "One of Olivia's teachers said the same thing, and I blew it off. But...it kind of makes sense."

"Has she done anything else like it since?"

"Well..."

"You don't have to answer that, Nat," Levi said before turning to stare at Willow. "I thought you didn't like psychology?"

She shrugged. "I don't particularly want to do it as a profession, but with all those years of school studying, it kind of comes out once in a while." Turning her attention to his sister, she smiled sadly. "I'm sorry, Natalie. I spoke out of place. I hope I didn't offend you."

"Are you kidding me? For starters, I'm not easily offended. And honestly, we've thought about talking to a child psychologist about it."

"Is she aggressive?"

"Definitely not. Not in a hurtful way. But the tree costume incident was really just the beginning. Any time there's a project that both she and Penny are involved in, things...happen. We attributed it to her just not being...you know, graceful, but I have to wonder if there's more to it."

"Hmm..."

"Hmm?" Levi repeated. "What the hell does *hmm* mean?"

"What are you getting all pissy for, Levi?" Natalie demanded. "Hmm means hmm. Stop being difficult." Then she focused on Willow again. "Don't mind him. He's a little over-protective of his nieces."

"Well, that's nice..."

"Do you think we should talk to a shrink?"

"Oh, uh..."

"Nat, stop! Willow doesn't know Olivia. Hell, she doesn't know you! Why would you ask a complete stranger for advice like this?"

Willow stiffened slightly. She never saw Levi so uptight before and it suddenly made her feel a little uncomfortable. Putting some space between the two of them, she felt her cheeks heat and wished there was someplace she could go to be alone.

The Sullivan siblings continued their heated discussion and Willow caught some movement by the stairs. Slowly, she leaned over and noticed a little girl who had to be around six or seven staring at her. The house was a small Cape Cod, and the staircase was tucked in the corner without much light so she couldn't quite make out if she was purposely hiding or just maybe being a little nosey about the raised voices.

Natalie stormed off to the kitchen and Levi followed her, and Willow figured she might as well go introduce herself to whichever daughter this was.

"Hi," she said, walking toward the staircase. "I'm Willow."

"I'm Livvy."

"As in Olivia?" Willow asked for clarification, and the girl nodded. "Well, it's very nice to meet you, Olivia."

"Are you Uncle Levi's girlfriend?"

It was way too complicated to try to explain their relationship, so she simply nodded. "We're on our way down to Florida and Levi thought it would be fun if we stop and visit. I hope that's okay."

"Are you going to Disney World?"

"Oooh...I wish. We're going to visit my grandmother for her birthday, so no Disney on this trip. But I would love to go! I haven't been there in years!"

"I want to go, too," Olivia said. "I want to ride the *Frozen* ride!"

"What? I didn't even *know* there *was* a *Frozen* ride!"

Olivia looked up at her with big blue eyes and nodded. "Uh-huh! You ride a boat and everything!"

And as if of one mind, they both started singing *Let*

It Go. Olivia jumped off the step she was on and began to twirl as she sang. She reached out her hand and Willow took it as they both started singing even louder. By the time they got to the final chorus, they each struck a dramatic pose before collapsing on the couch laughing.

"You are so cool, Willow!" Olivia cried. "No one ever sings along with me! Penny says she's too old to sing any Disney songs, and mom has a terrible voice, so…"

"Hey!"

Willow's eyes went wide as she turned her head and saw Natalie and Levi standing in the doorway watching them. "Um…"

"Mom! Did you hear us? Willow knows *all* the words! She even did all the movements Elsa did! Isn't that cool?"

Willow's cheeks heated, and she couldn't believe everyone was looking at her like…like…She looked up and saw Olivia smiling from ear to ear just like Nat and Levi.

"Um…"

"That's amazing, sweetheart!" Natalie said, hugging her daughter. She looked over at Willow. "That was very impressive! I can't keep track of all those songs. They are way more complex than the Disney movies from when I was a kid."

"Willow's a pro at them," Levi said, giving her a sly wink. "She admitted that in the car."

"Really?" Olivia asked. "Do you know the songs from the new *Frozen* movie?"

Nodding, Willow said, "My girlfriends and I saw that in the movie theaters like three times!"

"Wow! You are so cool!" Olivia declared. "Want to come up to my room and see my Elsa costume?"

"Sure!" Standing, she looked at Levi and Natalie and

shrugged. "We'll be back down in time for dinner. I promise."

And with Olivia laughing and tugging her hand, Willow followed the girl up the stairs.

"So...this is serious, huh?"

"What's serious?"

"You and Willow. It's serious, right?"

Levi sat down at his sister's kitchen table and groaned. *This so wasn't a good idea...*

"Nat, I explained the situation to you. I'm just helping Willow out with her grandmother. She didn't want to let her down or have to deal with her folks being judgy toward her. It's no big deal."

Placing the spoon down on the counter that she was using to stir the pot of sauce, Natalie turned and smirked at him. "Look, you're a good guy. We all know that. You'd give anyone the shirt off your back."

"Right, so..."

"However," she quickly interrupted, "this is the first time that favor extended to bringing a girl home with you."

"I'm not bringing her *home*, Nat. This was just a practical move–a way to save some money on the trip."

"Why are you so worried about money? The pub's doing fantastic, you just bought that ridiculous sports car..."

"It's not ridiculous," he countered. "It's just something I kind of always wanted."

"And you're looking at buying a house! You're doing great financially, so why volunteer to sleep on my floor for the night and bring Willow with you?"

Sighing, he rubbed his forehead and tried to stay calm.

"Willow was insisting on paying for the trip since I was doing her a favor. She...she thinks I'm a bartender."

"You *are* a bartender."

"No, she thinks that's all I am. She doesn't know I own McGee's."

"Well, that's stupid. Why don't you just tell her and then spring for a hotel with real beds for the two of you?"

"You wouldn't understand."

Sitting down in the chair beside him, his sister simply said, "Try me."

"Willow is...well...she's not in a particularly good place right now," he began carefully. "She's got a degree she doesn't want to use, she doesn't really have a job..."

"She's unemployed?"

"Sort of?" Then he shook his head. "She walks dogs. Like a lot of dogs."

"What's a lot of dogs?"

"Picture every cartoon or commercial you've ever seen where a person is walking an almost comical amount of dogs at one time. That's Willow."

"Wow, good for her! She's a tiny little thing, but she must be strong!"

He never thought of that.

"And she's a part-time nanny."

"Well she's wonderful with kids. I've never seen Olivia bond with someone that quickly."

Nodding, he explained, "Anyway, her folks are pressuring her to buckle down and get a position with a practice—preferably theirs up in Seattle..."

"Seattle? Is that where she's from? Because her accent is totally a New York one."

"No, she's born and raised on Long Island. Her parents moved there...I don't know when." He paused. "The thing is, she's probably the sweetest woman I've ever met, and she's a little lost right now. She made up a boyfriend so her grandmother wouldn't worry about her so much and here we are."

"You sure about that?"

"What do you mean?"

"Levi, there's obviously a bit of interest there," Natalie said with a knowing smile. "On both ends."

That was brand new information.

"Seriously? You think Willow's interested?"

Her smile turned mischievous. "You mean you hadn't noticed?"

"Well..."

He was interrupted by some loud thumping over their heads and the sound of Willow and Olivia singing something else and laughing hysterically.

"*Moana,*" Natalie said. "*How Far I'll Go.* Another favorite of Olivia's."

"Ah."

"Okay, before we get all teenage girl gossipy here, let's go back for a minute. Why do you say she's lost and what does any of this have to do with you not telling her you own the pub?"

"She doesn't know what she wants to do with her life and it's an issue for her right now. I think she feels comfortable with me because she doesn't see my job as being intimidating. I'm relatable, you know?"

Nodding, Natalie said, "I guess. But with all the getting to know you time the two of you have had, how has it not come up?"

"Anytime she mentions me talking to my boss, I just nod," he said solemnly. "She's opening up to me and sharing so much of herself and...I don't know, I don't want to do anything to jeopardize it. I'm afraid if I tell her, she'll look at me and be..."

"Intimidated."

"Exactly."

"Well, damn. That's both commendable and stupid all at the same time."

"I wouldn't say stupid..."

"Look, you need to be honest with her. If this thing goes beyond being her fake boyfriend for the week, it's not going to look good that you lied to her. And it's a silly thing to lie about."

"Nat..."

"What? I'm serious! It's not like you've got a wife and kids back home or anything. Now that would be a big lie– the kind you don't get over. But having a good job? Owning a business? Um, yeah. I'd be okay if someone admitted that to me."

"I'm sure Jeff would love to hear you say that," he teased. "Speaking of my brother-in-law, when's he going to get home?"

"Any minute. And don't worry, I gave him the head's up on this whole crazy relationship thing."

"Levi? You awake?"

The house was pitch-black and everyone had gone to bed about an hour ago, but Levi had been staring at the ceiling ever since. He was on the floor, and Willow was on the sofa beside him. Her soft whisper made him practically jump right out of his sleeping bag.

"Yeah," he whispered. "You okay?"

"Yeah. I'm having a little trouble sleeping."

Join the club.

Sitting up, he focused on her. It took a minute for his eyes to adjust, but then...there she was. "Do you need more pillows? Blankets?"

But she shook her head as she propped herself up on her elbow. "I wanted to thank you."

"Really? For what?"

"For introducing me to your family. This has been a really good day." She let out a soft hum that sounded far sexier than Levi imagined she meant it to. "I wish we didn't have to rush out of here in the morning."

"Well, we need to stay on schedule to get to your grandmother's, right?"

"I know." She paused and yawned. "But I had a lot of fun tonight. Your nieces are so sweet."

"And they loved you. Seriously, Willow, you were great with them."

"Can I tell you a secret?"

"Sure."

"One of the reasons I don't want to go into psychology is because..." She sighed. "I studied child psychology, and it made me really sad."

"Sad? Why?"

"I love kids. Like...I know I said earlier that I had no idea what I wanted to be or do with my life, but I really love working with kids. Just...not to analyze them. I hate to see a child in pain—physically or emotionally."

"I imagine that would be rough."

"But the thought of teaching them or playing around and making them laugh? That's something I could really get on board with."

"Willow, that's amazing. Why not go into teaching? Or...or...being like a nanny or something? The way you were today with Livvy was a bit on the Mary Poppins side."

She let out a low laugh before changing the subject on him. "Tell me about the sister we're staying with tomorrow."

"Katie." Leaning over slightly, he rested his arm on the couch. "She's the oldest; married to Aaron for about a dozen years. My nephew Brandon is their only child. He's ten and a total riot. I don't think he's into Disney songs, but he is all about sports. The kid is crazy gifted in baseball. Katie said she thinks he's on track to go pro."

"At ten years old? Seriously?"

He couldn't help but laugh quietly. "It seems weird to me too. I mean, a lot can happen between now and when he's eighteen. But they are doing everything they can to keep him on track. You know, as long as he continues to have an interest in it."

"Wow."

"I know." He was about to say more when he felt Willow's hand gently glide over his. His throat went dry, and he wasn't sure if he should acknowledge it at all. Then she wove her fingers with his and he saw her lie back down. "Any chance you know how to play ball?"

She chuckled. "Remember the gym teacher story?"

"Oh yeah," he said with a soft laugh of his own. "You think you can go to sleep now?" he whispered.

"Mm-hmm."

When he went to pull his hand away, Willow held tight.

"This is the sort of thing couples might do," she said sleepily. "We'll have to move up a level tomorrow."

Was he dreaming?

Starting to sweat?

Clearing his throat quietly, he asked, "Up a level?"

"Mm-hmm. Hand-holding will only get us so far around Gammy. She's very affectionate. She's going to expect to see us snuggling up together on the couch and kissing." A soft giggle was out before she spoke again. "I don't know what we can do about the snuggling while we're driving, but we should definitely practice kissing."

For a moment, Levi couldn't respond.

Was she fully awake?

Did she have any idea what she was saying?

"Um...sure," he said gruffly. "Yeah, uh...we can do that."

"Mmm...thank you, Levi. You're a great fake boyfriend."

And that's when he felt it. Willow's soft lips on his cheek. He closed his eyes and stayed utterly still.

"I'm sorry," she said softly, her breath warm against his cheek. "I thought you said we needed to practice."

Turning his head slightly, Levi reached up and cupped her cheek with his hand. This wasn't the way he had planned their first kiss to be, but maybe it was better that it was late and dark and...this.

"Don't apologize," he whispered.

"But...you seemed tense, like you didn't want me to kiss you."

The darkness of the room, the quiet of the house, and the soft tones of their voices made this all feel so intimate that it was hard to remember it wasn't real.

"Oh, I want you to kiss me, Willow. And I really want to kiss you."

Her voice was barely audible as she said, "Really?"

His hand moved to gently wrap around her nape as he moved in and touched his lips to hers. Kissing was something Levi loved to do-he loved the slow build, the teasing before completely sinking into it. But there was a shyness here that he never felt before, and just knowing what he did about Willow, he didn't want to take it too deep too fast and scare her off.

Little did he know that she would be the one to do it.

Yeah, one minute things were slow and a little timid, and the next she was shifting on the couch to get closer and using one of her hands to mimic his.

It would be wrong to crawl up on the sofa with her, right? To cover her body with his and just...

Willow let out a throaty hum, and the decision was made.

Levi slowly got up on his knees and cupped her face with both hands as he tilted his head and teased her tongue with his. The kiss was deep and wet and so damn good. Her arms went around him as she shifted to sit up. The darkness meant every move was a mystery, every touch was a surprise, and all of it was a turn on.

He lost track of how long they stayed like that. One kiss led to another and then another, and their touches were mostly from the shoulders up. At one point, he let his hands roam up and down her back, but he stopped before he gave in to the temptation to grab her ass and give it a gentle squeeze-something he'd been dying to do for months.

Ever since the day she fell in front of the pub and he picked her up.

When they finally broke apart, breathless and aroused-well, he hoped they were both aroused-they rested their foreheads against each other.

"Wow," she whispered. "That was..."

"Yeah. For me too."

"I don't think we'll have a hard time convincing Gammy or anyone for that matter that we're dating."

Swallowing hard, he gently argued, "Well, that doesn't mean we shouldn't keep practicing just to be sure."

"True," she said, her nails slowly raking through his hair.

"Plus, it's really dark in here. It could be quite different with the lights on."

"Oh...I hadn't thought of that."

"You know what that means, don't you?" he quietly teased, wanting badly to dive back in for another taste of her lips.

"What?" There was wonder in her voice and Levi could imagine her eyes going wide.

"It means tomorrow we'll have to be sure to try this again in the light of day. Will that be okay?"

Her laugh was the sweetest sound as she rubbed up against him a little and playfully nudged his nose with hers. "Does that mean we have to stop now?"

"Hell no." Then they were done talking for a while.

6

"Maybe you should ring the doorbell again."

"Willow, I rang it four times. She's not here."

Yeah, that was becoming more and more obvious, she thought. There were no cars in the driveway, no one was answering the door, and...well...that was it.

"What do we do now?" It was a stupid question to ask considering Levi had his phone up to his ear. With nothing to do, she took a few steps away to give him some privacy and thought about all the things she'd learned about Levi today.

They had only gotten halfway through their thirty-six questions yesterday–mainly because they were both easily distracted by the things they were seeing while driving. After saying goodbye to Natalie, Jeff, and the girls–and belting out a lively rendition of *"Never Had a Friend Like Me"*–they got on the road. They had hit some minor traffic and instantly held hands and it was something she was enjoying more and more.

But not as much as the kissing.

Oh, good Lord, the kissing.

In all her wildest fantasies about what it would be like to be with Levi, nothing prepared her for the reality. His kiss was all-consuming and positively panty-melting.

And if they hadn't been in his sister's living room in the middle of the night, she would have totally jumped him.

Repeatedly.

Okay, think of something different before you embarrass yourself in the middle of his other sister's front yard.

Once they had gotten back on I-95, she had asked him to sing with her, but he declined, so she decided they'd go back to their falling in love list of questions.

They had settled in and Willow found out if Levi could talk to anyone in heaven, it would be his maternal grandfather. They used to hang out together all the time, and he had passed away two years ago.

His celebrity BFF would be The Rock; something she didn't see coming at all. Ryan Reynolds was his second choice.

And one she could completely get on board with.

The most childish thing he still loved to do was watch Bugs Bunny cartoons. Or any of the old Saturday morning cartoons. She had to agree with him that they were all awesome and she wouldn't mind a good cartoon marathon sometime.

As for her, she'd love to talk to her Nana Ruth. She died when Willow was fifteen, but they used to have so much fun together. She was very artsy and was always painting pictures and redecorating her house. It was always a surprise going over there and seeing what was going to be different.

It was the reason she had redecorated her childhood bedroom a dozen times before moving out when she was eighteen.

Her celebrity BFF was the same one she would have lunch with–Anna Kendrick. Levi didn't even ask her to expand upon that.

As for the most childish thing...well...it was watching all the Christmas specials every year during the holidays. Not the new ones. The old ones. The classics. The cartoon Grinch, Frosty the Snowman, Charlie Brown, and all the Claymation specials. It just wasn't Christmas without them.

"You could have called, Kate," she heard Levi saying. "Yeah, I realize it couldn't be helped, but we would have made other arrangements." He paused. "I didn't say I thought I was king or that I expected you to wait on me!" More pausing. "None of this matters and I'm not trying to pick a fight with you. Willow and I will just go to a hotel. It's fine."

Okay, so we aren't staying here tonight.

"What's the code?"

And...yes, we are.

Willow watched as Levi punched the code in on the door panel and then opened it.

Who needs to leave their spare key in a fake-looking rock when you have technology?

"Thanks, Katie," he was saying as she stepped in behind him. "I appreciate it." He paused. "Of course, I promise!" Another pause. "One time! One time I left a wet towel on the floor when I stayed here. Let it go!" He groaned. "And you wonder why I don't visit more often." Then he laughed. "Love you too. Tell Aaron I hope his mom feels better."

When he hung up and slid his phone into his pocket, she could tell he was more than a little twitchy.

"Everything okay?"

Raking a hand through his hair, Levi sighed loudly. "Yeah. They had to leave town unexpectedly."

"So...family emergency?"

He raked a hand through his hair. "Yeah. Aaron's mom fell. She lives in Atlanta, which is almost four hours away, so they're staying there tonight."

All she could do was nod.

"She left food for us in the refrigerator, and there's always takeout, so..."

It was early yet, and she was tempted to say they should just get back in the car and keep driving, but...

She remembered her conversation with him from late last night.

They still had a whole lot of practicing being...close to one another to master. And hopefully that included a whole lot of getting close and kissing. And touching. And...wherever else that may lead.

There are worse ways to spend an evening...

Of course, there was no way for her to blurt out, "Oh, hey...since we're alone in the house, want to make out?"

And boy oh boy, did she want to make out with Levi.

Oh, God. Do people even say make out anymore?

Besides him being an incredibly nice guy who loved his family, he was funny, a great conversationalist, and he had amazing hands.

"You okay, Willow? You look a little flushed." Levi looked around. "It is a little warm in here. Let me check the thermostat and see what's going on." And he walked away before she could comment.

Alone with her thoughts again, she had to wonder how to broach the subject of...making out.

Should she just politely ask him to kiss her? Go up and kiss him on the cheek to thank him for getting them through another day of driving?

Or you can just grab his face and kiss him.

Just like you did last night.

Yeah. That one would require a level of boldness she just didn't have.

Mainly because it was still broad daylight out.

Last night she felt bold because she couldn't really see him and he couldn't see her. If he was shocked or repulsed by her actions, she couldn't see his face to know. There was something empowering about the whole cover of darkness thing. But in the light of day, she was way more uncertain of herself and wasn't quite sure what she was supposed to do.

"I'll go put your bags in the guest room," he said with a smile as he walked by.

Maybe I could be a little bold...

Staring at his denim-clad butt had her sighing with appreciation because Levi had a fine butt. Something she hadn't noticed until a few weeks ago. Most of the time they were around each other, they were in the pub, and he was usually behind the bar. Once he had offered to be her fake boyfriend, and they started spending time together, Willow found she was noticing all kinds of things about him.

Like his butt.

It was amazing what some good lighting could do.

Oh, that reminds me...

"Hey, Levi?" she called out, following him down the hall where he went.

"Yeah?"

"So, I was thinking about the pub."

"McGee's?"

"Yeah."

"What about it?"

"The lighting."

He put her bags down next to a bed that was so high she was going to need a step stool to get in it. Her eyes went wide before the sound of Levi clearing his throat distracted her.

"Right, the lighting. I think if the pub took on a more rustic chic vibe, using the mason jar lights could really make a great impact. You do a trio of them over each table with soft light bulbs, and I think it would be amazing!"

With a low chuckle, Levi shook his head and walked out of the room. "You seem to have an obsession with the lighting at McGee's, Willow. Why is that?"

She trailed after him and had to think about it. He had a point; she did seem to spend a ridiculous amount of time thinking about the interior of the place. That was...new, but somehow very comfortable.

"I think it's because of Nana Ruth," she said and then plowed into his back when he stopped in his tracks.

"Nana Ruth? Your grandmother who died when you were fifteen?"

She nodded. "Remember when I told you how she was artsy and always redecorating?"

"Yeah..."

"Maybe I take after her? Maybe I just never had a muse before."

"The pub is your muse?"

Shrugging, she said, "I guess. I don't know how that all works. Are there rules as to what can be a person's muse?"

He took her by the hand and led her into the living room. This house was much different from Natalie's. Where Natalie's was cozy and very well lived in, this house was a little more like something out of a decorating magazine.

A boring one, but...she supposed it could be considered a classic décor.

"Why are you making that face?" he asked, and she groaned.

"Sorry. I was looking around and thinking about how different this is than your other sister's house."

"Yeah, Katie is a bit of a Type A personality and likes everything to be crisp and clean and..."

"White?"

He laughed. "Exactly."

The kitchen was white, the living room furniture was white, the walls were white...it was a little blinding.

"She must go crazy when she goes to Nat's place?"

"Believe it or not, they don't do that very often. We do family trips and meet at either a central location or everyone goes to my parents' place." He shrugged. "More often than not, it's at mom and dad's. They've got the biggest house with enough bedrooms for everyone. Well, almost everyone. Since I live close by, I just go home at night and either Brandon or the girls sleep in my old room."

"Does it bother you? Not being able to be there when everyone's visiting?"

His bark of laughter had her jumping. "Are you kidding? I get to escape at the end of the day! I usually look forward to going home. Although..."

"Although...?"

"I work so much that the reason I'm usually leaving is that I have to get to the pub. Sometimes I feel like I'm missing out, but most of the time I'm exhausted from chasing the kids around all day."

She frowned. "Why are you chasing them?"

"Because I'm fun Uncle Levi," he stated like it was obvious. "They want me to run around with them or play ball or just...play. My mom tells me she loves when I show up because I'll be guaranteed to exhaust them and they sleep better."

"Aww...that's kind of sweet."

"Well...I do what I can." He winked at her and she got a little swoony.

Slowly, she reached out and placed her hand on his knee. He didn't seem to mind, and she figured this was a start. "So, you're good with your nieces and nephews. Does that mean you want kids of your own someday?"

His eyes went a little wide, and she was quick to explain herself.

"You know...the questions. Well, not exactly the questions we've been using, but...it's just another fact I thought a girlfriend would know. You don't have to answer. Really. It's okay." She let out a huff of breath. "Some people don't mind other people's children but don't want any for themselves. It's not a big deal. I always babysat when I was younger and it was fun, but I didn't start getting the...you know, the *feeling* that I wanted them until recently. I mean, I'm not getting any younger, and I guess my biological clock is starting. Maybe I'm a little young for that and maybe that's not it at all. Hmm...maybe I should consider working for a preschool or a daycare or doing that nanny thing full time. Or...get a dog of my own. Maybe that would pacify my maternal instinct. *Oh my goodness!* I said pacify! Like a baby pacifier!" Her hands immediately flew up to cover her face, and she groaned. "Don't mind me. I think I'm just tired and rambling."

Floor? Please open up and swallow me now!

Maybe if I sit here long enough covering my face, he'll just walk away...

Willow was really freaking adorable when she was all rambling and embarrassed.

Not that Levi was going to mention that. He had a feeling she wouldn't appreciate the observation at all. But still, it was something about her that he was finding endearing.

It took a solid two minutes for her to peek at him through her fingers and all he could do was wave and smile.

And that broke the tension.

"In answer to your question," he replied as if she had never yammered on about biological clocks and pacifiers and dogs, "I definitely want kids of my own someday. That's always been part of the plan."

"Plan? You have a plan?" she asked and then groaned. "Of course you have a plan. You just said that." She mumbled something that sounded a lot like "Stupid Willow" and that he couldn't stand for.

"Hey," he began, placing his hand on her knee. "What's going on? You seem very nervous today. Did I do something wrong?"

"Kiss me."

"Um...wha...?" But he never got to finish because Willow had cupped his face in her hands and cut off his words with a kiss.

Words could wait, right?"

They were all alone and even though this was his sister's house, no one was going to interrupt them. Clasping Willow's hips, he hauled her into his lap until she was straddling him and then took control of the kiss.

This was what he wanted to do last night.

Hell, this was what he wanted to do all damn day, but they had a schedule to keep so they could get to her grandmother's.

But now that they were alone and there was no one around to distract them, he was more than willing to get to know her a little better.

Okay, a lot better.

Her hands raked up into his hair as she leaned forward and pressed her breasts against him. It was good to know that he wasn't the only one with fooling around on the brain.

They were both a little crazed and needy. Last night had been about slowly exploring–at least for the first minute–but this was...well, there was nothing slow about it. Hands roamed and groped, and their kisses turned a little wet and messy, but it was still freaking awesome.

Levi broke the kiss because he wanted to explore more of her. He gently bit her earlobe before letting his mouth travel down the slender column of her throat. She smelled like sunshine and felt so damn soft and warm that he couldn't decide where he wanted his hands or mouth to settle. She was a feast that was wrapped around him and he wanted all of her.

"Levi?" she said breathlessly.

"Yeah?" he said between light kisses along her collarbone.

"I...I don't think we'll have to be this...demonstrative in front of Gammy, but...oh, that's good." Her head fell back slightly. "I think...we're doing...just fine and...ooh, bite that spot again...totally believable."

And it was like a bucket of cold water being thrown on them.

This wasn't real.

At least...not to her. To Willow, they were just practicing–playing a part so they could fool her family and give them one less thing to criticize her for.

And to not worry her grandmother.

Well...shit.

His hands gently rested on her waist and he gave a little push to put some distance between them.

"Levi?"

He saw the confusion on her face and didn't want to come off as sounding all butt-hurt because he lost sight of what they were doing.

Or rather, what they were supposed to be doing.

She reluctantly climbed off his lap even as she continued to stare at him. "Are you okay?"

"What? Oh, yeah. I'm fine. You were right, I don't think we'll have any problem convincing your grandmother about our relationship. We'll be fine." Standing, he turned his back to her and quickly adjusted the growing erection in his jeans until he hoped it wasn't too noticeable. "So what should we do for the rest of the day? Since Katie isn't here, I'm not sure whether we should eat the food she prepared or maybe go out someplace?"

She blinked up at him several times as if not quite understanding what he was saying.

"Or we can get back in the car and keep driving," he suggested. "I still don't think we should knock on your grandmother's door at ten tonight, but we can get even closer if you're interested."

"You don't want to stay here tonight?"

"I didn't say that."

"You...you want to keep driving?"

"I just thought..."

Scrambling off the couch, Willow walked into the kitchen and started pacing, and Levi had no choice but to follow her.

"I'm just giving us some options."

"Really? Because it sounds a lot like you don't want to be alone with me."

"Seriously? And you think my solution to that would be to get us back in the confines of the car with only inches between us?"

Again, she just blinked at him for several long moments. "So I don't express myself well! *Gah!* What do you expect? You kiss me until I'm stupid, and then you expect me to be able to form a coherent thought or even full sentences?" She let out a cute little growl as she continued to pace. "Maybe other girls you've gone out with are more mature or more...more...I don't know...maybe they don't get all stupid and floopy over a kiss, but I do! At least, I do now! I never did before, there? Are you happy? God, why are you badgering me?" Then she took off down the hall to the guest room.

And again, he followed.

He found her in the room talking to herself and he leaned against the doorjamb until there was a break in her one-woman conversation.

It took almost five minutes.

"I think there's been some sort of misunderstanding here—or, at the very least, some confusion."

Clumsily, she climbed up on the bed and stared at him.

Cautiously, Levi stepped into the room. "I was under the impression that you just wanted us to practice...you know...kissing so that if we had to do it in front of your family that we'd be comfortable with each other and believable," he began carefully. "But that wasn't why I was kissing you, Willow, and once you reminded me of why we were doing what we were doing, I...I took the hint and backed off. I really hope I didn't offend you or freak you out. And if I did, I'm sorry, and I promise to keep to just hand holding once we get to your grandmother's place."

"Wait...you wanted to kiss me?"

He nodded.

"And not just for practice?"

Now he shook his head.

She nibbled on her bottom lip as she seemed to consider his words.

Or...his wordless responses to her questions.

"What if...what if I said that I wanted to kiss you too? And not just for research purposes?"

Could he really be this lucky?

Taking another step closer to her, he grinned. "Then I'd have to ask if you mind if I sit beside you on the bed and pick up where we left off."

She let out the most feminine giggle he had ever heard, even as she scooted back on the bed and patted the space next to her.

Crawling up on the bed, he took her in his arms and gently lay back on the mattress with her, and it was so much better than the sofa or Natalie's floor.

There was something slightly comical about this whole thing—it was like being a teenager back in high school where it felt forbidden to be making out with a girl on a bed. Although there was no fear of his parents or hers coming home and surprising them, there were enough similarities that it made him smile.

Willow pulled back and looked at him. "What's so funny?"

"Nothing. Why?" he murmured, leaning in to kiss her throat.

"You were smirking." The words came out, but she was arching to give him better access to her skin.

"I was just thinking...this was a lot like...being in high school."

She laughed even as she rolled to pull him on top of her. "How often did you get lucky like this in high school?"

Instead of answering right away, he gave her a very thorough kiss. Lifting his head, he said, "I never got lucky like this. No other girl compares to you."

Ugh...way to sound creepy and a little...intense.

Luckily Willow didn't comment on it and cupped his head and steered him back in for another kiss.

And another.

And so many others.

The next time Levi noticed anything, the room was dark. Glancing at the bedside clock, he saw it was almost eight. Reluctantly, he rolled away from her and sat up. "Wasn't it just barely five a few minutes ago?"

With a soft laugh, Willow sat up and attempted to smooth her hair. "That's what I thought." Her stomach growled loudly, and she groaned. "Oh, my God...I'm sorry."

"For what? Being human?" Jumping off the bed, he held out a hand to her and helped her down. "Come on. I'm starving too."

And not really for food...

"Let's see what Katie left for us. Or we can get something delivered. It's up to you."

"Why don't we see what she made and then decide."

"Smart girl."

Her hearty laugh was infectious, and once she calmed down, she said, "I'm not so sure about that. After all, who invites someone they barely know on a weeklong trip to hang out with her family while pretending to be her girlfriend?"

Levi hauled her in close and kissed her soundly. "A really smart girl."

7

"Quick! What're three things we have in common?"

They were less than fifteen minutes away from Gammy's house and Willow was starting to panic. Their thirty-six questions had gone out the window yesterday, and now she was afraid her family was going to look at them and know this was all a sham.

Unless they asked her to make out with Levi.

But somehow, she didn't think she'd get that lucky.

Just like she didn't get lucky last night.

After kissing and touching for hours, they had eaten the rotisserie chicken and salads Katie had left for them, then watched some re-runs of *Friends*. At eleven, Willow had gone and taken a shower and was totally prepared for Levi to join her in bed and take things to the next level, but he had turned her down.

Sweetly, but turned her down nonetheless.

She had stared at the ceiling for hours and tried not to take it personally. His theory was that he didn't want to make love to her in his sister's house, and she had to admit, once he put that out there, he had a point.

Not that it made her feel better.

And neither did the cold shower she took this morning.

Levi had mentioned having to do the same, but...well, that one made her feel a bit better, but only marginally.

He was holding her hand and driving at a very leisurely pace. Grinning at her, he asked, "Three things, huh?"

Forcing images of Levi naked in the shower from her mind, Willow nodded. "Yup."

"Okay, we both like kids."

"You should probably avoid mentioning that if anyone asks."

"Why?"

"Because I have a feeling that will have my family–especially Gammy–pushing for you to put a ring on my finger."

Ugh...why did I just say that?

Open mouth, insert foot...

"Gotcha," he said, interrupting her thoughts. "So...we both love sushi, have similar taste in music and movies, and share a love of baked goods." He glanced toward the coolers in the backseat. "Speaking of, are there any brownies left?"

"Hmm...I think only one."

"Any chance I can have it before we get to your grandmother's place?"

"Seriously? It's barely lunchtime!"

"Don't worry. I won't spoil my appetite." Winking, he continued to smile, and she knew she couldn't say no to him.

Too bad he didn't have the same problem with you...

Twisting in her seat, she grabbed the cooler and pulled out the last brownie and decided she might as well be a total glutton for punishment and fed it to him.

Piece by piece.

And he licked her fingers with each bite.

It would be wrong to ask him to pull over, right?

Beside her, Levi let out one of those low, sexy laughs. "I can totally read your mind, Willow. And if we hadn't promised your grandmother that we'd be there for lunch, I would be totally open for a detour."

She wanted to fan herself.

Or put the icepack from the cooler down her pants.

The GPS noted how they were three miles from their destination and for the first time since this whole crazy charade started, she wasn't looking forward to seeing Gammy. What she was looking forward to seeing was Levi.

Naked.

And sweaty.

And possibly handcuffed to her bed.

Gasping, her hands flew to her mouth as if she said that out loud.

"You okay?" he asked, concerned.

"What? Oh...yeah. I just realized..." *That I have a very dirty mind.* "I realized I forgot the birthday card I had bought for Gammy."

Lame, Willow. Very lame.

"Do you want to stop at the store and grab one?"

"Uh...no. It's okay. Really. I have the gift, and I can just mail her the card when I get home."

He didn't look like he quite believed her, but luckily he didn't push her on it. Instead, they drove the rest of the way in silence. Once they pulled into Gammy's neighborhood and turned onto her block, all of her nerves threatened to bubble to the surface. Her breathing got a little shaky, and she immediately began smoothing her hair and her shirt and her jeans and...

The car stopped moving and Willow looked around and noticed they weren't in Gammy's driveway.

"This isn't the right house."

"Yeah, I know, but you're kind of freaking out over there, so I figured you maybe needed a minute to calm down before we actually go to the right one."

"Oh, well..."

That was incredibly sweet.

How was it that Levi was so in tune with her? Little things that she didn't think anyone ever noticed about her, he did.

Okay, don't think about that now too or you'll officially break into the mother of all anxiety attacks!

Easier said than done.

"I just...I need a minute."

He turned to face her and took both her hands in his. "What's upsetting you? You've been fine until now."

"What if this doesn't work? What if they know we're lying? What if they all figure out I'm just a fraud who had to ask a friend to pretend to date her because I'm so pathetic and undatable?"

His blue eyes went wide. "Undatable? Willow, what the hell are you talking about?"

Why did I have to open this particular can of worms now?

Letting out a weary sigh, she looked up at him. "Levi, I realize we haven't known one another very long, but...did you ever see me with a guy on Friday nights?"

"Well, no. But that doesn't mean you're undatable. I just thought Friday nights were girls' night."

"Yeah, no," she replied. "I haven't had a proper date in over six months and most of my relationships end because... I'm the girl everyone is friends with–the girl who guys date to pass the time until they can date the girl they really wanted in the first place."

"How is that even possible?"

"It's happened more times than I can to admit."

"Wow."

She nodded. "I know. And the thing is, most of the time, I knew it. Like I could tell they weren't super interested, but I figured that would change over time." She paused. "It never did."

"Why would you keep doing that to yourself? Didn't you see the signs? Any red flags?"

She looked at him sadly. "Levi, I'm like a red flag factory. Trust me." Groaning, she hung her head. "And now you probably wish you never signed on for any of this."

Kissing her hands, he simply did what Levi did best.

He smiled and made sure she was okay.

"For your information, I do not regret for one minute any of this. I have loved getting to know you, and the last two days have been a blast." Another kiss to her hands. "Now let's go get some time with your grandmother before your parents show up. That's what you wanted most, right?"

Well, that and an orgasm or two last night would have been nice, but...

"Yeah," she said instead. "Definitely."

"You sure you're good to go? Because if you need a few more minutes, we can do that too."

"Nope." She shook her head. "We've driven all this way, let's go and do this."

Levi straightened and drove them the rest of the way—all five houses worth—to her grandmother's. Gammy was walking out the front door grinning from ear to ear before the car even came to a complete stop.

Smiling, Levi looked at her. "Showtime!"

"And then there was the time when Willow bell and I went to Colonial Williamsburg and dressed up and learned how to make soap!" Gammy laughed and looked over at Levi. "Have you ever been there, Levi?"

"Um...once. In my senior year of high school we took a class trip there along with Busch Gardens."

"Oh, what fun! I bet that was a wild time for your chaperones!" Gammy said.

And yeah, she had insisted on him calling her Gammy.

Which just felt weird.

He was a grown man, and that was the kind of endearment that...well, that a grown man shouldn't use.

Especially one who just met her.

"Where did you go on your senior trip, Willow?" Gammy asked as she rose from the dining room table to get them more food.

Because clearly the platter of sandwiches along with potato salad, coleslaw, macaroni salad, chips, carrots and celery, and sweet tea wasn't enough.

I probably shouldn't have eaten that brownie...

Or licked the icing from Willow's fingers...

"We went to Niagara Falls," Willow said, smiling. "It was so much fun. I have a picture of a group of us straddling the line between the US and Canada somewhere. I never thought about going back or anything, but we definitely had a good time."

"I bet you did," Gammy said, placing a plate of cookies on the table before sitting down again. "So, Levi, Willow tells me you're a bartender."

He nodded.

"What's your specialty?"

"I don't really have one," he said lamely. "It's a pub, so it's a lot of basic stuff. Nothing too fancy. It's not that kind of clientele."

Willow frowned at him. "We were talking about that on our way here," she said. "The people that go to McGee's aren't the college crowd, but they're not the kind that hangs out at wine bars either. Still, there is a massive collection of beers they serve."

"I never acquired a taste for beer," Gammy said. "Give me a good Old Fashioned or just some vodka neat and I am a happy woman." She winked. "The bartender at the country club makes the best Old Fashioned I've ever had. You'll have to try it at the party, Levi."

He nodded again but didn't want to admit that he wasn't a big whiskey drinker. Honestly, he wasn't much of an alcohol drinker, period. He enjoyed all kinds of beers, but...that was it.

Probably not the smartest thing a pub owner can admit.

So he didn't.

"What about you, Willow bell? You still drinking your rum and pineapple?"

Reaching for a cookie, Willow nodded. "I am. And Levi makes it just the way I like it-the perfect ratio of rum to pineapple. Totally yummy."

"Yes, he is!"

"Gammy! Behave!"

"What? You think I don't appreciate a handsome young man just because I'm 75?" Gammy winked at him. "You'll fit in nicely with the Romeos. They're going to take you to lunch tomorrow while Willow and I go get our nails done."

"Um...what? Who am I going out with?"

"The Romeos," Gammy repeated like he had no reason to question her.

"And they are...?" he prompted.

"They're a group of wonderful men who live here in the community."

"And they're called the Romeos because...they're single and date a lot?" He glanced at Willow for help, but she was trying not to laugh while eating her cookie.

Gammy considered him for a moment. "Now that would be a much more interesting way to describe them, but Romeo stands for Retired Old Men Who Eat Out."

He thought about that for a minute. "But wouldn't that spell..."

Willow held up a hand to stop him. "Don't waste your time. It's what they call themselves, even if it's not what it spells."

"When they talk about themselves," Gammy explained, "they say retired old men eat out. But I'm a retired English teacher, and it just sounded wrong to me. I'm probably the only one who adds the 'who', but I can't help it. You can ask them about it when you have lunch with them tomorrow. They're very excited to meet you." She laughed with glee. "I think they're just excited to have such a handsome young man join them—like you'll improve their image."

"Gammy! Don't let them use Levi like that!"

"And what would you have me to, Willow? It's not like Levi can come and get pedicures with us!"

"Men get pedicures all the time," Willow challenged.

"Not this man," he murmured, unsure which of his options were the lesser of two evils.

"Nonsense. Levi is going to go to lunch with the boys. Your father may go too. I thought it would be nice if we invited your mother to join us at the spa."

He tuned out after that because he felt like he might break out in the same kind of panic attack Willow had earlier in the car. Not only was he going to be forced to go out to eat with a group of retired old guys–and complete strangers–but he was going to have to deal with Willow's father too? This wasn't part of the plan! They hadn't prepared for this kind of scenario. They were supposed to be together at all times–projecting a united front! Now what was he supposed to do?

As if sensing his internal freakout, Willow reached under the table and squeezed his knee. It was only mildly reassuring, and he couldn't wait to get her alone so they could figure out how to get him out of Gammy's plans.

"Oh, my goodness! It's time for Shirley and me to go get the mail," Gammy said as she stood. "Willow, why don't you and Levi get settled, and I'll be back in around thirty minutes, okay?"

Willow stood and began clearing the table. "No problem. Take your time."

With nothing else to do, Levi stood and helped her clear the rest of their lunch stuff, and once Gammy was out the door, he stopped. "We need to talk."

She sighed loudly. "Yeah, I know. She mentioned sending you out with the Romeos, but I didn't think she was serious. I'm sure we can get you out of it."

"How? It's not like I'm going to fake a headache or anything like that."

"Lunch won't be so bad–probably only an hour of your time. And all the restaurants in the town square are amazing. See if you can get them to take you to the kosher deli. The food is so good!"

"This isn't about the food choices," he commented.

"What am I supposed to talk about with a group of old guys?"

She put the last of the dishes in the dishwasher and straightened. "I don't see why this is bothering you so much. You're a bartender, Levi. Talking to strangers is in your job description."

"Yeah, but...I talk to them for the amount of time it takes to make a drink, I don't sit down and share a meal with them!"

"Okay, I didn't think of that..."

"And then there's your father getting thrown into the mix."

She waved him off. "He'll be so busy psycho-analyzing everyone in the group that he won't have much time to focus on you. If he even goes." She was walking across the room and toward where their luggage sat by the front door before he could respond.

The house was small–some would say cozy–but most of it was just one open space. Gammy's bedroom was off one side of the kitchen and he guessed the guest rooms were on the opposite side. Following Willow, Levi walked over and grabbed the rest of their bags and followed her to the...

Only other bedroom.

As in...one room.

One bed.

"Um...Willow?"

"Hmm?"

"Is there another room that I'm just not seeing?"

"Nope. Just this one. Why?"

She didn't seem the least bit bothered by this, and then he realized why should she? She had to have known about this from the moment they started making plans to come here together. Was it possible that she...was interested in sleeping with him *before* the whole fake relationship thing?

"Actually, I tried to talk Gammy out of this," she explained, interrupting his thoughts. "She thought she was doing me a favor by not having a problem with us sleeping together. I told her it wasn't necessary, but...well...you can probably tell already how she can be."

Okay, she was not *interested in sleeping with me...*

Kind of a hit to the ego, but...whatever.

"Anyway, if it bothers you, we can trade-off—I'll sleep on the floor one night, you sleep on the floor another. Unless you have a better idea."

Yes, for us to both be in the bed and naked.

"I think we can handle sharing the bed," he said, hoping he sounded casual. Taking a step closer to her, he put the bags down and kept moving until he was directly behind her. Slowly he reached out and put his hands on her hips and whispered in her ear. "We almost shared a bed last night."

Tilting her head, she hummed softly. "But someone turned me down. I took that to mean you weren't interested."

Turning her, Levi saw just a hint of hurt and uncertainty there and knew he needed to reiterate all the things they talked about last night. "Willow, me turning you down last night had absolutely nothing to do with you and everything about feeling weird about being in my sister's house." His hands rested on her hips again, gently kneading them. "I want you; you have to know that. But I'm not going to take advantage of our situation. And trust me, with your grandmother essentially across the hall from us..."

"Her room is on the other side of the house," she

explained and then grinned. "And she's a little hard of hearing, so…"

"Willow…"

"Okay, I know what you're saying, and as much as I hate to admit it, I agree. It's weird. This isn't the time or the place for anything to happen between us." She nibbled on her bottom lip–something he loved seeing. "But that doesn't mean I'm happy about it."

"Believe me, I feel the same way."

"Really?"

"I do," he said, reaching up to caress her cheek. "But just in case you need a little more convincing, let me show you." Leaning forward, Levi captured her lips with his and poured everything he had into kissing her. It probably wasn't the smartest thing to do, considering her grandmother wouldn't be gone long, but it was important for him to show her how desirable she was and how much he wanted her.

In the back of his mind, Levi knew the next few nights were going to be torture–to lie in bed with Willow and not make love to her, but…they could possibly change their plans for the trip home. Originally, they figured they'd stick to the same accommodations they used on the way down to Florida and stay with his sisters. But now? Now he was going to book them at a couple of hotels along the way and see about dragging out their road trip a little longer.

Whoa…getting a little ahead of yourself, aren't you?

Levi really wished his inner voice would shut the hell up.

"Yoo-hoo! I'm back!" Gammy called out. "Turns out, Shirley went to the post office earlier with Dorothy! So I'll just go tomorrow while we're out!"

Reluctantly, Levi lifted his head and saw Willow shaking hers. "She's going to be a handful. I just know it."

"Oh, there you two are! Oops! Am I interrupting?"

Willow took a step back and Levi's hands dropped to his side. "No, you're fine, Gammy," she said.

"Well, just so you know, there are condoms in the linen closet."

"Gammy!"

"What? I told you weeks ago, Willow bell, I'm not a prude. I always keep them in the house." Then she winked at Levi. "You never know when they're going to come in handy."

"Shoot me now," Willow murmured, hiding her face in her hands.

"Oh, stop. You're a big girl now and talking about sex shouldn't embarrass you." Shaking her head, Gammy continued to explain things that no one wanted her to. "Sweetie, you might not believe this, but I keep them in the house for me too."

All Willow did was groan.

"Not that there's any chance of me getting pregnant." She laughed heartily. "Heaven forbid! But did you know, Levi, that retirement communities have some of the highest STD rates in the country?"

He choked a little as he shook his head. "Uh...no. I wasn't aware of that."

"True story! I'm telling you, there are a lot of swinging singles here, and they all thought since the threat of pregnancy was gone that they were safe. No one gave a thought to how often or how many different partners they were going to have or that we aren't too old to get syphilis or chlamydia!" She shuddered dramatically. "I had a very dear friend who..."

"Gammy, please," Willow plead. "I don't think Levi needs to hear about the sex lives of your friends. And honestly, neither do I."

"Oh, poo. You're no fun." She turned to walk out of the room but turned around at the threshold. "Just remember, condoms in the closet. Tootles!" Closing the door behind her, they could both hear Gammy's laugh.

"So like I said...she can be a handful," Willow said wearily, sitting down on the bed.

Moving beside her, Levi laughed. "That was a definite first for me. Neither of my grandmothers ever openly talked about sex in front of anyone—not just me. I always considered them to be asexual. But your grandmother really just... I mean...I never..."

Patting his leg, Willow rested her head on his shoulder. "You'll be traumatized a few more times before we leave. Trust me."

8

"You two have a good night! There are clean sheets on the bed, but...don't worry about dirtying them up! Nighty-night!"

Willow quickly closed the door–and locked it–before leaning against it with a weary sigh. "I am so sorry."

Levi was taking all the decorative pillows off the bed while laughing quietly. "She's a pistol, that's for sure."

"I didn't think she was ever going to let us go to bed!" Pushing away from the door, she helped him with the rest of the pillows and then with pulling the comforter down. "I know we didn't discuss this but, which side of the bed do you prefer?"

"Prefer?"

"Yeah, when you're home and in your own bed, which side do you sleep on?"

"I sleep in the middle."

"Okay, no preference then." She walked around to the opposite side where he was standing and climbed onto the bed. "I sleep on the right side. I hope that's okay."

His smile was slow and sweet. "It's totally fine."

They had each taken turns showering and getting ready for bed almost two hours ago, so there was nothing else to do but...get in the bed. Willow felt mildly self-conscious, but considering Levi had seen her in her pajamas for the last two nights, she was okay with that. It was the fact that he was going to be sharing a bed and blankets with her that was mildly freaking her out.

Do I snore?

Talk in my sleep?

Thrash around and throat punch?

Oh, God! Why would I even put that thought out there?

Levi was wearing a pair of athletic shorts and a t-shirt like he had the previous nights, but when he walked around to the other side of the bed, his hands went to the hem of his shirt.

"Um...what are you doing?" she demanded.

"Just...taking my shirt off. It's a little warm in here."

Relaxing slightly, she replied, "Yeah, Gammy doesn't believe in using the air conditioning to its full potential. I can go adjust the thermostat." Jumping from the bed, Willow left the room and did just that. No doubt she'd hear about it in the morning how the house was freezing, but... she'd live.

Back in the room, a shirtless Levi greeted her from the bed, and she swore her ovaries sighed.

Down, girls...

Closing the door and locking it again, she walked around to her side of the bed and carefully slid under the blankets–all the while praying she wasn't drooling at the sight of Levi in her bed.

Because a shirtless Levi was...well...it was pretty damn fantastic.

They sat side by side, shoulder to shoulder in silence for a solid minute before Levi exhaled loudly .

"This shouldn't be awkward, right? I mean, we've known each other for months, and we've been getting...you know...closer...in the last few days. And we slept next to each other—sort of—at Nat's house." He turned his head and looked at her. "This is going to be okay."

Wordlessly, she nodded.

Smiling, he leaned in and placed a soft kiss on her lips and that made her instantly relax. Within minutes they were shifting until they were completely lying down, and it felt so good to be half-naked with him. Levi was warm and hard all over.

All. Over.

Last night when they had fooled around on the bed was nothing compared to right now.

Maybe it was because they were both barely dressed. Or maybe it was because it was still a bit forbidden for them to be doing this.

But Willow strongly believed their reaction to each other was full-throttled lust.

It was the longest foreplay possibly in the history of foreplay, and if they ever got the chance to be in a bed that wasn't owned by one of their family members, she seriously suspected that they would be out and out explosive together.

And I really hope I get to test that theory out soon!

One large hand reached up and cupped her breast, and, luckily, he was kissing her and that muffled her moan of pleasure. While she knew Gammy wouldn't be able to hear them from her room, she wouldn't put it past her to be nosy either.

Stop thinking of your grandmother, you dork! You have this incredibly sexy man in bed with you! Focus on that!

And as Levi slowly moved down her body–with both his hands and lips–all of Willow's attention went with him.

"I must say, Willow. Well done."

It was really hard to relax in the massaging chair while getting the world's greatest foot rub when all your grand-mother wanted to do was talk about sex.

The car ride over had been hell.

The only silver lining was that her mother had opted out of getting pedicures–she thought the salons were too unsanitary.

I wish I had thought of that...

"Gammy, please..."

"All I'm saying is I..." She paused and seemed to consider her words. Reaching over, she held one of Willow's hands. "Now, don't be upset with me, but..."

"But...?"

"But I was beginning to think you made him up."

Eyes wide, Willow had no idea what to say. Her mouth seemed like it was moving, but no words came out.

"You were always so vague on the phone whenever we talked about Levi, and at first, I thought you were just being shy. Then I thought you didn't want to share because the relationship was new and you didn't want to jinx it." She sighed. "But after a while, I thought he was a figment of your imagination, and honestly, I didn't want to embarrass you by calling you out on it."

Maybe I can go for a bikini wax and get away from this.

"When the two of you pulled into my driveway though,

hoo-wee! I got a glimpse of Levi and thought, what a lucky girl you are!"

Seriously, hot wax all over my crotch would be less painful...

"And his hands! Oh, my...he has the kind of large hands that you know can make you tingle in all the right places!" She shook Willow's hand excitedly. "Is he a good kisser?"

"Gams, I'm really not comfortable talking about this with you. Or anyone, really. What Levi and I have is...private."

"Sweetie, there's nothing wrong with sharing just a little bit. It's all harmless fun. I mean, I'm 75 years old. It's not like I haven't been where you are. I mean, your grandfather–God rest his soul–was a wonderful husband and a fantastic lover..."

"OH MY GOD!" her hands flew over her ears.

"Sex is a healthy part of life! I'm not asking for specifics, just a general idea. Although, I'd be lying if I said I didn't wish for you to have a fantastic sex life too. You're young and pretty and have such a curvy little body! Honestly, I wish my boobs were still..."

"Lalalalala!" Willow cried out as she stuck her fingers in her ears.

Gammy swatted at her arm. "I never would have pegged you for a prude, Willow. I have to say, I'm a little disappointed." And with a dramatic sigh, she turned her attention to the nail attendant who was massaging her feet. "That feels wonderful. Thank you."

They sat in silence for several minutes until Willow couldn't take it anymore. "Okay, Gam, here's the thing," she began carefully. "I'm just not used to...you know...talking sex with anyone other than my friends. My mother never talks about it..."

"Your mother's too uptight."

No argument there...

"You know what I'm saying. We never did this before and..."

"You never brought a sexy boyfriend here before."

"We never did this before," she repeated for emphasis. "And I'm not comfortable this."

"Would it help if I told you a little about my sex life?"

Oh, dear God...

"Remember the night I beat you at *Words With Friends* and I mentioned I was going out with Donald?"

"If I say no, can we change the subject?"

"No."

"What if I say yes? Then can we change the subject?"

"I'm ignoring you and telling my story," Gammy said stubbornly. "Now, I wouldn't say that Donald is my steady beau, but we do out together once a week, and he has been known to spend the night."

Groaning, Willow turned her head and rested it on her hand.

Again.

"Viagra is a game-changer, let me tell you."

"I really wish you wouldn't."

"But I really miss the spontaneity, you know? Sometimes it would be nice to just be able to...you know...do it whenever we wanted rather than waiting those pesky thirty minutes."

Another groan.

"One time, Donald took two pills instead of one!" She laughed joyously. "Now *that* was a memorable night!"

"Levi's an amazing kisser! And his hands are a little rough and scratchy, and I love the way they feel against my skin! And the sex is the stuff of fantasies!" Willow blurted out loudly and then noticed the entire nail salon had gone quiet.

Dammit.

Gammy gave her a knowing grin. "I knew I'd wear you down."

"Gammy..." she whined.

"The stuff of fantasies, huh? Bravo!"

"Yup. Fantasies."

Mainly because that's the only point of reference I have where sex with Levi is concerned...

"I'll say it again, Willow. Well done. I think he is absolutely perfect for you."

Okay, maybe now they could have a serious, sex-free conversation.

"How do you think he'll do around mom and dad?"

"You know I love your father like a son..."

"Gammy, he *is* your son."

"I know, so then I can say this without anyone judging," she said primly. "My son is far too rigid and snooty. I think he's going to look down on Levi because of his profession." When Willow went to comment, she held up her hand to stop her. "If your father would sit and talk to Levi first before asking about his job, you might stand a chance. But you know how he can be. He'll grill the poor boy first."

"That's what I'm afraid of."

"Although I must say, bartending does pay well. Johnny, one of the Romeos, used to be a bartender at one of the big hotels in Vegas. His place here in Florida is one of three homes he owns. There's big money in it."

"Maybe in Vegas. I'm not so sure about Long Island."

"Willow, Levi's car is brand spanking new and goes for a pretty penny. And when I talked with him last night while you were in the shower, he seems like he's doing more than okay. Did you know he's looking to buy a house?"

"Um..."

"You know what that means, don't you?"

"Um..."

"It means there could be wedding bells in your future! Oh, how exciting!"

"Um..."

"I'll have to grill the boys later at my birthday party and see if Levi happened to mention to any of them if he's planning on proposing," Gammy said seriously. "And I promise not to tell you even if I know. Something as important as that should be a surprise."

"I guess..."

Beside her, Willow knew her grandmother was still talking, but all she could think about was why Levi hadn't shared with her that he was looking to buy a house. That was a pretty big thing. In all of their pre-trip times together when they were really playing the getting to know you game, they had talked about where they lived. She had told him about her tiny apartment and how much she wished she had more space and more privacy, and all he had mentioned was how he had lived in his condo for the last five years and it was essentially one big man cave.

"Willow, you're frowning, dear. Don't do that. It will give you wrinkles. And we don't want that for our party later!"

No. I guess we don't.

"You want to make some real money, Levi, you need to

leave the island and head out to Vegas! I made a very good living tending bar in the casinos. Lots of big tippers!"

Levi nodded at Johnny and had to remember not to mention how he owned the pub. It would be wrong to admit that to anyone before he finally admitted it to Willow.

He was out to lunch with five...Romeos. They were eating at the kosher deli Willow had mentioned, and he had to admit, the food was good and the company wasn't so bad either. The old guys welcomed him like he was one of their grandsons, and he was actually having a good time. Willow had been worried all morning about it and tried to come up with excuses so he wouldn't have to go, but now that he was here, he was glad he hadn't backed out.

No doubt Willow was going to be surprised.

Willow.

She was turning him upside down and inside out, and if he didn't get her alone soon, he swore he was going to spontaneously combust. There were only so many cold showers he could take.

Sleeping beside her was...okay, it wasn't all sexy time and touching.

It turns out that when in a bed, Willow tends to sleep diagonally. He woke up that morning holding onto the edge of the bed for dear life. And she hummed in her sleep. Some of it was just tuneless hums, others were more...erotic sounding.

And he seriously hoped those were because she was dreaming of him.

Mainly because whenever he did manage to sleep last night, Levi sure as hell had dreamt about her.

"Willow and Irene are very close," Donald said, changing the subject. "I swear, Irene talks about her all the time, and it means the world to her that the two of you are going to be here for her party tonight."

"It meant a lot to Willow too," he said, smiling.

"We're glad you came with her," Tom, another one of the Romeos, chimed in. "We all adore Irene, and we think the world of Willow…"

"But…?" Levi prompted.

"But her folks are hard to be around," Johnny replied. "They're nice enough, but they don't seem to know how to relax, and both Willow and Irene tense up around them. Hopefully that won't happen tonight since it's a party."

"And you'll be there to protect Willow," Donald said.

"Protect?" he repeated. "Is it really that bad?"

Vinny, who looked like he could have been in the movie *Goodfellas*, spoke up. "Every time I see the two of them when they come to visit Irene, I want to take them for a nice walk and tell them how things are supposed to be." The man not only looked like a Goodfella, but he sounded like one too.

Levi swallowed hard.

Note to self: Don't piss off Vinny.

"How has Willow described them to you?" Barry, the last of the Romeos, asked.

"I think she's been very careful in how she talks about them. It didn't take long for me to figure out that they stress her out and that I was going to have to be a buffer for her. I hate it for her." Shaking his head, he went on. "Believe it or not, I felt guilty talking about the relationship I have with my parents because I didn't want her to feel bad."

"You're close with your folks?" Tom asked.

"Yeah. Really close. And we stopped at two of my sisters' places on the way down here, and I could tell it took her a little while to relax and understand our relationship.

The one between each of my sisters and me. We laugh and joke around one minute and then we'll fight the next. I think she found it weird."

"Poor kid," Donald said. "Irene worries about her. Tell me, has she found a job yet?"

"Not really. She's babysitting and doing the dog walking business, but...that's just filling the void temporarily." He paused. "I don't get it. She's really good with kids. Why would her parents push her into getting a degree in something she didn't want?"

"Once you meet them, you'll understand," Johnny said with a hint of disgust. "The first time I met them and Irene mentioned what I did for a living, they both looked at me like I smelled of something offensive. Now I just like to taunt them with it."

Oh, God...

"So...I should be worried," Levi said nervously, looking around the table.

"That depends," Vinny said, giving him a level stare. "Are you ashamed of what you do?"

"Hell no," he replied firmly. "I love what I do and I'm good at it."

"Okay then," Vinny said with a nod of approval.

"But just to play it safe, maybe I should avoid talking about my job and maybe just...praise Willow, right?"

"It can't hurt," Barry replied. "But they won't let you get away with that for long. They like to analyze people. They'll observe your body language, the way you speak, and want to ask you questions about things that really aren't any of their business."

"Well, in their defense," Tom interjected. "He's dating their daughter. They're going to want to put him under the microscope based on that alone."

There was a murmured agreement amongst the Romeos, and for the first time since he offered to help Willow, he was beginning to regret it.

What if he made things worse for her with her parents? What if they pissed him off and he told them off? Or worse, what if he blurted out the truth about...everything to them and hurt Willow?

He groaned.

"Yeah, we feel ya, buddy," Johnny said, clapping him on the back. "The only silver lining here is that you only have to deal with them tonight, right? You and Willow are leaving in the morning?"

"We hadn't set a time to get on the road. We were sort of playing it by ear."

"Trust me," Donald said. "Don't let them talk you into meeting them for brunch or anything. Irene will completely understand if the two of you need to cut out early. Tell them you need to get back to work or convince Willow to tell them she has a job interview. It will be best for everyone."

"But...what about Irene?" And yeah, it felt weird to be calling her that after twenty-four hours' worth of calling her Gammy. "Is it fair to leave her to deal with them?"

"Oh, she can handle herself," Tom said with a hearty laugh. "Right, Don?"

Levi was shocked to see the old guy blushing, but he gave Levi a reassuring grin. "Her son is a bit of a pompous ass, but he certainly doesn't disrespect his mother. And I'll let her know what we talked about, so if the two of you suddenly have a reason for heading out early in the morning, she'll play along. That's one of the best things about Irene, she's always got your back."

And Levi didn't doubt that for a minute.

"So now we'll all play the over-protective grandfather,"

Tom began seriously. "Are things serious with you and Willow?"

"Oh, um...this is all still kind of new. We've only been together for a few months."

"And how'd you meet?" Barry asked.

Now it was Levi's turn to blush. "It was a Wednesday afternoon, and I was at the pub. I was cleaning the front window and I see this cute brunette walk by. She was smiling and looking up at the sky, and then she tripped and fell on the sidewalk."

There was a bit of laughter from all of them.

"Sounds like Willow," Johnny said.

"Yeah, well, I ran outside and helped her. She was all scraped up, and I carried her into the bar and sat her down before running back outside and getting the things she'd dropped. After I came back in and got her cleaned up with the first-aid kit, we started talking, and...that was it. I was hooked. She started coming to the pub on Friday nights with her girlfriends and we just...progressed from there."

None of it was a lie, so he didn't have to feel bad.

"She's a good girl," Vinny said, now more menacing than before. "You make sure you treat her with respect."

"Oh, for the love of it," Tom huffed. "Want to tone it down, Godfather wannabe! Geez! Why are you trying to scare this kid?"

"I'm not!" Vinny argued. "Just making sure he does the right thing!"

"Right," Donald said with an obvious eye roll. "Like you're the guy who knows about doing the right thing. Pfft."

"What are you saying, Donny? You got a problem with me?"

Uh-oh...

"I'm just saying, Vin, that you are known for causing trouble and not doing the right thing. Leave the kid alone!"

It took Levi a minute to realize he was the kid.

"Guys, really, it's..."

"I've never been convicted of anything!"

"Not for lack of trying..."

"You don't know what you're talking about!" Vinny shouted, coming to his feet. He turned his attention back to Levi. "You just make sure you treat her right. Understand?"

All he could do was nod and felt himself sag in his seat a little as Vinny walked away.

"That guy," Donald murmured. "He can be a real hothead. Sorry, Levi."

Still unable to find any words, Levi just nodded.

"We all share his sentiment." This came from Johnny. "We've just all got manners."

"Yeah. I hope this little scene didn't ruin lunch for you," Barry said with a sympathetic grin. "Vinny goes off at least once a month like that. It's nothing personal."

"Oh...uh...okay."

The remainder of the meal was spent talking about the party and all the things the Romeos had bought for Gammy...er, Irene. They were a great bunch of guys–very different personalities–but honestly, it felt like he had gone to lunch with all his favorite uncles.

Well...Vinny was still a little too scary for his taste, but up until the end there, he had been okay to hang out with as well.

When the check came, they all fought over who was paying, and eventually, Johnny won. He winked at Levi. "I always win."

And there wasn't a doubt in his mind that it was true.

Out in the parking lot, everyone was saying goodbye, but Johnny hung back and walked with Levi to his car.

"Can I ask you something?"

Shrugging, Levi said, "Sure."

"You own that pub or are you just working there?"

It was the last thing he expected anyone to ask. Keeping his focus straight ahead as they walked, he said, "Why do you ask?"

Johnny stopped, and Levi had no choice but to do the same. "Levi, come on. Unless you come from a wealthy family, there's no way a bartender from Long Island is making enough money to drive a car like this."

Something in his expression must have given him away because Johnny placed a hand on his shoulder and gave him a reassuring squeeze.

"Your secret's safe with me."

"Thanks."

"Can I ask why you're not telling anyone? You afraid Willow's only with you for the money?"

"What?" he cried. "No! Hell no!"

"Then what? I never owned my own place, but if I did, I'd be bragging about it to anyone with ears!"

"Yeah, well...normally I do. But with Willow...I don't know...I think one of the reasons she even gave me a chance was because she felt like she could relate to me. If I mentioned I owned the pub, she might have felt..."

"Different."

"Exactly. But not like she would have dated me for the money..."

"No, no, no...I get ya. Willow really is a sweet kid, but she's a little insecure," Johnny said, a hint of sadness in his voice. "I fully blame her parents."

So do I...

"Anyway, it didn't seem like a big deal not to bring it up when we first started hanging out. But now it's..." He let out a long breath. "I don't know how she'll handle it."

"Can I give you some advice?"

"Sure."

"Tell her before somebody else does. It will make thing much harder for you if she finds out for herself that you've been lying to her."

"It's not really lying..."

"It is. By omission. Just sayin'." Then he clapped Levi on the back. "Okay, time to go home and nap so I can stay awake long enough to enjoy Irene's party. I'll see you there!"

"Thanks, Johnny. And thanks for lunch."

The old guy smiled. "Any time, kid. Anytime. You take care of yourself and Willow."

Levi stood rooted to the spot while Johnny walked away, and he could only hope that this party went as smoothly as lunch did.

9

"ARE YOU SURE THIS LOOKS OKAY?"

"You look beautiful."

Smoothing her hair down, Willow swallowed hard and looked around the room to try to spot her parents. Luckily, they were running late, and it gave her a few minutes to get settled before she had to face them.

She startled when Levi reached out to hold her hand. It wasn't like it should have, they'd been holding hands for almost a week already, but in the moment, she wasn't expecting it.

"You're going to have to relax. All our hard work at making things look natural will go out the window," he murmured softly against her ear. His warm breath gave her chills, and she wanted to drag him to the nearest dark corner and kiss him senseless. Actually, she wanted a few minutes alone with him all afternoon to do just that, but it had been non-stop chaos.

After their pedicures, Gammy decided she needed a manicure too and treated Willow to one. After that, they went out for lunch at one of Willow's favorite restaurants–a 1950s themed diner before going to get their hair done.

Well, Gammy got hers done. When the stylist suggested that Willow should shorten her hair, she had immediately backed out and said she preferred to do her own. It had earned her so many judgy looks, but she held her ground and only had to sit in the salon for ninety minutes while everyone glared at her.

Super fun.

Back at the house, they found Levi on the phone. It sounded like he was talking to someone at the pub and she thought it was rude for them to be calling him while he was on vacation. Wasn't he allowed to take any time off for himself? Why couldn't the boss handle things without him?

Although...that was probably a good thing for Levi. It meant job security and all that.

Willow had gone and taken her shower first before doing her hair and makeup. Then Gammy needed her help getting ready while Levi went and took his shower. It just seemed like they didn't have more than two minutes to themselves and most of it was spent with him telling her about his lunch with the Romeos.

Which, thankfully, went better than her sex-talk filled pedicures with Gammy.

Something she was definitely going to share with him tonight once they were alone in their bedroom.

Their bedroom.

She really liked the sound of that.

And she'd like it a whole lot more if they could actually do more than just making out like horny teenagers.

"Willow, sweetheart. There you are!"

She jumped at the sound of her mother's voice and spilled white wine down the front of her.

Levi was quick to get her a handful of napkins to help her clean up, and all it really accomplished was giving her a few extra minutes before greeting her parents properly. Once she was somewhat dry, she looked up at her parents and smiled.

And noticed their focus was fully on Levi.

"Hey, Mom. Hi, Dad," she said, kissing them each on their cheek. "How are you?"

"We're fine, dear. Just fine," her mother said, her eyes still trained on Levi. Finally, she held out her hand. "And you are...?"

"Oh, um..."

"Levi Sullivan," he said, reaching out and firmly shaking first her mother's hand and then her father's. "It's nice to finally meet both of you. Willow's told me all about you."

It was a miracle how he said that like he meant it.

"It's a pleasure to meet you, Levi. I'm Marilyn Andrews, and this is my husband, Paul." Then she turned her attention back to Willow with a small frown. "At least it wasn't red wine."

"Do you want me to take you back to the house so you can change?" Levi asked, and she had never been more thankful for anyone in her entire life.

"That would be amazing. Thank you."

"Is that really necessary, Willow?" her father said in his usual disapproving tone. "We all know you're prone to spills, and it's not going to be an obvious stain. You don't want to ruin your grandmother's party by leaving."

"We won't be gone long," she murmured. "Gammy's house is less than ten minutes away. I'll be back before the salad is served."

"It's nonsense," her father stated firmly before taking a

sip of his own wine. "So tell me, Levi, how long have you been dating my daughter."

Willow groaned and hoped Levi would stick to the script and...

"We've been together for three months, Mr. Andrews. Your daughter is an amazing woman. But if you'll excuse us, I know she'd feel much better if she could change into something dry." He squeezed her hand. "We'll see you both at dinner."

She was speechless and offered her parents a small smile before they walked away.

"We should let Gammy know where we're going so she doesn't worry," he said to her with a confident smile.

And at that moment, he absolutely solidified himself as her knight in shining armor.

They walked across the room and gave Gammy a quick update and were out in the parking lot before she knew it. It wasn't until they were in the car that she spoke. "Thank you."

"For what?"

"Levi, you...you...you totally got me out of an awkward situation without letting my father intimidate you. I've never seen anything like it before. Most people just kowtow to him."

"One thing you should know about me, I don't kowtow to anyone." He grinned. "Okay, my Nana is probably the only one I would, but...she's barely five feet tall and intimidating as hell. I tend to do whatever she asks."

She couldn't help but laugh. "That's kind of adorable."

"Glad you think so." They pulled out of the parking lot and began heading back to the house. "Do you even have another outfit to change into or are we just going to drive around to kill some time and let your father stew a bit?"

And that just made her laugh harder. "Oh, my goodness! I never would have even thought to do that!" Playfully swatting at his arm, she admitted, "I actually brought three different outfits with me."

"Three? Seriously?"

"Mm-hmm. I wasn't sure what kind of mood I'd be in and I wanted to have options."

"Okay then. New outfit it is!" They drove in silence for several minutes. "Are you doing okay?"

"What? Sure. I appreciate you helping me like this!"

"No, I meant...about before. Your parents. You doing okay with all that?"

"Pfft...that was nothing. The real challenge will be while we're sitting at dinner. No doubt we'll end up sitting right by them. Did you see how long that table was? Around twenty people are coming and I can guarantee that we'll still be right beside them."

"I can make sure that doesn't happen..."

"Levi, I can't avoid them all night. Trust me, I've tried that tons of times before and it never works."

"You never had me with you." He winked at her, and for some silly reason, it made her feel better.

"Maybe we need a codeword."

"For what?"

"For when I'm feeling stressed. I'll say the codeword and you'll know I need to either distract them or get away."

"Willow, I hate to break it to you, but no codeword is necessary. Case in point—we're in the car, aren't we?"

"No, I mean..." And then it hit her. "Why you devious little genius! I didn't even think of it like that!"

"Yeah, you've told me enough about your relationship with your parents, and I've gotten to know you well enough that I can tell when enough is enough."

"I don't know if I'm thankful or embarrassed."

"You don't have anything to be embarrassed for. They're the ones who should be."

"But if we needed a codeword, what would it be? It couldn't be anything too obvious – like saying something like pineapple or meatloaf would be way too obvious."

He laughed softly. "Why does it have to be food?"

"It doesn't! I was just throwing words out there. Why, what would you use?"

"If you said pineapple, I'd think you were ordering your favorite drink."

"Oooh...good call."

"Food would be good though, the more I think about it. It would be easy to direct the conversation toward that if we needed to."

"Exactly."

"How about...mango?"

"Mango?"

He nodded. "Yeah. It's not a food that comes up often, and I think it would be obvious only to us that it was code for 'get me the hell out of here'." So what do you think? Will that work?"

"Definitely." She paused. "But hopefully we won't have to use it."

They pulled into Gammy's driveway and as much as she would have loved to take advantage of their alone time and have him help her with her zipper–or something remotely sexy–now wasn't the time.

She reached for the door handle and turned to look at him. "Levi..."

"Go." His voice was gruff and his expression was beyond sexy. "I think we both know if I go inside with you, we won't get back to the party until the cake was being served."

"It's a little scary how easily you can read my mind," she said softly, her gaze lingering on his handsome face.

"You're very expressive, Willow. Your face gives you away every time."

"Oh. Um, I should..." Just as she was turning to get out of the car, he reached out and stopped her.

"It's one of the things that makes you most attractive," he said with a lopsided grin. "I've enjoyed learning all kinds of things about you based on your expression."

Her cheeks heated because her thoughts were suddenly going in the direction of all the things she'd rather be doing with him rather than going back to the party.

Leaning forward, he rested his forehead against hers. "And we can discuss all these wicked thoughts later. While we're in bed." Placing a soft kiss on the tip of her nose, he whispered, "Go. I'll wait here."

And this time, she listened and quickly ran into the house.

The sooner they got back to the party, hopefully the sooner it would all be over and they could crawl into bed together.

Stripping as soon as she closed the front door, Willow ran and changed into party dress number two. She looked longingly at the bed once she was fully dressed and ran her hand over it. "I never thought I'd be so anxious to go to bed. My punishment as a child has now become my reward for putting up with my parents." Checking her reflection one last time, she murmured, "Oh, how times have changed."

"Levi, there you are."

Great. Here comes Mr. Personality...

With a smile plastered on his face, Levi shook Paul Andrews' hand. Again. Glancing around the room, he made sure Willow was nowhere nearby and, hopefully, enjoying herself. He spotted her dancing with Barry and figured they had at least three to five minutes before she'd be done. Longer if any of the other Romeos cut in.

"We didn't get a chance to really talk earlier," Paul said, his expression bland.

"With dinner for twenty, it's a little difficult to focus on any one conversation." Truth was, Levi had managed to put a little distance between the Andrews' and Willow.

With a little help from Gammy and Donald.

"It was a little rude of my mother's friend to force people to change seats."

Levi shrugged and casually slid his hands into his pockets. "Your mother didn't seem to mind, and since it's her big day, who are we to argue, right?"

The pinched look on Paul's face told him the guy was on to him. "I would never make a scene at a family event," he said evenly. After taking a sip of his wine—and seriously, did he ever put the glass down?—he continued. "So tell me about yourself. Willow mentioned you work in a bar."

"A pub, actually."

"There's a difference?"

Nodding, Levi explained, "Bars tend to be a bit loud and boisterous with dance floors, pool tables, dartboards, and dance floors. Pubs, on the other hand, are a little more casual with a somewhat quieter atmosphere and serve a full menu of food."

"And you're a bartender?"

He nodded.

"And…?"

"And…what?"

"So that's all you do? Make drinks?"

It would be so easy to put this guy in his place, but just like he thought earlier, Levi knew he needed to be honest with Willow about his position first before he blurted it out to prove a point to her father.

"There's more to it than that. But more importantly, I love what I do and I'm good at it. And that's the important thing, isn't it? Having a job that brings you joy?"

"Having one that supports you and allows you to have money in savings for retirement and other incidentals is also important." Another sip of wine. "And one you can take pride in–and one your significant other wouldn't be ashamed of."

Levi nodded. "I agree whole-heartedly, Paul."

And yeah, he enjoyed how much more Paul's face pinched up.

"I make a great living, drive a brand-new car, and have money in savings." He shrugged. "My folks come in often and are very supportive of me."

Every word was the truth.

"Of your being a bartender? Really?"

"Well, it's not like I'm dancing on the bar shirtless," he joked.

"I don't think you're a very good influence on my daughter."

"And why is that?" His fists were clenched in his pockets, and it took every ounce of control to not use them to pound on this guy.

"Willow's…struggling right now and…confused. She had the opportunity to join a very successful psychology practice, and she's refusing. I realize now that her hanging out with someone who doesn't have a...*real* job is adding to her confusion. She sees you being okay with being laid back and thinks that will work for her." He let out a snort of derision. "Babysitting and walking dogs. She has a college degree! She needs to be using it!"

"Why? It's not something she wanted," Levi stated. "Seems to me that makes it nothing more than an expensive piece of paper."

"Willow's always needed prodding. She never would have made up her mind. If left to her own devices, she would have skipped college and ended up...waitressing or something. Probably at your pub!" Then he shook his head before taking another sip of wine. "No, she's too clumsy to that."

It would be wrong to punch him...

"If that's what she wanted to do, I'm sure she'd make it work. And there shouldn't be anything wrong with that. It's not a Fortune 500 company or a snooty psych practice, but when I go home at the end of the day, I feel good about the work I've done and the people I've met."

"By helping them feed their alcohol addiction?"

Okay, now the gloves were going to have to come off.

"Are you addicted to alcohol?" Levi challenged.

"Excuse me?"

He nodded toward the glass of wine in Paul's hand. "That's your third, right? Now, according to *your* logic, the bartender here is doing nothing more than holding a lowly position and assisting you in your over-indulgence of alcohol." Crossing his arms over his chest, he added, "Maybe it's time to put *you* under the microscope, Paul. Or maybe there's someone in your practice you can talk to."

With narrowed eyes, Paul sneered, "I do *not* have a drinking problem."

"And bartenders aren't responsible for people's addiction." He paused. "Granted, I'm sure there's a small percentage of patrons who come in to drink that shouldn't, but I keep an eye on all of them while I'm behind the bar and if I think they've had enough, I cut them off. I wonder if the guy serving drinks tonight will offer the same service to you?"

Walk away! Walk away before things get even more heated!

"Now if you'll excuse me, I'd love to see about dancing with my girl. It was nice talking with you." There was no way he was going to shake this guy's hand again, but he couldn't resist one last zinger. "Oh, and maybe switch over to water for a bit. You know, to stay hydrated." And with a small wave, he walked away.

Willow was dancing with Donald, and Levi had absolutely zero qualms about cutting in. "May I?" he asked, knowing his smile was a wee-bit forced.

"Absolutely," Donald said, taking a step back. "See you two at dessert."

The band was playing a slow ballad and as soon as Levi had Willow in his arms, he rested his cheek against hers. "Mango."

"Hmm?"

"Mango."

She pulled back slightly and looked at him like he was crazy. And then...the lightbulb when on. "Oh, no. What happened?"

Levi repeated the conversation he just had with her father. "I'm really sorry, Willow. I know I should have held my cool a little longer, but..."

"Dad knows how to push people's buttons. Trust me, it's like his gift."

"I should probably go and apologize."

Shaking her head, she pressed in closer. "Nope. No way. He'll be expecting that. I say we enjoy the rest of the party–the Romeos have our backs and will keep us away from my parents when we sit down for cake–and then we just have to get through breakfast."

"Yeah...about that..." He explained the advice he had gotten earlier. "I'd totally understand if you don't want to– you know, if you want more time with Gammy before we get on the road."

"Levi?"

"Hmm?"

"We're not leaving until Monday, so..."

Oh, shit. He had completely forgotten about that!

His nervous laugh was out before he could stop it. "Well, then I've really gone and made things awkward, huh?"

Luckily, she laughed with him. "Are you kidding? If anything, you made it more interesting."

"Somehow, I doubt that."

"And Levi?"

"Yeah?"

"Thank you."

Now it was his turn to look at her like she was crazy. "For what?"

"For sticking up for me. Gammy tries, and I know all her friends are always praising me when my folks are around, but...this was the first time someone really stood up for me, so...thank you." She placed a soft kiss on his cheek and he wished like hell that he had punched the old guy in the face. It just about gutted him that he had done so little and yet it meant so much to Willow.

"I'll always stick up for you. And trust me, after that

conversation, I won't let you be alone with them. Not while I'm here."

The music died down and it was announced that it was time to sing Happy Birthday to Gammy. Willow took him by the hand and led him across the floor and over to where the massive cake had been wheeled out. The closer they got, Levi realized it wasn't a cake at all. It was a tower of cupcakes.

"Oooh...cupcakes," Willow said with awe. "How fun and totally Gammy."

"She...likes cupcakes?"

"Loves them! Goes back to her days of teaching. Whenever there was a birthday for one of her students, there were always cupcakes. She hates a regular cake."

"What? How is that possible? They're essentially the same thing."

Looking at him sympathetically, she said, "Are they? Because a cake is usually one flavor, a filling, and the icing. But a cupcake tower like this offers a bunch of possibilities." They stepped closer. "See? There's yellow cake with chocolate icing, yellow cake with vanilla icing–which, to me, is a little boring, but...whatever–chocolate cake with vanilla icing, chocolate cake with chocolate icing..."

"You're beginning to go a little Forrest Gump on me, Willow. I can see the different varieties."

"There are literally a dozen different varieties on here and way more than twenty people can eat–unless we each have two or three. And I am totally on board with that."

Before he could respond, Gammy stepped up beside them as the bandleader cued the guests to start singing. A small portion of the cupcake tower had candles, and once the song was over, she blew them out and grabbed the microphone to make a speech.

"I cannot thank all of you enough for coming to celebrate with me today. It means the world to me." She smiled out at her guests. "Some of you traveled a long way to get here, and I just want you to know that it made my day that much more special. We all live so far apart now but I love that you took the time from your busy schedules to get here." She turned her attention toward him and Willow. "And I don't know if you've all had the chance to chat with my beautiful granddaughter Willow and her handsome, handsome, *handsome* boyfriend, Levi!"

He groaned as he closed his eyes and shook his head.

"I didn't even *think* she'd have a microphone," Willow murmured.

"I am thrilled the two of you drove all the way here and chose my birthday party to make your debut as a couple at a family event!"

"Oh, Lord," Willow sighed.

"Now, I want everyone to eat a couple of cupcakes, have a few more drinks, and remember to call an Uber if you drank too much!"

Maybe it was Levi's imagination, but it seemed like Gammy looked directly at her son, and he had to fight a smirk because...how awesome would that be?

"Enjoy!"

All around, guests lined up to help themselves to cupcakes while coffee was being poured at around the massive table. Levi and Willow followed the group, and when she handed him a plate, he wondered if cupcakes would be a good option to have at the pub–like an addition to the dessert menu. It was something to think about.

Back at the table, he was relieved when they kept their same seats and were still separated from Willow's parents. He helped her by adding cream to her coffee and she helped him find his wayward cloth napkin. They were already like one of those couples who had been together for years rather than weeks, and it made him feel pretty damn good.

He examined the cupcake he'd picked–it was red velvet cake with cream cheese icing. Picking it up, he peeled the paper off of it and noticed Willow picking up her fork. "You're going to eat your cupcake with a fork?"

"Um...I was. Why? Do you think that's weird?"

"Well...I wouldn't say weird, but...why not just pick it up and eat it...you know...normally?"

"So it is weird."

"Willow..."

"Okay, fine," she said, picking up her chocolate cupcake with vanilla icing. "Here goes..." Taking a bite, she hummed with appreciation, and when she looked at him, he couldn't help but smirk. Her eyes crossed, and she cursed.

There was a dollop of icing on the tip of her nose.

"Uh...Willow..." He handed her his napkin, and she yanked it from his hand even as the cupcake fell from the other and landed in her lap.

Now he felt bad.

She wiped furiously at her face while he reached for her fallen cupcake, and he thought that was that.

Then her hand reached under the deep-vee neckline of her dress and she looked like she was cupping her breast.

"Uh..."

"Cake. In. My. Bra," she huffed. "I mean...*how?* How do these things only happen to me?"

"I'm sure you're not the only one..."

"Do you see anyone else here feeling themselves up, Levi?" she hissed and tossed the wayward piece of cake on the table. "Oh, God...people are looking."

"They're not."

But...they were.

Taking the napkin from her, he gently wiped the last tiny trace of icing from her nose before placing a soft kiss on her lips. He felt her relax as she kissed him back.

"Thank you."

"My pleasure," he murmured, giving her one more quick kiss before straightening. "And FYI, next time there's rogue cake to be fished out of your cleavage, let me know. I'll gladly handle it."

Luckily that did the trick, and she was back to enjoying herself.

And eating the remainder of her cupcake with a fork.

Out of the corner of his eye, he saw Mr. Andrews grab another glass of wine while rejecting the coffee. It was clear Levi wasn't all-that off-base with his accusations. Guys like that never think they're the one with the problem, and he had to wonder if it was part of the reason the old guy was so hard on Willow.

It wasn't something he was going to bring up to Willow tonight, or possibly ever. It wasn't his place, and for the rest of the night, he wanted them to enjoy themselves.

Once dessert was finished, they danced a little more and joked around with some of Gammy's friends when he noticed Willow yawning.

"Tired?"

"It's been a long day. More mentally exhausting than physically, you know?"

"Really? I thought you and your grandmother went and got pampered all day."

Rolling her eyes as they swayed to the music, she said, "We did, but it was far from relaxing." Then she told him about all the sex talk and the incident at the hair salon.

"Wow. Yeah, none of that sounds relaxing at all."

"Exactly. Plus, my feet are killing me. I'm not exactly a dressy kind of girl. Once a year, I can put on heels and that's it. All the massaging my feet got earlier was for nothing." With a pout, she shook her head. "I'm going barefoot all day tomorrow."

"Tell you what," he said, his voice low against her ear. "When we get back to your grandmother's place, I'll give you a foot rub. What do you say?"

"What do I say? Can we leave now?"

That was exactly what Levi was wondering. But...

"Don't you think it would look bad if the youngest people here were the first ones to leave? Plus, Gammy drove here with us."

"Well drat. I forgot about that."

Just then, Gammy and Donald spun by. "You kids having fun?" she asked, smiling from ear to ear.

"We are! Everything has been wonderful, Gam." Willow's words were interrupted by another yawn. "Sorry!"

"Nonsense, you're allowed to be tired. I ran you ragged today!"

"Just a bit..."

"Donald's going to take me home later. So if the two of you want to go, you don't have to wait on me." Smiling up at Donald as they continued to dance, she added, "And you probably shouldn't wait up either."

Levi met Willow's gaze and saw she was just as uncomfortable with that information as he was.

"Okay, then. So...would you mind if we hit the road?" Willow asked.

"Not at all! You two deserve some alone time!" She winked, and when Donald spun her around one more time, she waved. "And don't forget, condoms in the closet! See you in the morning!"

Willow shuddered slightly in his arms and all he could do was chuckle softly. "Mango," she muttered against his chest. "Mango, mango, mango!"

Holding her close, he said, "That was going to be my line."

With a sigh, she looked up at him. "So then we're in agreement. We are free to go and we should go, right?"

"Absolutely." Hand in hand, they walked across the room to the table where Willow grabbed her shawl from her chair. Levi kept his hand on the small of her back while looking around to see where her parents were at. It wasn't likely that they'd be able to leave without saying goodbye to them, but he was hopeful it was all they were going to have to say.

Wishful thinking and all.

"Are you leaving, dear? We barely had a chance to talk!" This coming from Willow's mother as she approached them.

Turning, Willow faced her mother and kissed her on the cheek. "Parties aren't exactly the best place to sit and chat." She smiled at Levi as he placed her shawl over her shoulders. "If you had come with us today for a little spa time…"

"Oh, you know I hate that kind of thing. So many germs." She visibly shuddered. "I don't know why you would even subject yourself to them."

"It was a nice time to sit and chat," Willow said, ignoring her mother's comment. "Gam and I made a lovely day of it. You could have joined us for lunch, too."

"You know how your father is. He wanted to play some golf and relax before the party."

The image immediately came to mind of Paul Andrews enjoying a few cocktails at the country club after his golf game.

Willow shrugged. "Will you be joining us for brunch tomorrow? Gammy's really looking forward to sitting down with the family before we all have to leave."

Mrs. Andrews eyed him before returning her attention to her daughter. "It's on the calendar, so we'll be there."

"Oh, okay then. Great. I guess we'll see you in the morning," Willow said before kissing her mother on the cheek again.

"It was a pleasure to meet you, Mrs. Andrews. I hope you have a good night." Levi wasn't surprised when her wan smile was her only response, and he hoped they could make their escape unnoticed.

"Willow," her father called out when they were in the lobby. They both stood still and waited for him to walk over. "A little early for you to be leaving, isn't it?"

"Actually, no," she said, but Levi could hear the slight tremor in her voice. "It's been a very full day, and the party is winding down. Gammy was the one to suggest we go home."

His gaze narrowed at her and then Levi. "You should stay until the end of the party. It's the proper thing to do."

Levi was about to step forward and say...something, but Willow beat him to it.

"Oh, really? And is it also proper to get drunk and be surly to all the guests?" she asked, and there was no disguising the sarcasm in her tone. "Maybe *you* should consider calling it a night, too, Dad." She paused and looked at him with mild annoyance. "Or at the very least, have some coffee. Oooh...there's one of the waiters! Maybe I should call him over for you?"

Paling, Paul muttered a gruff "Goodnight" to them before turning and walking away, and it was hard to tell who was more shocked by her act of bravery.

"Come on," she said, smiling. "You promised me a foot rub."

His bark of laughter was out before he could stop it. "Willow, you got it!"

10

"What song would totally embarrass you if people knew you loved to listen to it?"

"Okay, but you can't tell anyone..."

Willow made a zipping motion across her lips.

Levi let out a long, dramatic sigh. "I listen to Mariah Carey's 'All I Want for Christmas Is You' year-round." He shook his head. "I love that song."

She knew her eyes went wide but fought the urge to giggle. "Okay, wow. That was...not what I was expecting."

They were lying in bed, in pajamas, facing each other. Only one small lamp was lit and even though no one else was home, they were talking softly. It was almost as intimate as all the kissing and touching they'd done last night, but for some reason, she wanted to talk to him right now more than anything.

"Although...I sort of got hooked on Wham's 'Last Christmas' after seeing the movie by that name last year. I could probably listen to it year-round and not get tired of it."

"I also really love Taylor Swift's 'Lover'."

"Wow."

Nodding, he said, "Yeah. I know. Now it's your turn," and reached for her hand and linked their fingers. "And it better be really embarrassing."

"Trust me. It is."

"Well?" he prompted when she didn't share right away.

"Ugh...all right. It's the Pina Colada song." She huffed. "There. I said it." Flopping onto her back, she closed her eyes and waited for him to laugh.

"So...you like Pina Coladas."

Turning her head, she looked at him. "And getting caught in the rain."

It was pointless not to laugh at that, and while they were both cracking up, Levi pulled her into his arms and kissed her on the head. "That is awesome. And surprising. That's a really old song!"

"I know, right? I can't even tell you when I heard it for the first time or why it stuck, but it's on my playlist and I swear I listen to it several times a week."

"Good to know."

"New topic...did you ever have one of those themed birthday parties when you were a kid?"

"Guys don't do that."

"Oh, please," she said with a snort. "Yes, they do. And I'm talking about when you were young–like ten or younger."

"I was really into trucks, and one year my mom did everything with them–the plates, the cups, the cake...she even made a bunch of kid-sized trucks out of old cardboard boxes so my friends and I could sit in them and watch a movie in the living room."

"Aww...that's adorable!"

"Did you?"

"I have always loved Disney princesses, so I had several parties with a princess theme."

"Really?"

"Yeah, why?"

"After everything you've told me about your parents and after meeting them tonight, I can't quite envision them doing something whimsical like that."

"Only on birthdays and holidays," she admitted. "And trust me, they looked uncomfortable with it."

"Did your siblings want parties like that too or did they come out of the womb as academics?"

The imagery was enough to make her laugh. "No, they were normal kids too. And really, they're normal now. They just chose very challenging careers. And believe it or not, they both love them. I don't think they felt the same pressure as I did growing up. It's probably harder on me because..."

Levi placed a finger over her lips. "No negative stories. We were going for funny childhood memories and embarrassing things like that."

She nodded.

"What was the best Christmas present you ever got?"

"That's easy. I got a treasure chest filled with costumes– well, princess dresses and all the accessories. I was a different princess every day of the week. It was awesome!"

"Awesome? You must have been really young."

"Not as young as you'd think..."

His eyes went wide. "Um...are we talking under the age of ten or over the age of twenty?"

"I plead the fifth."

"Now I'm even more curious!" He hugged her closer. "Come on...tell me!"

But she held firm. "Sorry. No can do."

"Willow..."

"Most embarrassing thing you've ever worn–either by choice or your parents made you."

"Hmm...we went to Disney when I was around eight. I had a mullet and was dressed in this whole khaki outfit with a matching hat–like one of the tour guides on the Jungle Cruise."

"That sounds so cute!"

"And I also had on a fanny pack."

"Yeah, that ruined it."

"Yup. What about you? And it can't be anything princess related."

"Well, duh. How can I be embarrassed about wearing something I love?" she asked, feigning sarcasm. "But I did go through a bit of a goth phase in high school. There are some pictures of me, Donna, and Jen, where you would think it was Halloween, but...it wasn't."

Levi pulled back and looked at her in shock. "No way! There is no way you were goth. I don't believe it."

"The next time the girls and I come into McGee's, ask them. I think Donna even has one of the pictures on her phone."

"Oh, believe me, I am totally asking her that."

Resting her head on his shoulder, she asked, "Do you believe in fortune tellers or psychics or tarot cards?"

"Not quite the direction I thought we were going in, but...okay." He sighed. "I've never had any personal contact with anyone who claims to be...what's the word...clairvoyant, but I think it's possible. What about you?"

"I totally believe in them."

"Really?"

She nodded. "A friend of mine took me to get my cards read when we were in college and it was so spot-on. Not the usual generalization that you hear about, but a lot of specifics. But then I went to one on my own back home and it was a total waste of money. She was so off on everything that I almost left in the middle of the reading."

"Why, what did she say?"

"That I was going to be a lawyer because I like to argue. That is the total opposite of who I am. If anything, I never make waves."

Kissing her forehead, he said, "Well, no one's right all the time. Maybe she was just having an off day."

"Maybe. Still, it was very disappointing."

Sort of like how you can lie here with me half-naked in your arms and not even remotely try to cop a feel...

"What were you hoping to find out?" he asked after a few moments.

"To know that I'm not going to grow old alone," she admitted and immediately wanted to kick herself. "To see if maybe she could give me some hope that I was going to figure out what I was going to do with my life."

"Willow..."

Yeah, yeah, yeah...no negative or deep thoughts...

"She wouldn't give me the winning lottery numbers either, so that didn't seem fair. She could have lied and said it was possible..."

"I think I'd probably spend the first few minutes trying to prove they were a fraud–like thinking crazy shit and then asking them to tell me what I was thinking."

"So you don't *really* believe."

He shrugged. "Like I said, I don't have any experience with them to make that call."

She opted to leave out the part that she was supposed to meet the love of her life when she was at her lowest point and then have three kids. No need to freak him out.

Besides, how much lower can my life get?

Although...she peeked up at Levi and wondered if he could possibly be the love of her life. With a quiet sigh, she immediately pushed that thought aside. How can someone be the love of your life when they're obviously just a good guy helping a friend out? That was friendship, not love.

Maybe she was getting too confused by this whole situation. Lines were getting blurred, but...if all she had was this week with him, did she really want to waste it talking herself out of what she wanted most?

They lay there in companionable silence, and Willow snuggled closer, enjoying the warmth of his body, the feel of his scratchy jaw...pretty much everything about him.

What's not to like? He's a good friend, an excellent fake boyfriend, he put up with the craziness that is my family and the Romeos...

She knew they had discussed this—all the reasons why fooling around beyond what they had done last night would be wrong. This was her grandmother's house and all, but...

Shifting a little, she rubbed her legs against his until they were tangled together, and with a soft hum, she placed a hand on his chest.

"Willow..." His voice was barely a whisper, and she couldn't tell if it was a warning or a plea.

Tilting her head, she looked up at him, she cupped his jaw and saw him swallow hard. "We could talk about our first crushes, or we could maybe...stop talking."

His eyes closed as her fingers caressed his jaw, his lips.

"It's your call, Levi."

"No fair, Willow. You know I want you. I've wanted you for a long time."

She gasped. "Really?"

He nodded before slowly moving forward until Willow

rolled onto her back. "Yeah. Really." Then his lips claimed hers and she was more than okay with waiting to ask any more questions–even though she suddenly felt like she had a million of them. Raking her hands up into his hair, she held him to her while he completely consumed her.

It didn't take long for him to cover her body with his and for Willow to wrap her legs around his waist. It felt so good–the feeling of the weight of him on top of her–and it no longer mattered where they were or whose house it was. She wanted this.

Wanted him.

And thanks to Gammy and her closet full of condoms, she knew she could have him.

Honestly, Levi knew there were reasons why they shouldn't be doing this, but for the life of him, he couldn't have remembered even one of them right now. With Willow beneath him, wrapped around him, the only thing he could focus on was finally being free to touch her the way he wanted to.

And he wanted to in a dozen different dirty ways.

Slow...you've got to take things slow.

Wait...why?

He deepened the kiss–or maybe she did. All he knew was that Willow's hands had a tight grip on his hair and her legs had an even tighter hold around his waist. It was almost impossible to move, and he desperately wanted to. The need to touch her and be touched by her was almost over-whelming, and he'd rather deal with the brief disappoint-ment right now of breaking their connection than waiting much longer to do what he wanted to.

Lifting his head, he stared down at her breathlessly.

"I'd ask if you're sure, but..."

"I'm sure, Levi. So very, very, very sure."

It was hard not to smile. Her face was so serious, and her words were so firm and unlike anything he'd seen of her until this very moment. "I thought we were going to..."

Her hands continued to rake through his hair as her eyes scanned his face. "I thought so too. But...this just feels right, doesn't it?"

Ah...there it is. The uncertainty.

Can't have any of that.

"It does," he said, his voice gruff and sure. With a curt nod, he said, "Do you really think we'll have the house to ourselves all night? I'd hate to have an awkward encounter with your grandmother and have her walking in while we're...well...you know."

With a sexy little laugh that was part giggle, part moan, she said, "This is the first time I'm experiencing this kind of a situation with her. Most of the time I come to visit she refrains from...sleeping out. Actually, I don't think it's something she would normally do while anyone's here visiting. I have a sneaky suspicion that she's doing it to give us a little privacy."

"Okay, but..."

"She was trying to get all the details about our sex life out of me earlier, and it was the most awkward conversation ever. And in the middle of the nail salon, no less!"

"Yeah, okay. But..."

"I mean, why would she think I'd share that kind of information? And for that matter, why would she want to know?" She shuddered dramatically. "It's one thing to discuss your sex life with your friends, but I don't think it's particularly proper to talk about it with your family. That's just weird." She paused and looked up at him. "It is weird, right? Or do you think I'm way off-base here?"

"Willow..."

"I mean, just because I don't have that kind of relationship with my mom or my sister, doesn't mean that it's like that for everyone else. Do you ever talk about sex with your father?"

"What?! No, why?" Then he paused. "You mean other when he gave me the sex talk when I was a teenager?"

"Well...yeah. Like do you ever share with him any information about the women you sleep with?"

"Oh, God..."

"Or what about your sisters? Do you ever try to get advice from them?"

"Why would I go to my sisters for sex advice?" he cried, horrified at the very thought of it.

"There's no need to freak out, Levi. It was just a question."

"And it was just a question when I asked if you thought we'd have the house to ourselves for the night." And it took her several moments of him staring at her pointedly for her to understand what he was saying.

"Oh. Right. Sorry." She let out a nervous laugh. "Um... basically, I can't say with any great certainty that she'll really be gone all night." Her smile was slow and filled with all kinds of promises. "We'll just have to make sure to play it safe and lock the door."

Finally! We're back on track!

With a surge of energy, Levi jumped off the bed and opened the bedroom door. The linen closet was right there, and he nearly ripped the door off its hinges in his haste to get it open. The hallway was dark, and he fumbled around for a moment before he found the box of condoms. It took less than a second for him to grab it and walk back into the bedroom–locking the door behind him. Why bother with picking out a packet or two when he could just take the whole box and place it next to the bed.

Talk about being optimistic...

Willow was exactly where he'd left her, and she looked like some sort of sexy vixen–her dark hair in disarray on the pillows, her nightshirt hiked up to reveal a pair of pastel pink panties. His mouth went dry and all he could do was stand at the foot of the bed and stare at her.

"Um...Levi?"

"Hmm?"

"Are you ever going to come back on the bed?"

That was a loaded question if he'd ever heard one.

Slowly, he crawled up and over her. Bracing his hands on either side of her, he held himself up like that while staring down at her.

She was beautiful–the perfect combination of sweet and sexy and pure temptation to him. From the moment they met, Willow had intrigued him. At first, it was her innocence and his need to protect her. Then it was her wit and personality that drew her to him as a friend. But the woman lying beneath him, looking up at him with sensual hunger, was everything he ever wanted wrapped up in one amazing package.

"I won't break. I swear."

Her soft words broke into his thoughts, and he gave her a lopsided grin. "How did I ever get this lucky?"

One of Willow's hands gripped his hair hard. "You haven't." Then her grin turned a little wicked. "Yet."

He was torn between diving in and ravaging her–if that was something people even said anymore...

Damn Romeos in my head!

But it was a battle between ravaging her or savoring. Both held major appeal, and it took Levi all of three seconds to realize that Willow was the kind of woman you savored; took your time with.

Slowly, he lowered his head and gently pressed his lips to hers. They sighed simultaneously as they sank into the kiss, and after that, it was all small touches that turned to grasps. Sweet kisses that turned heated. They worked together to get her nightshirt off and then his boxers.

Taking her panties off, however, was all on him.

Levi didn't want her help, he wanted to take his time and kiss her stomach, her hips, her thighs, and everything in between. And when Willow's hands sank into his hair again and held him in place, he was more than happy to oblige.

She tasted sweeter than any dessert and he intended to get his fill of her.

Willow cried out his name, and he was determined to make her do that several more times before the sun came up.

"Levi?"

"Hmm?"

"Are you awake?"

He wanted to chuckle at the question, but honestly, he was beyond exhausted and couldn't be sure if he was awake or asleep. Still, it seemed safe to reply, "Yes."

"Can I ask you something?"

"Sure."

"Do you think it would be wrong to leave tomorrow instead of Monday?"

The conversation he had the previous day with the

Romeos about getting out of Dodge sooner rather than later came to mind, but he wasn't really thinking clearly enough just yet. Turning his head, he glanced at the clock and saw it was four in the morning. He and Willow had made love twice, and in between, they had talked about everything and nothing all at the same time.

It was probably one of the greatest nights he could ever remember.

Shifting against the pillows, he attempted to sit up slightly, but Willow rolled toward him and rested her head on his chest.

"I'd ask why you want to leave, but I think I have an idea," he said around a yawn. "I'm not sure it's something you should try to decide right now."

"I know I'm just avoiding the inevitable, but...who could blame me."

I know I can't...

"Just the thought of going to brunch with them exhausts me," she went on. "And after the way we ended things after the party, I know I'm going to catch all kinds of grief for it."

"To be fair, I encouraged it. So if there's any grief being thrown your way, part of it's on me. You won't have to face them or deal with them alone, Willow."

Part of him felt so bad for her–that her parents caused this level of anxiety that she was awake at four in the morning obsessing over it. But the other part of him wanted to encourage her to go and stand up for herself. She hadn't done anything wrong; she had simply voiced her own disapproval with their behavior rather than the other way around.

"You shouldn't have had to deal with it at all..."

Rolling her onto her back, he placed a soft kiss on her forehead. "Hey, I went into this whole thing with my eyes open. You never held back on all the possibilities we might have to deal with where your folks were concerned. We are in this together, Willow. I promise."

He heard her soft sigh. "Levi," she began quietly. "I don't want you to think...you know...because of...um...this, that you need to do more than you already have. You've been amazing. And not just...you know...here."

Wait...what the hell was she trying to say?

"Willow..."

"I just want you to know that I appreciate you and I don't expect anything more from you. What happened here tonight between the two of us was...well, it was incredible, but I'm not asking for any promises or for any extra...how can I say this...like extra boyfriendy things when we're around everyone at brunch or...whenever. So if you wanted to skip brunch, that would be okay too."

Pushing off of her, Levi sat straight up. His eyes had adjusted to the darkness, and he could make her out in the moonlight. "What are you saying, Willow? That you don't want me around your family tomorrow? Today? Whatever the hell day it is!"

Sitting up, she clutched the sheet to her chest. "I just don't want you to do anything you're not comfortable with, that's all. I just didn't want you thinking the sex tonight changed anything."

Mentally counting to ten, Levi did his best to calm down before he spoke again. "I hate to break it to you, but the sex did change things."

"Oh," she murmured.

"As a matter of fact, it changed everything."

"Oh."

Why did she sound so miserable? Was it possible he had read all the signs–and orgasms–wrong?

He figured he might as well ask while they were having this...whatever this was...kind of talk. "Can I ask you something?"

"Mm-hmm."

Swallowing hard, he asked, "Would you prefer if I didn't touch you again? Was tonight just about...curiosity or passing the time? Did it mean anything to you?"

She was quiet for several moments. "That was three."

"What?"

"Questions. That was three questions."

She was the most infuriating woman sometimes...

"Can you answer at least one of them?" his voice was so low and so gruff, he barely recognized it himself.

The silence was deafening, and it took everything he had not to rush her.

"No. No. Yes."

It took a minute for him to realize what she meant.

Relief washed over him in waves. "Okay, then."

"I'd really like it if you touched me now," she whispered, and Levi was one thousand percent on board.

11

"Isn't this nice? All of us together for brunch!"

"Mother, we were all together at your party last night," Paul said wearily, rubbing his temple. "I had to reschedule to a later tee-off time because you pushed back what time you wanted us here."

"Well," Gammy said, not looking the least bit put out, "I stayed up later than I had planned and didn't get home until after eight this morning. A girl needs some time to get ready, you know."

Paul groaned while Willow and Levi fought the urge to laugh.

Although, there had been an awkward moment earlier when Gammy had first gotten home that wasn't the least bit funny at the time.

Levi took his turn in the shower after Willow had finished, and when she walked out into the living room as Gammy was walking in the door, it was hard to say who scared who more.

"Oh my goodness, Gam, you scared me!" Willow had cried, hand over her heart.

"Did you and Levi finally get to have sex last night?" Gammy asked, breezing across the room.

"What?!"

"Don't even try to deny it. You're all glowy right now. I knew you wouldn't do it if I was in the house. Donald was such a dear to let me stay with him." She paused and chuckled. "Although I did thank him properly, so I don't think he minded too much."

"Gams," Willow said with a sigh. "TMI. I keep telling you, stuff like that is TMI."

"Nonsense! There's no such thing!" She fluttered around the kitchen, making herself a cup of tea. "I saw the way you and Levi were looking at each other all afternoon and during the party and knew you were a little tense because of your parents so..."

"So you shouldn't have stayed out all night for my sake!"

"Oh, trust me, it wasn't *all* for your sake. I got a good bit out of it myself, if you know what I mean." And with a sassy wink, she turned her back and wiped down the countertops. "Donald is a very thorough and enthusiastic lover. I bet Levi's the same way."

You have no idea...

Feeling herself blush from head to toe, Willow had excused herself and ran back to her bedroom to get ready.

And had avoided her grandmother until everyone arrived for brunch.

Why didn't I leave when I had the chance?

Oh, right, because Levi said she would later regret it.

Sadly, he was right. As much as she wanted to avoid having another uncomfortable conversation with her father, she would hate cutting her visit with her grandmother short. As it was, they only got to see each other once a year, and her grandmother wasn't getting any younger–no matter how impressive her sex life was.

"So, Levi," her mother began, and Willow fought the urge to groan. "We didn't get the opportunity to speak with you much last night. Why don't you tell us about yourself?"

He was about to speak when Gammy interrupted.

"Hello? Birthday girl here! As much as I have loved getting to know Levi, this is supposed to be *my* day, remember? I don't want this turning into some psycho-analyzing session, Marilyn."

"I was merely expressing an interest in the man who is dating my daughter. It's only natural to be curious about the kind of person he is. Especially since she's driving alone with him across the country."

"Mom...that's a little bit of an over-exaggeration," Willow argued mildly. "I told you, Levi rescued me when I fell. He helped me out, and we started talking, and then we just...clicked." She smiled at him and saw him wink. Facing her mother again, she added, "Today is about Gammy."

"Yesterday was about her, as well," her father murmured, pouring himself another cup of coffee.

"It's her weekend," Willow countered. "This is a milestone birthday, and we should be talking about what's new with her and what she has coming up. Any trips planned, Gammy? I thought I heard you talking about a cruise."

"Oh, yes!" she replied, grinning from ear to ear. "It's going to be fantastic! It's one of those Flower Power cruises that cater to people of my generation and all the entertainment is music groups from the 60s and 70s! I can't wait! My girlfriend Dotty planned the whole thing for us. There's fifteen of us going and it's a seven-day cruise that leaves right out of Fort Lauderdale! I'm telling you, it's going to be a blast!"

"Surely it's not going to be the real artists from the groups performing," Marilyn said with a hint of disbelief.

"Well, not *all* of the original members, but yes, a lot of them are still around and still performing. There are going to be a few tribute groups and shows, but...who cares! It's the whole feeling of the cruise that's important! Free love, good vibrations, flower children...it's going to be quite the scene! The whole group of us have been scouring thrift shops and making our own clothing so we'll fit in. You should see me in my bell-bottoms! I look just like I did when you were a boy, Paul!"

Her father groaned.

Gammy turned and looked at Levi. "Have you ever gone on a cruise, Levi?"

"Why is it okay for you to question him and not me?" her mother asked, plainly miffed.

"Because we're talking about cruises, Marilyn. I already know that you and Paul and Willow have gone on them. I don't want the poor boy to feel left out. Sheesh!" She smiled at Levi. "So? Have you ever cruised anywhere?"

"I have, actually," he replied. "My family and I have done several. We've cruised to the Bahamas, Mexico, and the Caribbean. A couple of years ago, my folks did an Alaska cruise. I would have loved to go with them because Alaska is a bucket-list destination for me."

"Why didn't you go?" Gammy asked.

"For starters, it was their anniversary, and they didn't invite any of the kids or grandkids, and I couldn't take the time off from the pub even if they had."

Willow saw him squirm in his seat and wondered why.

"No backup bartenders?" her father asked, and she wanted to slug him. Why was he fixating on what Levi did for a living? Why couldn't he just be normal and look at him as a person and not a profession?

"There was a...um...a change in management around that time, and it wouldn't have been right for me to take off. I've been there the longest, so..."

"That's very commendable, Levi," Gammy gushed. "So many young people don't have any real commitments to their jobs. If they're not the boss, then they just don't care. Such a shame." And with a tsking sound, she took a sip of her tea.

The oven timer went off and Willow jumped to her feet, thankful for the distraction. They had a wonderful frittata baking, and it was the last item they needed before serving. She put the oven mitts on her hands and felt Levi come up beside her. "I've got this," she said softly, blushing at his heated gaze.

"Nonsense. You don't need to do everything yourself. I'm here to help."

"And I appreciate it." Pausing, she went and pulled the frittata from the oven and placed it in its warming basket. "But I know you're just trying to get away from the table."

"Was it that obvious?"

"Only to me." She kissed him on the cheek. "And Gammy, probably. No biggie."

Together they worked to put the rest of the buffet on the table—muffins, chocolate croissants, bagels, assorted cream cheeses, butter, breakfast sausage, and the frittata. It was way more food than five people could possibly eat, but it was all Gammy's favorites. When the last plate was set, Willow straightened and smiled. "Hope everyone's hungry!"

Luckily, after that, the conversation turned toward Gammy's Mahjong group and local retirement community gossip. Then it went to the new golf cart she wanted to upgrade to. After that topic was exhausted, her parents talked about what was new with Willow's siblings and that eventually led to what was new with them in Seattle. It was only a matter of time before all eyes were on her.

Awesome.

Now would be the perfect time for her to spill something or maybe choke on a muffin, but for the first time in her life, she was getting through a meal without incident.

Seriously, Universe?? You couldn't have helped me out when I fell on my face in front of Levi? Or when I fell off the stage in my third-grade play and showed the whole school my Little Mermaid underpants??

"You know, Willow," her mother began, "we just moved into a larger office space and have several offices for you to choose from. Fully furnished."

She studied the muffin on her plate for a few moments, mentally counted to ten, and prayed for patience all before raising her head and giving her mother a serene smile. "Thank you for the offer, but I'm still not interested in moving to Seattle or joining the practice. I'm sure you'll have plenty of candidates to rent out the space to."

"Willow," her father chimed in with a much less pleasant tone than her mother. "We've tried to be patient with you. It's time for you to stop being difficult and settle into a career. You can't keep being irresponsible!"

"Paul," Gammy interrupted. "Now is not the time..."

"Mother, this isn't a damn Norman Rockwell painting. We all fawned all over you yesterday and most of the morning. Five minutes of talking about how your granddaughter is behaving like an ungrateful child isn't going to hurt anyone."

Um...really? Because I'm kind of hurt...

"With all due respect, Mr. Andrews," Levi said evenly, but Willow immediately stopped him.

"It's okay, Levi. I got this." Then she looked at her father. "How exactly am I being irresponsible or ungrateful? I'm not asking you to help support me, nor have I been disrespectful toward either you or mom. I've never lied to you; I never wanted to go into psychology. I said I wanted to work with children and you pushed for child psychology rather than letting me go into early childhood education or…or…anything that I wanted to do! Did Gammy force you into psychology?"

"That's not the point…"

"Actually, Paul," Gammy said, leaning back in her chair and crossing her arms over her chest. "Willow has a very good and valid point. If you'll remember, you getting a psychology degree was *not* what I wanted for you."

"Yes, I know, Mother, but if it were up to you, I would have gone to clown college or majored in basket weaving. The only thing you were vocal about was…" He stopped mid-sentence as if he realized what he was saying.

Gammy's smile was a little smug as she stared at her son. "The only thing I was vocal about was finding your passion because without it, a degree was worthless."

Willow was fairly certain her jaw was on the floor and as her father stood and excused himself, she had to wonder what was going to happen from here.

They all watched as he stalked across the room, out to the lanai, and then out to the backyard. She was about to get up and follow, but again, Levi beat her to it. He bent and kissed her on the cheek and whispered, "Don't worry. I got this one."

Once the back door closed a second time, Gammy clapped her hands together and reached for a chocolate croissant. "So, Marilyn, how are the beds at that hotel you're staying at? Good for sex?"

And for the first time since she arrived in Florida, Willow was thankful for her grandmother and her sexcapades topics.

"Mr. Andrews? Are you okay?"

"This doesn't concern you, Levi. Go back inside."

It was tempting to laugh because, seriously, did this guy think he had the right to boss everyone around? "I will in a minute, Sir, but I just thought maybe someone should check on you." He paused and waited to see if he was going to respond, but when he didn't, Levi continued. "Things got a little heated and I imagine that happens a lot. Willow's mentioned..."

"Spare me, Mr. Sullivan. You've been dating my daughter for...what...a few months? You don't know anything about our dynamic. I'm sure Willow's made us out to be the bad guys..."

"No offense but...even if she hadn't, you managed to do that all on your own. It doesn't take a genius to figure out you're a bit of a control freak and that Willow's lack of interest in doing what you want her to is a real sticking point for you."

If looks could kill, Levi knew he'd be...well, he'd be slightly injured because Paul Andrews wasn't the least bit intimidating.

But it was cute how he tried.

"Don't try to play armchair psychologist with me, Mr. Sullivan. You're way out of your league."

"I'm not playing at anything. It's not hard to see and you

seem to enjoy taking every opportunity to let it be known to everyone. I don't see why you couldn't just let this be a pleasant family get-together for your mother's birthday. It really wasn't that hard of a thing to do."

"How dare you!"

Levi held up a hand to stop him.

"No, how dare you!" he snapped. "Like it or not, I care about your daughter. A lot! And I'm not going to stand by and watch you belittle her or bully her into doing something she doesn't want to do! As a parent, you should be happy that someone has her back, even if it's against you!"

"Excuse me if I don't want to take advice from you. Not only are you a stranger to this family, but you're not a parent. You have no idea what you're talking about."

"Actually...I do."

Paul quirked a dark brow at him. "Oh, really? Do you have a child? Is Willow aware of it because she hasn't mentioned that fact to her mother or myself."

Letting out a breath, Levi tried to relax his stance a bit– to try to diffuse some of the tension. "I have three sisters," he explained. "They're all older than me. I'm very close with my father and he's always been very open and honest about how important it was for them to find men who would protect them. Fight for them. Take care of them. Don't get me wrong, they had to date a lot of guys before they found the ones that my father approved of, but they did. And to this day, my father talks about how much he respects each of my brothers-in-law because he knows they look after my sisters the way he would."

They stood in silence for several moments and Levi was certain he had proved his point.

"How touching. Again, you'll excuse me if I'm not impressed. I know my daughter better than you and I know what she needs. You might think you do, but trust me, you don't."

"I hate to be disrespectful here, Mr. Andrews, but...I don't think you have a clue about what Willow needs. You don't seem to listen to her at all. I'm guessing you don't pay much attention to all the ways that she's gifted and talented."

Paul let out a mirthless laugh. "Gifted? Willow? Please. Levi, my daughter is a walking accident waiting to happen. Sitting in a chair in an office and taking notes is the safest place for her. Trust me."

Wow. Just...wow.

"I think you're wrong."

Another mirthless laugh. "I don't really care."

"Okay, this is getting us nowhere. What would make you feel better? If Willow just took a job with a psych practice? Even if it made her miserable?"

"Life isn't about things being all sunshine and unicorns, Mr. Sullivan. Life is about being responsible; about taking care of yourself financially."

Ah...now we're getting somewhere...

"Look, as far as I know, Willow hasn't asked you for money, and she hasn't asked for any help from you to help her find a job. She has–repeatedly, mind you–told you she's not interested in joining your practice or any practice. You're not going to intimidate her and you're not going to bully her and bend her to your will. Why not just be a supportive parent? Maybe with a little encouragement, Willow can find the perfect career for her."

"Is that what your parents did for you? Offered encouragement so you can just do whatever you want?" Paul sneered.

"As a matter of fact, they did."

"And I'm sure they're so proud of their son, the bartender."

Ducking his head, Levi hid a smirk before looking up again. "You seem to be fixated on my career choice. I think it's comical considering our conversation last night."

Target hit!

Paul paled slightly, and, at that moment, Levi decided to do something he had sworn he'd never do.

"Well, they're proud of the fact that I'm happy. And when I was just a bartender, they were supportive of that too." He took a step toward Paul and lowered his voice to a gruff, menacing tone. "And they were equally supportive of me when I became the owner of that pub. You see, that's what parents do–their love isn't based on the level of career I chose, just on the fact that I'm their son and that I'm doing okay. Maybe you should try that sometime." He turned to walk away but stopped. Looking over his shoulder, he added, "Maybe one of your fancy textbooks can offer a study on the importance of loving your child where they're at rather than where you want them to be. You should look into that."

This time he did start to walk away, but at the door to the lanai, he said, "Or maybe you should find someone to talk to about it–your incessant need to control your daughter. You know, like a psychologist or something."

Then he opened the back door and walked back into the house.

It was after midnight, and Willow was breathless beside him. They had gone to bed over an hour ago, and the minute the bedroom door had closed, she had pretty much attacked him.

And he hadn't put up much of a fight.

It had been wild and frantic and...mostly quiet. Willow had put her hand over his mouth and warned him not to be too loud; otherwise Gammy would be knocking on the door wanting to know if they were having fun.

Just the thought of that was enough to keep him from uttering even a small peep.

"Not that I'm complaining," he said, still trying to catch his own breath, "but what brought that on?"

"You are a total knight in shining armor," she said quietly, resting one hand on his chest. "I thought that about you the day we met, and this trip totally confirmed it. Especially today."

Levi had refused to discuss what he and Paul had talked about out in the yard, but the difference in the man's demeanor when he rejoined the group had been hard to miss. He apologized to Willow and his mother before asking his wife what she wanted to do for the rest of the day. The look on Marilyn's face had pretty much said it all–that was something her husband never did.

He felt like a damn superhero.

Even though no one talked about it, the look of appreciation he received from all three Andrews' women told him everything he needed to know.

And he loved it.

Especially what was happening right now.

"I really didn't do anything, Willow."

That's it. Sound modest...

Turning her head, she looked at him. "I'm not going to ask you for specifics, Levi. But you accomplished more in those five minutes alone with my father than any of us have accomplished in...well...my entire life! I swear, I think he's finally let the idea of me moving to Seattle go! I feel like a ginormous weight has been lifted off of my shoulders and it's all because of you."

"Willow..."

Now she lifted up on one elbow to look at him. "No, I'm serious, Levi. I was so nervous about this trip and everything you've done has made things easier. Better. I don't know how I can ever repay you."

"I'm not looking to be repaid. I did it because..."

Shit. How do I say this without freaking her out?

"I know. You did it because you're a nice guy and we're friends. I get that," she said, interrupting his thought.

Um...friends?

"Friends?" he repeated.

"Well...yeah." Then she giggled. "Okay, so maybe we've ventured into the friends with benefits territory, but the bottom line is that you're this amazing man and I'm incredibly grateful to you."

"Willow," he groaned.

"Oh, stop." She placed a soft kiss on his chest. "You seem like the kind of guy who doesn't like people fussing over you or praising you publicly, but it's just the two of us here, and you should know that I think you're incredibly awesome." She yawned. "You're like the perfect guy, Levi. Some woman is going to be very lucky to be your real girlfriend."

Then she lay back down and cuddled up next to him. Levi contemplated correcting her, but she was yawning and getting comfortable and he wasn't sure now was the time.

Crap. She still saw this as them pretending to be involved. Fake relationship. Fake lovers.

Little did she know the only thing fake was...well, the

fakeness. They had two days worth of driving starting tomorrow morning. That meant he had two days to convince her this wasn't pretend.

This wasn't because he was doing her a favor.

When he heard her soft snore, Levi slowly stretched and reached over to the bedside table for his phone. Even though it was late, he knew he could send a few quick texts without it being a big deal. As much as he hated to let Willow go, he carefully pulled his arm out from under her and pulled out his messenger app. With a small smile, he sent a message to both Katie and Natalie that he and Willow wouldn't be stopping and seeing them on their way home.

Levi: Change of plans. Willow and I are taking some detours, and making a few other stops on the way home. Thanks for letting us stay with you last week and hopefully we'll be seeing you both again soon. I'll call when I get home and make sure everything's okay at the pub. Love you guys! Xoxo

---

Once he put the phone down, he turned out the light and wrapped his arms around Willow again.

It took less than a minute for him to fall asleep.

12

"So there's no plan."

"Nope."

"No...scheduled stops."

"Not a one."

"What about gas?"

"Well, that's a given, but I don't have it scheduled."

"Potty breaks?"

"Same thing."

"Hmm..."

"Hmm...what?"

"Any time I've ever driven to Florida and back, there's been a plan. Places we always stop."

"Any of them exciting?"

Willow didn't even have to think about it. "No. Gas and a hotel for the night. That's it."

Levi glanced over at her with a grin. "Were there places you wanted to stop but weren't allowed to?"

"Oh my goodness, yes!"

"Okay, then. That's what we'll do. Any place you want to stop at, we will."

"What if it's for a snack?"

"Done."

"What if it's for a tacky roadside attraction?"

"Even better."

"Can we stop and get some Florida oranges to take home? Peanuts and peaches in Georgia? Stop for tacos at South of the Border in South Carolina?"

Beside her, Levi laughed as he merged onto the highway. "Willow, we can do all of that and more. It doesn't sound like any of those are particularly time-consuming. Are we still aiming to make this a two-day trip or can we extend it to three?"

"We really need to keep it to two, unfortunately. I really need to get back to work and I'm sure you do too. That just means longer driving time. I hope that's okay."

"You know, you never did try and get behind the wheel."

Closing her eyes, Willow's head fell back against the seat. "I was hoping you didn't notice that."

"No worries, no pressure," he said smoothly. "However...this is going to be a lot of driving..."

Opening her eyes, she twisted in her seat to face him. "Let me ask you something."

"Go for it."

"When did you buy this car?"

"Why?"

"I'm being completely serious here. How long ago did you buy it?"

"Um...about a year ago."

"Okay. And how much have you babied it since buying it?"

"Willow, I don't baby it..."

"Really? So you don't take it to the car wash once a week or make sure no one eats or drinks in here?"

"If memory serves, we ate and drank in here the whole way down to Florida."

"Damn, I forgot about that." She paused and then smiled. "And you're telling me you didn't stop and vacuum the car after having lunch with the Romeos?"

"Um..."

"And have it washed?"

"Well..."

"And that the whole interior wasn't wiped down with some sort of vinyl protectant?"

"Okay, fine!" he cried with a laugh. "I'm a little obsessive about the car! I can't help it! I spent a lot of years driving an old pickup truck, and even though I loved it, this car is just...it's different. Besides costing a lot more than the truck did even when it was new, this car represents the fact that I'm an adult and not a kid anymore." After letting out a low growl, he continued. "And there's nothing wrong with wanting your car to be nice and clean and for it to smell good and shine and...and..."

Carefully, Willow reached out and placed her hand on his arm. "Okay, okay," she said quietly, soothingly, so as not to startle him. "I didn't mean to get you all worked up. Believe it or not, I was really just trying to get you to re-think the idea of me driving the car."

She watched as Levi took several calming breaths. "Why would I re-think it?"

"Levi, you've known me for a few months now and just spent a week with me. I'm kind of a walking disaster."

"That doesn't mean you drive like one."

She leveled him with a stare. "Seriously? Have you ever looked closely at my car?"

"Well...no..."

"Trust me when I tell you it has multiple scratches and dings everywhere. I have had about a half a dozen parking tickets, I get lost easily, and I've gotten pulled over twice for speeding and four times for going too slow on a highway."

"Seriously? That's a thing?"

Nodding, she said, "Yup. Trust me. I cried my way out of the speeding tickets."

"And the going too slow ones?"

"Same."

"Wow."

"Yeah, I'm not too proud of that, but, in my defense, I cry easily–especially when I'm stressed or scared. And there is nothing scarier than looking up and seeing those flashing lights in your rearview mirror." She shuddered. "So I think it would best for all of us if I...you know...didn't drive your car. At all. Like ever."

"Ever's a long time."

"And I'm sure you'd like to have your car for that long."

He shrugged. "I don't know about that. Maybe in a few years–or at least when it's paid off–I might be ready for something new. Something different."

"And you should be allowed to have that option. If you let me drive, that might be me making that decision for you."

"Willow, I won't allow you to speed, and I promise to prompt you if you're driving too slow."

But she shook her head. "Nuh-uh. No way. Not going to happen."

"What if I was too tired to drive and needed a nap?"

"Then you wouldn't be awake enough to make sure I didn't speed or hold up traffic!"

"Damn, you got me there."

"Driving is definitely not my strong suit." She paused and thought about it for a moment. "And long-distance driving is especially harsh on me. The speed things happened on road trips. Around town, I'm not terrible. Except at parking. Parking I'm terrible at."

His laugh was low and just a wee-bit sexier than she ever thought a laugh could be.

"Willow, you are definitely one in a million."

"You think so, huh?"

"Oh, I know so."

"It's because I'm such a dork, right?" she teased. At least, she hoped he realized she was teasing. There was no way she wanted him to agree with her being a dork.

Way to be a dork, dork...

"That's not what I was thinking," he said, and Willow let out a slow sigh of relief. "I meant because you are very open and honest about yourself. It's kind of amazing. Most people don't want to admit to having any flaws or are always trying to put the blame for the bad things that happen to them on other people. But you just own it and I think it's very cool."

"Donna and Jen say the same thing to me, but I always thought they were just being nice."

"I'm sure that's part of it, but it doesn't make it any less true."

Her hand smoothed down his arm until she reached his hand. Squeezing it, she said, "Thanks, Levi. You're a really great friend."

It felt wrong to say it, but...their trip was coming to an end and they didn't have to pretend anything anymore. Sadly, it was time to get back to the way things were before they left New York a week ago.

And she hated even the thought of it.

Not the part about going home–she actually couldn't wait to see Josh and all the dogs–but about things going back to the way things were between her and Levi. The thought of only seeing him on Friday nights and talking while he was working his shift filled her with such an overwhelming sense of sadness that she hadn't expected.

Although, to be honest, she hadn't allowed herself to think this far ahead. In all her planning for the week, Willow's main focus was on keeping her family off her back. Never in her wildest dreams did she allow herself to think about developing real feelings for Levi that had absolutely zero to do with friendship.

Oh, God...he's seen me naked! None of my friends have seen me naked! I always hide when I get changed!

Releasing his hand, she straightened herself in her seat again and sighed.

"You okay?"

"What? Oh...um...yeah. I just needed to get comfortable."

With the idea of us not being boyfriend and girlfriend anymore.

They drove in silence for several miles before Levi called out, "Hey, look! Florida oranges in one mile! Want to stop?" He looked at her with the biggest smile. How could she possibly do anything but smile back?

"Absolutely!"

Something was definitely up.

For the life of him, Levi had no idea what it was, but something was bothering Willow. He just hated that he didn't know her well enough to just know, and he wasn't sure if it was smart to push her to talk about it.

They had stopped for oranges.

A ten-pound bag of them.

Willow bragged about loving all citrus fruits and how she couldn't wait to get home and make herself freshly squeezed orange juice every morning.

He didn't have the heart to tell her it might take all of those oranges to make a decent glass of juice.

Now they were in Georgia and had just stopped for peanuts and peaches.

Luckily, not ten pounds of either.

"So...peaches not as big of a deal?" he asked as they loaded their latest purchases in the car.

"Yeah, not a huge fan of them. Like I'll eat one or two and be good to go. But I know Jen loves them, so I'll give the rest to her."

"And the peanuts?"

She shrugged. "I wanted to see what all the fuss was about."

Unable to help himself, he laughed. They were back in the car and he was about to back out of the parking spot, but he couldn't. "You wanted to see what all the fuss was about...peanuts?"

"Well, yeah. I can walk into any grocery store and buy peanuts like it's no big deal. And yet once you start driving through Georgia, there are these giant signs everywhere that make it seem like these are the greatest peanuts in the world. So I need to taste for myself and see what I think."

"Should I have kept them up front with us?"

"Nah, not in the mood."

For a moment, he could only stare. "So you're curious,

but not curious enough to try them right now. Do I have that right?"

"Yup."

If anyone asked him for one thing he learned about Willow this week, it was that she was utterly unpredictable.

And in a good way.

"Would you mind if I tried some?"

"Now?"

He nodded.

"Sure. Be my guest."

And there it was again. Some of her spark and light was gone.

So instead of reaching into the back seat and grabbing the peanuts, he turned toward her and stared until she returned his gaze.

It took almost a solid minute.

"What? What's the matter?" she asked.

"That was going to be my line."

Brows furrowed, she didn't respond.

"Willow, clearly something's bothering you. Is it me? Did I do something wrong?"

She looked like she was about to say something but changed her mind.

"I have no problem waiting you out," he explained. "I'm very patient."

"You're being ridiculous, Levi. There's nothing wrong. I guess I'm just a little tired and not looking forward to the long drive home. For some reason, it always seems to take longer." Then she shook her head. "And I know we're doing it in less time, but it already feels like it's going to take forever."

It made sense. Sort of.

"You're already missing your grandmother, aren't you?"

It wasn't a question. Over the few days they were there, Levi could tell Willow and her grandmother were very close. It was very sweet to see, and he knew they both wished they lived closer together.

Both sets of his grandparents had always lived close by. He never had to travel farther than the next town to see them. It was hard to imagine what life would have been like without them being so close.

If his grandfather had lived anywhere else and owned a pub, he had to wonder if he still would have followed the path he was currently on.

Wow...this is some deep shit. I need to lighten things up.

"Does she ever come back up to New York?" he asked, trying to get back to the topic at hand.

"No, not anymore. She loves to travel and so much of our family is scattered around now that I'm the only one left up there. It's easier to go to her. Usually I don't mind it. This was just a more stressful trip because...well...you know."

"For what it's worth, I think it all went perfectly. No one questioned our relationship and I don't think you're going to be getting any grief from your parents any time soon." He glanced over at her and winked. "At least, I hope you won't."

Her soft laugh made him hopeful that maybe they *were* lightening the mood. "I honestly can't say yes or no to that. No one's ever put my father in his place the way you did. This should be interesting to see how it all plays out."

"I have to admit, I'm kind of curious about it myself," he teased. "Just basing things on what I observed and not on the stories you shared with me, I'm thinking it's going to be interesting. How often do you talk to them?"

"I get a call from my mother once a week," she replied.

"It's a perfunctory sort of thing; like I don't think she's genuinely interested or concerned with what I'm doing, but she calls to see if I'm going to fall in line with what they want me to do."

"Okay, so let's be optimistic," he said, doing his best to sound positive. "Let's say they are now officially off your back. How does that make you feel?"

"Honestly?" she asked with a nervous laugh. "I don't know yet. It's all too new and too foreign of a concept yet."

"Oh, come on...don't you feel like you can take on the world? Just a little bit? Last night you said it felt like a ginormous weight had been lifted off your shoulders. You should be thinking about hitting the ground running when we get home and being free to explore all kinds of opportunities!"

Tilting her head, Willow blinked at him like he was crazy.

"What? I'm being serious here! I think all their negative comments and energy were holding you back. You're free now."

"Okay, that sounds a little dramatic..."

"Me? Dramatic?" He blinked at her innocently. "I wouldn't know the first thing about being dramatic. I leave that to my sisters, thank you very much."

"Sounds like something a brother would say."

And now he saw the impish grin peeking out that he was used to.

From there, they talked all about the things her brother used to do while they were growing up, and Levi realized for as crazy as her parents were, she had a fairly normal childhood. He felt a connection to her brother even though they had never met, mainly because they were both the only boys in their families. It wasn't often he met someone with the same family makeup as his and now he almost wished they could all get together sometime.

So not going to happen...

Just the thought of his mild-mannered, fun-loving parents hanging out with Willow's insane and uptight ones was enough to make him laugh.

And he did.

"What's so funny?"

Levi explained what he was just thinking, and luckily she laughed with him.

"I can't even imagine," she said, still laughing. "Although, to be fair, I haven't met your parents so I'll have to take your word for it. But based on your description, it would be incredibly awkward."

After that, the conversation flowed and Levi was confident that whatever funk she was feeling earlier had finally lifted. They stopped for lunch in Savannah, and Levi had been tempted to call his sister and see if she could join them. But after some discussion, he came to the conclusion that if they were going to stick to some semblance of a schedule and get in the most hours of driving for the day, they needed to keep their breaks short.

Once they were back in the car, Willow pulled out her phone and began checking their route. "I think at the pace we're going, we should consider stopping once we cross into North Carolina."

"And after we stop at South of the Border."

"Naturally."

Chuckling, he agreed and figured they'd simply play it by ear and see how they felt once they got there. "When we stop for dinner, we'll see what the area is like and where the nearest hotel is. How does that sound?"

"Like the perfect plan."

He wasn't quite so sure...

They were still in the parking lot of the diner they had eaten lunch at, and after several long moments, Willow looked over at him. "How come we're not driving?"

"Well, technically, there is no *we* in that. I've been doing all the driving. I think it's your turn."

"*What?!*"

"Come on. It won't be so bad. South Carolina is fairly easy to drive through. The roads are nice and smooth, the traffic's not that bad...I really think you should try to do some of the driving. Just for an hour. What do you say?"

He saw the indecision and panic on her face, but he knew this would be a good thing for her. Maybe if she tackled this–the whole driving thing–and succeeded, she'd have a little more confidence in herself.

Or...this could all go horribly wrong and you'll end up taking a Greyhound home...

Okay, thinking like that wasn't helping anyone, and Levi forced those thoughts aside.

Before he could change his mind, he climbed from the car and walked around to the passenger side. Pulling the door open, he reached in and took Willow by the hand. "You got this. I have faith in you."

"Levi..." she whined. "This is crazy! I'm telling you, this is the worst idea ever! Worse than anything you've ever done!"

He led her around the car and helped her get seated behind the wheel. For several minutes he helped her move the seat until she was in a good position, then he pointed out everything she could possibly need to drive. With a quick kiss on her cheek, he said, "You're all set!" before jogging around and getting in on the passenger side.

And that just felt weird.

Like...super weird.

Like...I don't like this weird.

But now that he'd opened his big mouth and made such a production out of making her drive, he was just going to have to make the best of it.

And pray nothing went wrong.

It took her almost five minutes to pull out of the parking spot and then out of the parking lot. Levi made sure to be supportive and encouraged her with every inch she moved the car.

It was exhausting.

They weren't far off of I-95, and he found himself holding his breath as she merged into traffic.

"You doing okay?" he asked once she was doing the speed limit and going with the flow of traffic.

She had a white-knuckled grip on the steering wheel and he was pretty sure she hadn't blinked in a solid minute, but...she nodded.

At least, he thought it was a nod.

"Willow?"

"Just...shush!" she hissed. "Don't distract me!"

"Willow, we've got like four hours between here and South of the Border. You can't expect me to be silent the entire time. That's crazy."

She glanced at him, and the car immediately swerved into the next lane.

"Willow!" Reaching out, he grabbed the wheel and waited for her to get back in her lane.

"I told you," she murmured. "I know myself, Levi. I know that I need to concentrate. At least for a little while. I'll let you know when you can talk."

He was afraid to even comment, so instead, he reached for the radio to turn it on.

"No!" she cried. "No music!"

"Um..."

"If you turn on the radio, I'm going to inevitably hear a song I like, and then I'll start singing along, possibly dance, and then the next thing you know, the car will be in a ditch! Or a tree!"

"How can you dance while you're driving?"

"Levi...please..." she whined.

"Okay, okay, okay." He made a zipping motion over his mouth and reached over and went to grab his phone.

"What are you doing? The GPS is on there! You can't just turn it off!"

It was obvious he'd made a mistake.

A horrible, horrible mistake.

"We're on I-95. We're not getting off of I-95. It's pretty much a straight run for the next 180 miles. You don't need the GPS. Trust me."

"I *did* trust you, and now I'm driving this big scary car and trying not to get us killed."

"Do you want to pull over and switch back?" he asked, feeling completely exasperated. "There's going to be a rest area when we cross into South Carolina. We can stop there and just forget this whole thing." With a loud sigh, he closed his eyes and slumped down slightly in his seat.

"And now you're mad at me," she huffed. "I told you, but did you listen? No! You would think you'd realize that I know more about myself than you do! Or that maybe you would appreciate that I was being protective of you and your car because that's the kind of person I am. Considerate. Compassionate. And...and...thoughtful. Here I was all concerned about your feelings and you didn't do the same for me. Wow. Just...wow. Thanks a lot, Levi."

"Now who's being dramatic?" he murmured under his breath.

"I heard that."

Arguing with her was pointless. So instead he said, "Just...drive, Willow. The rest area isn't that far away. I think we can do it without incident."

As soon as the words were out of his mouth, he wondered if he was lying to himself.

And prayed that he wasn't.

13

"Holy shit! Are we...are we alive?"

"I think so."

"I don't...I mean how...when..."

"I know. Think how I feel."

Levi scrubbed a hand over his face as he looked around in dazed confusion. He reached for the door handle and immediately stopped. "I can't get out over here."

"Well, don't think I'm going to move the car!"

Willow watched him swallow hard as he considered his options. "Okay, are you okay to get out?"

She nodded.

"You do that, and then I'll climb over the console and move the car."

"Levi, I'm..."

But he held up a hand to stop her. With nothing left to do, she slowly climbed from the car and took several steps back.

Inside the car, Levi was doing his best to twist himself into a pretzel to get into the driver's seat and she cursed herself for making him do it.

They had driven by the rest area three and a half hours ago. She had settled into driving, and felt like it would be okay for her to keep going. About an hour into her shift, Levi had dozed off. It would have been mean to wake him up and really, there wasn't any traffic and it was a fairly uneventful stretch of road.

So she kept going.

"Ugh...why did I keep going?"

The car door slammed, and she saw Levi moving the seat back to his position and felt bad all over again.

Everything was going just fine until she pulled off the exit at South of the Border. That was where they had agreed to stop and she was excited that she'd driven the entire way without incident. Levi was still asleep at that point and she figured she'd wake him up once she had parked.

The parking lot was crowded and Willow had been slightly twitchy as she maneuvered through the throngs of cars. She was confident that she could find a spot to park far enough away that she wouldn't be near anyone else. Then someone beeped at her and she jumped, hitting the gas pedal hard and ended up pulling a stunt that belonged in a *Dukes of Hazzard* episode–she sped up, jumped a curb, and spun the car 360 degrees and ended up pressed up against a pair of eight-foot-tall roosters.

Good going, Willow...

She was afraid to see what the passenger side of the car looked like. No doubt it was all scratched up and damaged.

Oh, God...how am I even going to face Levi–let alone spend another full day of driving with him?

The car started to move, and Willow took a few more steps back to give him room. When he turned the wheel and started to drive away, she was convinced he was leaving her there. Tears stung her eyes, and within seconds, she was full-on bawling. She was in the middle of the parking lot and managed to stumble out of the way of other cars and found a place to sit.

Beneath the giant roosters.

Glancing to her left, she saw a man walking his dog, and before she knew it, the dog was peeing on one of the roosters.

This is it. I've hit an all-time low. Surely there is nothing worse than leaning against a filthy peed on rooster in the middle of a roadside tourist attraction 600 miles from home...

Leaning down, her hands covering her face, she bawled some more. How was she supposed to get home? She didn't have her purse, her luggage, no money, nothing. Now she was going to have to call someone...Jen? Donna? Or, God forbid, her parents.

Oh, Lord...anything but that...

She could only imagine how *that* conversation would go. Any progress they had made thanks to Levi's conversation with her father would be completely undone, and then she'd have to move to Seattle. It was the only way to get out of this.

"I don't want to move to Seattle," she cried into her hands.

"Why are you moving to Seattle?"

Gasping, she looked up and saw Levi staring down at her.

"You're still here."

Frowning, he asked, "Why wouldn't I be?"

Slowly, Willow came to her feet, afraid she was seeing a mirage or that maybe she hit her head during the death-spin in the car and was hallucinating. "You left," she blurted out. "I watched you drive away!"

Gently, Levi grasped her shoulder and turned her a little to the right. "I parked the car."

She threw herself at him and wrapped herself around him and started crying all over again. "I'm so sorry! I am so, so sorry, Levi! You have to know that! And I swear I'll pay for all the damages! It may take a while since neither of my part-time jobs pays much, but I'll walk a hundred dogs if it helps! Or...or...I'll do dishes at the pub! Or mop! Or anything!" She hugged him even harder. "Just please tell me you forgive me and that we're still friends. Please! I would hate to think of us not being friends anymore!"

Levi returned her hug, and then carefully put some distance between them. Then, taking her by the hand, he began to lead her back to the car. "There's something you need to see."

"Oh, no..." she groaned. "It's bad, isn't it? I don't need to see it. I'll take your word for it. There's no need to..."

He stopped, and she walked right into him, because she was staring at the ground instead of where they were going.

"Willow..."

She scrunched her eyes shut and shook her head. "I can't. I can't look at it."

"Willow..." he said with a little more heat.

"I'm the worst. I get it! I'll sit in the back seat for the entire rest of the trip and I won't say a word. You won't even know I'm there! And I promise not to touch anything! Ever!"

"Willow!" he snapped.

And that tone had her stopping and opening her eyes.

He was smiling and motioning toward the car.

"What the...?" Slowly, she stepped around him and toward the car, unable to believe what she was seeing.

"There's...I mean...how...?"

"There are no scratches," he explained. "And no dents. No damage."

"How is that possible? I was a one-woman stunt show back there."

Leaning in close, he said, "And a good stunt person knows how to pull off a stunt without causing any damage."

Willow examined the car more closely, running her hand along the entire passenger side. "I don't get it. Those roosters are eight feet of solid concrete. How could they not scratch up the car?"

"Wait, are you actually upset that you didn't damage the car?"

The car felt perfectly smooth—the only marks were the smudges from her fingerprints. "No, that's not it. I'm just confused. I thought for sure...between jumping the curb and flying through the air and then...you know...the roosters..."

He chuckled softly. "Somehow you managed to miss the roosters. You got close, but...never touched them. Seriously, you were only a hair's width away, but it was enough to not even touch."

"Holy crap! This is great!" She threw herself at him again, but this time while laughing and feeling better than she had...possibly ever! "Seriously, this is amazing!" Her legs were around his waist, and he was laughing with her. Placing a loud, smacking kiss on his cheek, she repeated, "Isn't it amazing?"

Levi spun her around one more time before putting her back on his feet. "I'd say more like a miracle."

Her heart was racing, and she knew her laughter was verging on hysterics, but she couldn't believe her luck. "You have no idea how relieved I am! I was certain I had totaled your car – or at the very least done some serious damage!" She let out a long, shaky breath and tried to calm down. "And I am so glad you weren't hurt! How embarrassing would that be to explain– that you were hurt by a pair of giant concrete roosters!"

He cleared his throat and tried to look like he wasn't amused, but she knew he was. "Um, yeah. I'm glad I don't have to explain that to anyone. Ever."

Turning her back to the car, Willow leaned against it until she caught her breath. When she did, she looked over at Levi. "So I think we can agree that letting me drive is a bad idea."

Surprisingly, he shook his head as he moved in close. "No. Letting you *park* is a bad idea. Your driving is just fine. Smooth. So smooth that I fell asleep. I think that speaks volumes right there."

"Well, sadly, there's no way to allow me to drive without eventually having to park, so..."

"You've got a point."

"Anyhow...now that we've had our excitement for the day, let's go inside and do a little shopping."

"Seriously? You can think about shopping right now?"

"Levi, I'm going to need some time before I can get back in the car without suffering from PTSD or something. I say we do a little shopping, maybe grab a taco or two..."

"It's almost dinnertime. And I was hoping for something more than tacos."

"Consider it a pre-appetizer or just a snack," she reasoned. "Either way, I know it's too early for dinner, but I really do need some time before we get back in the car. Plus, you promised we'd stop here. What's the point in stopping if I don't get to explore?"

Sighing, he pinched the bridge of his nose, and she knew he was trying to stop himself from rushing her–or telling her she was crazy. Either way, she appreciated it. After a few moments, he said, "You're right. It would be silly to stop and not go in and look around. Although it really just looks like a gas station, some gift shops, and a restaurant. I don't see what..."

"There's miniature golf too, but don't worry, I really just want to look around and see what all the fuss is about. This place has been here since forever! There are billboards advertising it hundreds of miles away! Come on, where's your sense of adventure?"

She reached for his hand and began tugging him toward one of the buildings.

"Willow, I really don't consider a gift shop off an exit ramp to be an adventure?"

"Not even after the dramatic entrance we made to it?" she asked, feigning offense.

But he was on to her. With a dramatic sigh, he said, "You know what? You're right. Anyplace that warrants that kind of entrance is bound to be amazing. We should ask about them putting your picture up on the wall–like a parking lot hall of fame or something."

"Oh, my God! Do you think they'd do that? How cool would that be? I'd be famous!"

"Willow..."

"Yeah, yeah, yeah, I know. I'm just teasing."

They walked through the doors of the gift shop and she didn't know where to look first. It was all so bright and tacky and colorful, and she wanted one of everything! Releasing Levi's hand, she ran over to a display of sombreros and put one on her head.

"What do you think? Am I a hat person?" And with a laugh, she picked another one and walked over and put it on his head. "Yes! We totally rock these sombreros! Wait! Where's my phone? We totally need a picture!"

"It's probably still in the car–which is locked, so relax," he assured her. "But I've got mine right here."

Then, pulling her in close, Levi held up the phone to get a selfie of the two of them, and Willow knew it was going to be her favorite memory of the entire trip.

You're such a good friend.

Willow must have said that at least a dozen times over dinner and another dozen more while they drove to their hotel and booked a room.

With two beds.

Okay, fine, she was hitting him over the head with the fact that their fake relationship was over and so was the not-so-fake sexual part of it. He got it. He understood.

But that didn't mean he liked it.

How the hell was he supposed to go back to just being friends–and sleeping in the same room as her–after everything that had transpired over the weekend? Sure, he'd dated plenty of women who he went on to be just friends with, but he never had to spend the night in a hotel with them afterward either.

"Maybe I should have gotten us separate rooms," he muttered.

"Did you say something?" Willow asked as she came out of the bathroom, drying her hair.

Hoping he didn't look too guilty, he forced himself to smile. "Just commenting on how this is a nice room."

"It really is," she said as she walked across the room. She

sat down on her bed and looked at him. "I hate that you are the one paying, though."

"Willow, we've been over this..."

"I know, I know. But after everything that happened today..."

He held up a hand to stop her. "Staying at a hotel here in North Carolina made way more sense than trying to drive all the way to Richmond and going to Natalie's again. I don't care if I did nap earlier, I would have been cross-eyed by the time we got there."

"That's not what I meant."

"It's really not that big of a deal," he countered, hoping she'd just let this go. "I wanted to do this."

"But I was supposed to be the one paying for the trip. This was all for me and..."

"You bought me a sombrero and a taco," he said lightly. "We're good, Willow. Trust me."

The way she was frowning at him told Levi she wasn't buying it.

And then her loud huff pretty much confirmed it.

"What? What do you want me to say? I'm not going to apologize for this. I paid for the hotel. It's not a big deal. You can pay for gas the rest of the way home and all the meals if that makes you feel better."

He knew he'd never allow it, but she didn't need to know that.

"You're mad at me," she said after an uncomfortable minute.

"Um...what?"

She nodded. "You're mad at me. Admit it."

"Why would I be mad at you? I told you, we're good."

"Yeah, it's not so much what you say but the way you're saying it. You have a tone."

"A tone?"

She nodded again. "Yup. A tone."

Leaning back on his elbows on his own bed, Levi did his best to appear bored. "Okay, I'll bite, what kind of tone do I have?"

Willow tossed her towel down as she stood and tried to look intimidating.

It was sexy as hell.

Wet hair, hot pink flannel sleep shorts and a white t-shirt that was a little clingy, yeah, sexy.

And her nipples were hard so...that was also a little distracting.

"You're barely looking at me, Levi, and ever since we got to the room, you've been kind of short with me. Annoyed. If you wanted me to get my own room, you should have said so." With another huff, she turned and reached for the phone.

"What are you doing?"

"I'm calling the front desk to see if they have any other rooms available."

Groaning, Levi jumped up and put his hand over hers, preventing her from picking up the phone.

"Levi!"

"Willow!" he mimicked. "You don't need to get your own room. We're totally fine sharing one. We've been doing it for almost a week."

That and a whole lot more...

Yanking her hand out from under his, she took a few steps back–as if even been close to him was a bad thing.

And if that wasn't a message she was sending–loud and clear, no less–then he didn't know what was.

"I...I just don't want this to be awkward." She paused. "We only have to get through tonight and then everything will go back to normal." Then she looked away. "No big deal."

Only...it was.

"Is that really how you feel?" he asked.

A shrug was her only response, and rather than push her and make things even more uncomfortable than they already were, Levi raked a hand through his hair and stormed off to the bathroom.

"I'm going to take a shower," he murmured, slamming the door shut behind him. It was childish, and it wasn't really going to solve anything. It wasn't as if he was going to spend the night in there or sleep in the bathtub. All he was accomplishing was putting a little distance between them to give them each a little time to calm down. With any luck, Willow would decide to go to sleep early and then they won't have to talk to one another again until morning.

He turned on the hot water and then turned to look at himself in the mirror and grimaced. He was pissed, there was no denying it. After the whole incident with the car, he thought they were fine. They had joked around for almost an hour in the gift shop. He had stood back and watched as Willow breezed around the entire space and touched everything in there. She tried on hats, sunglasses, jewelry...she was literally like a kid in a candy shop. They had laughed and taken silly pictures, and after she had purchased about a dozen things, they had gone and grabbed a few tacos–they weren't his favorite, but they were still pretty good.

After that, they had walked out and taken a few pictures with the giant roosters before going to put gas in the car and heading to dinner. Willow had Googled local hotels, and they found one with a good rating that was only fifteen minutes from where they were. And the entire time, they had been happy and carefree and...two completely different people from the ones who were just snapping at one another.

What the hell changed?

The bathroom was steamy, and standing and staring at himself in the mirror wasn't getting him anywhere, so he stripped and stepped under the hot spray. It took several minutes for him to relax and a few more minutes for him to reach for the soap and shampoo. He cursed as he used the hotel brand that was stocked in the bathroom because he hadn't taken the time to go through his luggage.

Which reminded him...

He hadn't stopped to get himself a change of clothes either.

It wouldn't be the worst thing to throw his jeans back on for just a few minutes so he could get his suitcase. No big deal.

By the time he stepped out of the shower, he felt much better, and if Willow was still awake, he figured he'd be the one to go to sleep early. It wouldn't kill him to get a good night's sleep. Lord knew it had been quite a few nights since that had happened. Between Nat's floor, Katie's couch, and then sharing a bed with Willow, it was shocking he wasn't dead on his feet by now.

He toweled off and sighed as he picked his jeans up off the floor and slid them on. It was pointless to button them, so he scooped the rest of his clothes up and walked back out into the room. Willow was sitting on her bed...

Shit.

She was crying.

Well, she did warn you on the first day that she cried easily. Who knew she'd wait to prove that until now?

Walking over to his suitcase and fighting the urge to go to her, he asked, "You okay?"

With a sniffle, she looked up at him and her eyes went a little wide. "Um...yeah." But then she shook her head. "No. No, I'm not okay."

Levi pulled a pair of shorts out of his bag but didn't make a move toward her. "What's going on?"

It took her a minute to get herself together, and then she stood and faced him. "I hate this," she finally said. "I thought it was going to be okay, that I could handle it, but...I can't."

His heart started to race, and he began to sweat. Did he really want to hear the whole "Let's be friends" speech followed by the "It's not you, it's me" one?

Hell no.

"Willow..."

But she wasn't listening. Instead, she walked over to him and didn't stop until they were practically toe to toe.

She was killing him.

Before he knew it, one of her hands was on his chest. She wouldn't meet his gaze and he had to grit his teeth to keep from asking her what she was doing.

"I don't want our last night to be spent like this. Fighting," she clarified, studying his chest. "Ever since we met, you've always been so sweet and gentle and kind to me. I really thought I had blown it earlier with the car, but...even then...you were incredibly gracious."

Just say we're going to be friends and put me out of my misery!

Then those big, beautiful eyes slowly looked up at him and Levi knew he'd never be able to think of Willow as just a friend ever again. It wasn't possible. Hell, he had no idea how they were going to move forward from this, but...he'd put on a brave face and do the honorable thing and get her home without putting any pressure on her. And then...

well, then he had no idea what he was going to do. Probably bury himself back in his work like he had for the last two years.

If nothing else, she gave him an incredible break from the monotonous existence he'd been living for so long. He should be thankful for that.

Her hand smoothed down to his stomach and he couldn't help the low moan that escaped his lips. "Willow..."

Placing a finger over his lips, she shook her head. "We have one more night, Levi," she said quietly. "We agreed to be boyfriend and girlfriend for this trip and...the trip isn't over yet."

Um...say what now?

Looking down, he saw her swallow hard. "I'll get another room if that's what you want or I'll sleep in the other bed and never bring this up again, but...I really want–need–to be with you tonight." She paused when their eyes met. "Please don't turn me away."

Was she kidding him?

"Willow." His voice was low and rough, practically a growl. Slowly his hand came up and anchored into her damp hair. He saw the vulnerability in her eyes, the slight tremble of her lips. "I'd never turn you away."

"Levi, I..."

He didn't let her finish. It had already felt like an eternity since he'd tasted her. Touched her. Kissed her. Together, they slowly maneuvered themselves across the room until they fell onto the bed Willow had been sitting on earlier.

Not that it mattered. He had a feeling before the night was through, they'd use both beds and possibly other assorted spots and surfaces. Sleep be damned because if she was giving him one more night–one last night–he wasn't going to waste it sleeping.

Tongues dueled, hands grabbed and grasped and stroked, and it was a kind of glorious madness. They didn't have to be quiet because they were in somebody else's home or someone else's bed. This entire space was theirs to be as wild and as loud as they wanted to be.

And Levi was desperate to know just how wild and loud he could make Willow.

He broke the kiss long enough to whip her shirt up over her head and loved the sound of her soft gasp. Her breasts were perfect, and her skin was pale and as smooth as silk. He could touch her for hours on end and never get enough.

"Please tell me there's more of that," she whispered, breaking into his thoughts.

"Sweetheart, there is so much more of that coming, I promise you. I just don't even know where to begin."

"Can I ask you something?"

"Anything."

"Are you wearing anything under your jeans?"

His grin was slow and a little devious. "You tell me."

The instant she realized what he was saying, he felt her hand smooth down his back and then under his jeans to grip his bare ass.

And squeezed.

"Wow," she said breathlessly. "I had no idea you were commando under there."

"It wasn't planned, but...now I'm really glad I am."

"You know what would make me really glad?"

He shook his head.

"If you took those off and then got back on the bed with me. Please."

It was hard not to chuckle when she was being so polite.

Leaning down, he kissed her hard before jumping to his feet.

He quickly shucked off his jeans and stood before her completely naked. "Whatever it is you want tonight, Willow, is yours. Anything."

Pushing up on her elbows, she blatantly ogled him. "There's no risk of anyone interrupting us, right?"

"Depends on how loud we get."

Then he watched in stunned silence as she shimmied out of her shorts and panties before lying back provocatively on the bed. "Then let's see what we might have been missing the last few nights." She held out a hand to him, and he gladly took it. "I'm going to want everything, Levi. Everything you have to give." He crawled up over her and saw the mischievous gleam in her eyes. "And I'm going to be very vocal about asking for them."

"I'm a very good listener," he promised, letting his body slowly cover hers. The skin on skin contact making them both sigh. His erection was almost painful by this point, but he knew he was more than up for the challenge. And when he claimed her lips in a kiss that almost brutal, he knew he'd listen to whatever else she wanted to say.

Later.

14

THEY CROSSED into Suffolk County and Willow knew they were only thirty minutes from home. She yawned broadly and fought to keep her eyes open.

"You going to make it?" Levi asked with a hint of amusement. They had driven all day–almost twelve hours–and except for gas and bathroom breaks and going through the drive-thru's for meals, they hadn't stopped.

Another yawn.

"I don't know why I'm so tired, you're the one who drove all day." But...she knew why she was tired. They had only slept a handful of hours last night and she didn't regret that decision for one minute.

If she had thought the sex with Levi was incredible while they had been in Florida, it was nothing like it was last night.

Holy. Crap.

Without the limitations of having to be quiet for fear of waking anyone, Willow found herself to be extremely vocal in bed.

Something she never really had been in the past.

And she never even had to ask for anything–Levi just seemed to know exactly what she wanted and how to give it to her.

Hard and repeatedly.

Yum.

Her vocalness came more from her responding to what he was doing to her rather than asking for it, and those responses seemed to really spur Levi on. What she really wanted was to test that theory again but...unfortunately, she had made such a big deal about last night being their last night, that she didn't think there was any way to bring up the subject.

All day there hadn't been any hand-holding or outward signs of affection and she knew it was the right thing to do. They were playing a part for a short period of time and no matter how much she enjoyed it, she needed to remember that Levi had been doing her a favor. Well...she didn't think the sex was part of the favor, more like a perk, but still...it wasn't real.

Friends with benefits.

Briefly.

While pretending to be something they weren't.

But what if they extended their benefits just because? No reason. No favors. Just because they were enjoying themselves? Levi didn't seem interested in being in a real relationship and he worked all the time, so maybe offering him this sex with no strings option would appeal to him.

It couldn't hurt to ask, right?

Or it could totally hurt, and you'll be humiliated because he'll turn you down. Is that what you want?

She sighed.

Then yawned.

And heard Levi's soft laugh.

It was on the tip of her tongue to just blurt it out and ask him right now, but with them still having some time left in the car, she didn't want it to be awkward. However, she decided as soon as they got to her place and got out of the car, she was asking him and to hell with the consequences. If he turned her down, she could go into her apartment, close the door, walk into her bedroom, and scream into a pillow. No big deal.

And if he said yes, she could lead him into her apartment, close the door, take him to her bedroom, and scream into a pillow.

But for completely different—and sexy—reasons.

It's good to have a plan.

"So, um...do you have to work tomorrow?" she asked.

"Yeah. Definitely. I've been calling and checking on everything, but I really need to get back."

"Wow, your boss is lucky to have you. You're so dedicated to your job!"

All he did was shrug.

"I told Mrs. Moore—Josh's mom—that I'd call her when I got back. Her mother's been helping her out while I was gone, but she's older and it's hard on her to keep up with him so I'm sure she'll be relieved that I'm home."

"And the dogs?"

"Same." Then she laughed. "Not that Mrs. Moore's mother has been walking them, but I told everyone I'd call them when I got home."

"Why not just tell them the date you were getting back?"

"Honestly? I had no idea how this trip was going to go.

Maybe I was going to come back earlier than planned, or maybe I was going to have so much fun that I didn't want to leave?" She shrugged. "Everyone was cool with being flexible so..."

"Have you given any more thought to maybe going back to school to get your degree in early childhood education?"

"What?"

Looking at her, he nodded. "You know, so you can work at either the daycare center you told me about or just go into the field wherever you want."

"Levi, I...I wasn't really serious about that. I mean, how crazy would that be to just go back to school again after all the years I already went? And believe me, I didn't enjoy it at all the first time. Why would I want to go back?"

"Because now you'd actually be studying something that interested you and not something you were being forced to study. I bet that would make a huge difference. It's something to consider."

She groaned.

"I'm not trying to pressure you like your parents, trust me. I'm just offering a suggestion. I bet if you ran it by Donna and Jen, they'd agree."

"Don't play dirty, Levi."

"What's that supposed to mean?"

"It means don't you dare bring it up to them the next time we go to McGee's." Sighing, she turned her head and looked out the window, suddenly not feeling very chatty anymore. Levi must have taken the hint because he grew quiet as well.

By the time they pulled into the parking lot of her apartment complex, Willow was ready to go crazy. She couldn't wait to get out of the car, stretch her legs, and...speak. Yeah, that was a biggie right now.

Once the car was parked, they worked together to gather all of her things and Levi carried the bulk of them to her door. Willow unlocked it but didn't open it right away. Instead, she turned and faced him.

"I never should have said you'd play dirty."

He nodded.

"And I want to thank you for everything you did this past week."

"You're welcome." His words were spoken so softly that she barely heard them.

Good thing I'm focusing on his mouth...

"I know everything didn't go the way we planned, and... there were times when they were awkward..." She swallowed hard and forced herself to meet his gaze. "And some things were completely unexpected."

"Willow?"

"Hmm?"

"Open the door."

"What?"

He motioned to the door.

"Oh, right. Sorry." No doubt all the things he was carrying were getting heavy. Opening the door, she stepped inside and moved out of his way. With a weary sigh, she went on, "Anyway, I just want you to know..."

Before she knew what was happening, the door was closed, she was pressed up against it, and Levi was kissing her senseless.

And it was glorious.

Willow wrapped herself around him, wanting to climb him like a tree–which she pretty much did. With her legs around his waist, she pulled back and broke the kiss and breathlessly asked, "Um, Levi?"

"Trip's not over," he said before diving in to kiss her again.

If the theory worked last night, he didn't see why he couldn't be the one to use it today.

It was late, and he was exhausted, but leaving Willow simply wasn't an option. Granted, he knew he was going to have to eventually, but...just not now. Not tonight.

I should be checking on the pub! It's still open and I've been gone for over a week!

But he knew he didn't really need to. His manager was amazing and had been keeping him updated throughout the trip about everything that had been going on. It had been an uneventful week, and he was thankful for it. There would be plenty of time tomorrow for him to go in and sit in his office and deal with all the things he would have to deal with—paying bills, payroll, and ordering supplies. They had a first-rate computer system that handled most of that for him, but that didn't mean he didn't check, double-check, and triple-check on everything.

Tomorrow.

Right now, the only things he wanted to check, double-check, and triple-check were ways to make Willow come.

Because good Lord, was that an amazing thing to see, feel, and hear.

Yeah, one more night and he should be able to walk away and let them go back to the friend zone.

Just the thought of it nearly killed him, but luckily, Willow was sucking on his tongue and rubbing up against him so he was pretty much able to push those thoughts aside and focus on her.

They clumsily made their way to her bedroom, and he saw it was very feminine–some stuffed animals in a chair in the corner, lots of soft, pastel colors, and a ton of pillows on the bed. So many pillows that he wasn't sure where he was supposed to lay her down. He broke the kiss and stared down at the bed. She turned her head to follow his gaze.

"Floor," she said, climbing out of his arms and he wasn't sure if she meant her or the pillows. But once she was on her feet, she quickly swept all the pillows off the bed and onto the floor before whipping her shirt up and over her head.

"Fantastic idea," he murmured, stripping off his own shirt.

Maybe he should be questioning why she was so readily on board with what they were doing. Levi knew his reasons, but he was curious why he didn't need to explain himself more. All day yesterday and last night, Willow had been all about reiterating how they were friends–and seemingly, *just* friends–and yet here they were frantically stripping down together again.

In the blink of an eye, she was down to her panties and pressed up against him, kissing her way down his chest, grabbing the waistband of his jeans as she went.

"Pants, Levi," she whispered between kisses. "This will work a lot better without the pants."

She seemed to say that a lot.

Maybe he should...

His eyes rolled back into his head as she pulled his jeans and boxers down enough to start kissing below the belt.

One hand gently gripped the back of her head as all the breath whooshed from his lungs. Reaching around behind him, he did his best to balance against the bed without falling over.

But it didn't quite work out that way.

The comforter material was a little too slippery, and the hand that was on her head pushed her away as Levi lost his balance and slid.

He hit the bed; Willow hit the floor.

And they both burst out laughing.

It was the least sexy moment ever and yet...he loved it.

Forcing himself to straighten, Levi kicked off the rest of his clothes before he held out a hand to her and helped her to her feet. "You okay?"

"I'm fine," she said, still laughing. "But I'm really glad it's kind of dark in here. That was not a position I'd want anyone to see me in."

Banding his arm around her waist, he kissed her softly. "You, naked on the floor? I'll always want to see that."

"Levi..."

Tucking a finger under her chin, he leaned in and kissed her again, this time making sure she knew they were done talking for now. He was about to guide them both onto the bed when she went on the move again.

He kind of loved it when she did that.

This time nothing was stopping her from kissing every inch of him.

Every. Inch.

"Willow," he panted. "I think...I need...oh shit, that's good...maybe..."

She gave him a playful shove, and he fell back on the bed. He scooted up toward the headboard and got comfortable before Willow joined him. Straddling him, he realized she had gotten rid of her panties too. Before he could comment on it, she was kissing her way down from his chest again. Just when she was about to pick up where she'd left off, she raised her head and gave him the sexiest smile he'd ever seen.

"Just FYI, these walls have great insulation. We can be as loud as we want for as long as we want."

Which was perfect news because it didn't take long for her lips to wrap around him and cause him to roar with his release.

The room was pitch black and Willow was curled up next to him sound asleep.

Levi wished he was doing the same.

He was exhausted; that was a given. But he just wasn't sure what he was supposed to be doing right now.

You mean other than sleeping?

Sure, that was one option, but...should he leave now and make things a little less weird in the morning or did he stay and...deal with the weirdness?

Yawning, he knew the smart thing to do was deal with the weirdness. He had no right being out on the road driving when he was this tired. No need to be a danger to himself and anyone else on the road.

Decision made, he closed his eyes and started counting backward from one hundred.

Ninety-nine, ninety-eight...

And he was asleep.

The next time he opened his eyes, the room was bright, and he was alone. Sitting up slowly, he looked around and listened for where Willow might be. He smelled coffee and figured she was in the kitchen.

His limbs felt like they were made of lead as he climbed from the bed and slid his jeans and boxers back on. Shirtless, he made his way out of the room and toward wherever the kitchen was.

Last night, he had only seen the entryway and had a vague memory of stumbling across the apartment. In the light of day, it was much smaller than he thought it would be. There was one open living area with a small kitchen and...that was it. Other than the bedroom and bathroom, there wasn't much else. It was decorated in a style that totally screamed Willow, though, much like her bedroom. She was obviously a girly-girl, and he wanted to walk around and look at all her framed pictures, but...she was sitting at her little kitchen table watching him.

"Good morning."

She blushed and lowered her gaze. "Good morning."

"Did you sleep well?" It was inane conversation at best, but...he wasn't sure what he was supposed to say, nor was he awake enough to give it much thought.

"I did. It was nice to sleep in my own bed again." She smiled at him before motioning to the counter behind her. "There's coffee if you'd like some. They're the pods, and there are different flavors on the rack for you to choose from."

Thanking her, he walked over and scanned the selection, even though he knew he'd go for the basics. He wasn't exactly a flavored coffee kind of guy. There was already a mug out for him and a spoon, so there wasn't much he needed to do other than put the pod in the Keurig and wait the whole thirty-seconds. Once it was ready, he turned and sat opposite her at the table.

"I noticed you never put cream or sugar in your coffee," she said shyly. "That's why I didn't offer you any. But if you do want some..."

Levi held up a hand to stop her. "No, it's okay. This is fine. Thanks."

Then it was quiet.

Awkwardly quiet.

"Um...I don't want you to feel like you need to rush out or anything," Willow began, "but Mrs. Moore saw us get back last night and texted me early this morning. I'm going over there at nine to watch Josh."

Glancing around, he asked, "What time is it?"

"Almost eight. But like I said, don't feel like you need to rush. If you want to shower or do anything..."

"I'll probably just wait till I get home to do it. All my luggage is in the car, so..."

"Gotcha."

More silence.

He cleared his throat. "So, uh...you think you'll come to McGee's Friday night?"

"Oh, um...I guess so. Obviously I haven't talked to Donna and Jen yet, but..."

It was small talk.

Painfully awkward small talk.

"Right, well..." He took another sip of his coffee and tried to think of how to say what he wanted to say. Putting his mug down on the table a little too forcefully, he hissed as the hot liquid splashed on his hand. Willow immediately handed him a napkin. "Thanks."

"Levi..."

"Willow..."

They looked at each other and laughed at how they both started to speak at the same time.

"Sorry," she said. "You go first."

Now he was almost afraid to, but he knew if he didn't–if he left here without telling her how he felt–he'd regret it.

"Willow, you know I've always thought how amazing you are," he began and saw her expression fall a little. "I want you to know that..."

"No," she quickly interrupted. "Don't. Please."

"Don't what?"

Her shoulders sagged as she looked up at him with a sad smile. "I know what you're going to say, and if it's okay with you, I'd really rather not have to sit here and tell me what a good friend I am and how fun this all was...blah, blah, blah." She waved her hand around. "I know we talked about this back at the hotel and all and I get it. We're still friends, Levi. And...I'll be okay. Really. It's not your fault that I started to think of it as something more."

"Wait, wait, wait," he said, shoving the coffee aside. "Are you saying that...you'd like to be more than friends?"

She looked away, but not before he saw the flush of her cheeks. "Come on, Levi, don't make me say it. It's embarrassing enough..."

Reaching for her hand, she jumped and spilled her coffee. They both stood up, and when Willow went to reach from some paper towels, he stopped her.

"Levi, I need to clean this up!"

"Not until I say what I need to say," he said firmly.

With a huff, she looked at him, but her gaze kept straying to the coffee that was now dripping off the table and onto the floor.

"Okay, fine. We'll clean this up, and then I'm saying what I need to say!"

Way to sound firm, dude.

Together they quickly cleaned up the mess, but he didn't let her sit down. Instead, he took both of her hands in his and waited for her to look at him. "I want you to know that it's important to me for us to be friends."

She started to pull her hands away, but he held on.

"But I also want more, Willow. I realize it was all supposed to be make-believe, but...there were real feelings there for me. I don't want things to go back to the way they were before. I want to see where this goes. I want you to be my friend and my lover." He tugged her in close. "I want you to be my girlfriend for real."

Her eyes went wide. "Really?"

"Yeah, really."

"Oh, okay then." Her smile grew as she moved in closer. Levi released her hands, and her arms immediately went around him. "In that case, I'd really like to kiss my boyfriend good morning."

"And as your boyfriend, I'm totally on board with this."

Up on tiptoes, Willow pressed her lips to his, and it was the perfect kind of lazy kiss to start the day. And he couldn't wait to start more of them this way.

Things escalated quickly, and as much as he knew he needed to leave and she needed to get ready for work, that didn't mean they shouldn't commemorate this change in their relationship by doing...well...pretty much what they'd been doing for days.

But this time, they were both a little more vocal about how they felt toward each other. He realized they'd each been holding back a little bit of themselves and once they were breathless and lying beside each other, he turned to her and said, "Was it me or did that feel so much better than it has in the past?"

"You mean in the last four days?"

"Well...yeah."

"It did," she said with a soft hum, rolling toward him. "It was definitely better, and I didn't think that was even possible."

Chuckling, he replied, "Me, either. But just to play it safe, we should keep doing it. A lot."

"Right now?" she cried. "Oh, God, Levi, I don't know if my hoo-ha can take anymore. She needs a rest!"

"Your...what?"

Burying her face against his chest, she laughed. "Never mind! Forget I said it!"

As much as he wanted to tease her a little more, he saw it was getting late and knew she needed to get ready for work. Placing a kiss on the top of her head, he maneuvered away from her and stood up, pulling his clothes back on for the second time this morning. She was watching him hungrily, and it took all he had not to strip again and join her back on the bed.

"I really need to go."

"It was the hoo-ha, right? I ruined things. I swear I'm not really a huge dork! Just...give me another chance and I swear to say things in my head before I say them out loud!"

Laughing softly, he leaned down and kissed her again. "This has nothing to do with your hoo-ha–and yes, I know what that is–and everything to do with the fact that you need to go to work. And honestly, so do I. It's going to be a long day and I know I'm going to be swamped."

"Yeah, me too." She rolled over and sat up, pulling the sheet up to cover herself. "And I really need to shower and get caught up with all my dog peeps too. Then there's grocery shopping. Ugh...now I'm overwhelmed."

"Don't be." He slid his sneakers on and kissed her again. "I'll call you later, okay?"

She nodded.

"But...you can call me too if you want."

She smiled sweetly. "Okay."

Unable to help himself, he leaned in for one more kiss.

"Have a good day, Willow." When he turned to leave, she called out to him. "Yeah?"

"You're going to totally love having me as a girlfriend. I promise to take really good care of you."

One more kiss.

"You already have."

15

"What in the world is all this?"

"These are chocolate-covered bananas with marshmallows on the base," Donna explained, pointing to the platter in her hands.

"They look like penises."

"They're supposed to." She winked.

"Oh, my God..."

"And these," Jen added, "are Flirtinis and they are super yummy. You may have to ditch your boring Malibu and pineapple for them. Trust me."

"What's in them?"

"Okay, so it's very similar to your drink, but different. It's vodka, champagne, and pineapple juice. You'll love them."

"Oooh...I wonder if we dip the banana in the Flirtini if it tastes good?" Donna asked excitedly. "Let's check that out!"

"What is happening right now?" Willow asked as her friends made themselves comfortable on her sofa. "I thought we were going out?"

"Nah, we needed a girls' night in," Donna said, waving one of the chocolate banana penis things around. "We want all the details about your trip with Levi, and we don't want to hear it with him hovering."

"Levi doesn't hover..."

"Oh, please...," Jen said, snorting. "He totally hovers. There would be no way for us to talk about him if he was right there. That's why we decided to come over tonight and get all the details. This way, when we go to McGee's tomorrow night, we'll know how to be around him."

"*Be* around him?" she parroted, still not quite following this ridiculous conversation. "Why would you have to worry about that?"

Her friends looked at each other with knowing smirks before looking at her.

Here it comes...

Donna put the banana down and shifted a bit on the couch, her elbows resting on her knees. "We were hoping to ease into the subject, but...it's clear that you're not going to let that happen."

"Let what happen? I still have no idea what's going on!"

"Oh, Willow. Sweet, sweet, naïve Willow," Jen said, reaching out and patting her on the knee. "You had that delicious man all to yourself for a whole week and a day. Or two. I can't remember, but either way, you had a lot of alone time with Levi. Pretending to be your boyfriend. And you were pretending to be his girlfriend." She sighed dreamily. "I'm betting you have a lot of stories to tell about all the um...role-playing you had to do."

Oh, good Lord...

"And we're not talking about the boring stuff like hand-holding," Donna chimed in. "We're interested in hearing about what kind of a kisser he is and what he looks like with his shirt off."

Willow felt herself blushing from the roots of her hair to the soles of her feet. She knew they were going to have this conversation, she just hadn't expected it quite so soon after she got home. Hell, Levi had only left her apartment less than twelve hours ago after declaring himself her boyfriend, shouldn't she have been allowed a little more time before being forced to share all the sexy details?

"She's blushing," Jen observed in a not-so-quiet whisper. "You know what that means!"

"It means she found out a whole lot more than how Levi kisses and how he looks without his shirt," Donna replied.

"Think she's going to give us the details?"

"If we ply her with enough Flirtinis."

"I'm sitting right here," Willow said, groaning and doing her best to hide her face in her hands.

"Come on, Wills, don't get prudish on us. You know you want to tell us."

"Not like this," she murmured.

"Okay, fine," Donna said, miffed. "Have a penis banana while Jen pours you a drink. We'll talk about something else in the meantime. Happy?"

She reluctantly accepted the banana, but she didn't feel right about biting into it. "Um...do we have any other snacks?"

"I baked cookies," Jen said, reaching into her bag and pulling out a large Tupperware container. "Chocolate chip. The big and soft kind that you like."

Beside her, Donna smirked. "Big and soft cookies–bet Levi's wasn't big and soft." Then she laughed hysterically. "Or maybe I should say I hope it was big but not soft."

"Dude, you totally blew that," Jen said and then cracked

herself up. "I totally didn't mean that the way it sounded, but how freaking funny am I?"

Willow had to admit they were pretty funny and found herself laughing too. "You two are utterly ridiculous, but I love you."

"Seriously, Willow, we are going to need details. All the blow by blow," Jen stated and instantly started laughing again. "OMG, how do I keep doing that?"

"Um...maybe because you have sex on the brain?" Donna replied.

"Oh, and you don't?"

"Okay, okay, okay," Willow interrupted, holding out her glass. "Someone fill me up!"

"That's what she said!" both friends said before falling back in another fit of laughter.

It's going to be a long night...

Letting them laugh, Willow poured herself a Flirtini and grabbed one of the cookies. They really were her favorite–especially when they were still warm and gooey like this. She eyed the kitchen and considered getting herself a glass of milk and saving the Flirtini for later, but... she'd make it work.

Once her friends had calmed down, and they were all settled in their seats eating cookies and drinking, Willow finally felt ready to share a little about her trip.

"So...it was a good week," she said, popping the last piece of cookie in her mouth. "A really good week."

"How was Gammy?"

"She's a pistol. I swear, if she was here right now, the three of you would have had a blast together. She poked and prodded at me about Levi too. Only she did it over mani-pedi's. She got me all relaxed in the big massaging chair while getting my feet rubbed and then started asking about our sex life!"

"Go, Gammy!" Jen said, nodding with approval.

"At that point, did you and Levi *have* a sex life to be talking about?" Donna asked.

"Do we really have to talk about this?" she whined.

"That means no," Jen commented dryly.

"Yeah, yeah, yeah, whatever," Donna huffed. "But do you have one now? And if so, did you tell Gammy about it? Was it weird? TMI?"

"Trust me, Gammy still doesn't quite get the meaning of TMI. If anything, she was the one providing the TMI. She has a new boyfriend and..."

"No one cares!" Jen cried, and then her hands flew over her mouth. "Sorry! I'm so sorry! That was mean."

"Geez, it's like a mob mentality in here," Donna murmured. "Shame on you. Dissing a sweet little old lady like that." She batted her eyelashes at Willow. "Me? I love Gammy. So she has a new boyfriend, huh? Is he nice?"

"He's a Romeo."

"Oh, so like a player? A...what did they call them back in the day...a Casanova?"

"Is that a thing? Like a real word?"

"Of course it's a real word! When have you ever known me to make up a word?"

Willow let the two of them argue that out for another couple of minutes and helped herself to another cookie.

"Hey! Why are you having another cookie?" Donna accused. "Why aren't you eating the banana I gave you?"

"Um...yeah. I'm not putting that in my mouth."

Jen nearly choked on her drink as she started laughing.

"Of for the love of it, just say it," Willow said wearily.

"That's what she said," she murmured and then shook her finger at Willow. "You take all the fun out of it when you tell me when to say it!"

"Sorry."

"Fine, but to make it up to me, you have to give us all the details about your time with Levi. All of them!"

Maybe it was the Flirtini or the sugar high from the cookies, but suddenly Willow didn't mind sharing some of the details with her friends–not all of them. Some things were just between her and Levi. But she told them about their practice at holding hands and then kissing and then sharing a bed when they got to Gammy's. By the time she got to the part of the story when Gammy had chosen to go home with Donald so the two of them could be alone, they were both sitting on the edge of their seats.

"So, you guys really did it?" Donna cried. "Was it amazing? Incredible? Awkward?"

Smiling, Willow finished her drink and said, "All the above. But then it got better. Way better. Off the charts better!"

"Oh my God! This is totally awesome!" Jen said, practically bouncing in her seat. "So...what happens now? Are you guys back to being just friends? Friends with benefits?"

"I just assumed that we'd go back to the way things were before we left..."

"Assumed? You what happens when you assume, Willow."

She frowned. "No. What?"

Trying to hold back a laugh, Donna said, "You make an ass out of you and me!"

"Lame, Donna. Completely lame. Where'd you hear that joke, fifty years ago? Maybe you should..." Jen never got another word out because Donna shoved one of the penis bananas in her mouth.

All serious conversation stopped right then and there as the two of them made a mess of what was left of the bananas. Reaching out, she grabbed the cookie container and moved it out of the way. There was no way she wanted to see those go to waste. She felt a little gipped at having her story interrupted, but for now, she was okay with it. She'd tell them about where she and Levi were at when the time was right and everyone had calmed down. But for now, it was perfect just relaxing and laughing with her besties.

An hour passed by and they were all beyond tipsy when the conversation finally came back to the topic of where she and Levi left things.

"Well..." she said with a hiccup while giggling. "We are no longer faking it."

Which caused even more hilarity.

"Oh, no! Did you have to fake it in bed with him?" Jen cried, practically falling off the chair as she laughed. "Faking it is the worst!"

"Fake it till you make it," Donna hummed, smirking.

"Wait, fake what till you make what?" Willow asked.

Groaning, Jen slapped Willow's leg. "Why must you always question these things? Don't you think we know what we're talking about?" She took a long drink of her Flirtini before slamming the glass down on the coffee table. "Because we do!"

"Do we?" Donna asked.

"Do we what?"

"Know what we're talking about?"

Willow shook her head and knew she had to put a stop to this. Jumping to her feet, she whistled loudly to get their attention. "Okay, to be clear here, Levi and I are officially dating! Boyfriend and girlfriend. For real! No fake dating! No faking anything! The sex is great, he's amazing, and I'm incredibly happy! Can we please move on? Sheesh!"

Two pairs of wide eyes stared back at her.

"Geez, relax, *Mom*," Donna murmured.

"Yeah, you didn't have to yell. We were just having fun. No need to get all testy."

This time, they all laughed.

"Levi, the tap's on the fritz again!"

"Levi, the fire inspector is here!"

"Levi, your accountant is on the phone!"

"Levi, Dex broke a tray of dishes!"

Yeah, and that was all in his first twenty-four hours of being back at the pub. He was exhausted–or should he say *still* exhausted–and it didn't look like he was going to be catching up on his sleep any time soon.

It was Friday night, and he knew Willow and her friends were on their way in, but there was no way he was going to be able to find time to be alone with her. There was just too much to do. When he had agreed to go away with her, he really felt like it would be okay to leave the pub for a week, but now he knew why his grandfather rarely took any vacations.

And he knew his staff was amazing and nothing that happened was due to anyone being incompetent. There was just a lot of things going on at all times.

Okay, and maybe he wasn't the best at delegating everything yet, but that would come in time, right?

Either way, he was a little frustrated and more than a

little disappointed that he wasn't going to get to spend any time alone with Willow.

Of course, he could ask her to hang out until closing time–which was midnight–and maybe she wouldn't mind waiting while he did the books and handled everything that needed to be handled. She would understand and maybe even enjoy learning a little more about his job. Or maybe...

Oh, right...she thinks this is just a job.

"Shit."

Yeah, he was going to have to come up with a way to tell her about that.

It wasn't like he lied about it, not exactly. More like a lie of omission, and it was really done because he didn't want her looking at him any differently. Now that he knew her better, he knew it was a mistake. Willow wasn't the kind of person to see him for anything except who he was. She wouldn't have felt intimidated, she would have still been his friend.

And his girlfriend.

But after he admitted how he lied–and his reasoning–he couldn't be so sure.

Why didn't I speak up sooner?

"Hey, you."

Turning, he saw Willow standing at the bar smiling happily. He drank in the sight of her. Funny how it had only been yesterday morning when he last saw her, and he was already a little crazed with missing her.

Stepping around the bar, he did a quick check and saw she was there alone; no friends. "Hey, yourself," he said gruffly, taking her in his arms and kissing her like he hadn't seen her in weeks rather than days.

Or...a day.

When they broke apart, Willow rested her hands on his

chest and let out a very sexy little sigh. "Wow. A girl could totally get used to that kind of a greeting."

"I'll see what I can do about that," he teased and helped her onto one of the barstools. "So, where are the girls?"

"Oh, they're meeting me here. They figured I'd want to stay and hang out with you until you got done for the night." Then she paused and nibbled her bottom lip. "But if you're going to be too busy, I don't have to do that. You know...no pressure. If you've got too much to do, I can leave like I always do. No big deal. I mean, we weren't dating the last time we all came here on a Friday night and I never stayed until closing time so I have no idea what it is that you have to do, but I'm guessing it's a lot since you're always here and you checked in with your boss so much while we were away. And..."

"Willow?"

"Hmm?"

"You're rambling," he said, kissing the tip of her nose. Taking a step back, he kept his hands at her waist, feeling better just touching her this innocently. "So, how was your day?"

"Oh, my goodness, have we gotten that domesticated already?"

"What?"

"The whole 'hi, honey, how was your day?' thing. It's sweet, but it just feels like something long-time couples might say."

"I disagree. I look at it as something you should say to anyone who means something to you. You should be interested in how they are and how their day went." He kissed the tip of her nose again. "So there."

Willow reached up and cupped his face and kissed him briefly on the lips. "Okay, then. My day was pretty great."

"Oh, yeah? What's up?"

"Well, Mrs. Moore, Josh's mom, just got a promotion at her job and wants to hire me as a full-time nanny!"

"Really? That's amazing!" Lifting her out of her seat, Levi hugged her and spun her around. "Congratulations!" Once she was back in her seat, he asked, "But what about the dogs?"

Smiling, she reached for his hand and squeezed it. "I love that you thought of them too."

"I know how much you love them."

"That I do. And Mrs. Moore knows it as well, and we talked about it, and we agreed that I could still do it with Josh in the stroller. I might not be able to take them all out at one time like I do now, but in shifts. It gives Josh time outside, and it means I don't have to let anyone down or scrambling to find new walkers for their dogs. It's a win, win." Her smile grew and he could feel the excitement practically vibrating off of her.

"This calls for a celebration!" Stepping around the bar, he held up a finger. "I'll be right back." Stepping into the back room where they kept all the wine and champagne, he found the best bottle he had and went back to get her approval.

"Oh, my goodness! Champagne?" Her laugh was pure feminine joy, and he loved knowing he was the one to make that happen. "Can we chill it a little and then save it for when the girls get here?"

"Absolutely."

After that, Willow sat at the bar and chatted with him while he made drinks and even joked around with the staff when he was busy.

She fit.

He'd dated women who made demands on his time or

who weren't pleased when he wasn't giving them his full attention, but not Willow. He had a feeling she would be comfortable coming and hanging out here more than just on Friday nights. But eventually he was going to have to find time to take her out on actual dates–especially if she was going to be a full-time nanny.

As she told him more about the position, he could see just how it was the perfect fit for her too. There was a lightness to her–a joy–that hadn't been there a few days ago. Like she'd finally found her calling. He could only wonder if she had spoken to her parents about it yet. Judging by her mood, she hadn't. He hoped they didn't crush her enthusiasm.

"Hey! There are the new love birds!" Donna called out as she approached the bar. Levi watched with amusement as she hugged Willow before turning to him with a knowing smirk.

So clearly Willow told them about us...

He hoped she didn't share *too* much.

"Willow and Levi, kissing in a tree. K-i-s-s-i-n-g," Jen sang as she stepped up next. Winking at him, she said, "Hey, Levi. So, um...what's new?"

He rolled his eyes before stepping around the bar and putting his arm around Willow. "Cat's out of the bag, huh?"

"Oh, yeah," she said with a soft laugh. "They got it out of me between penis-shaped chocolate-covered bananas, Flirtinis, and big and soft cookies."

There were so many things in that statement that needed clarification, but...he opted to simply nod and smile. "Awesome."

"Do you serve Flirtinis here, Levi?" Donna asked.

"Flirtinis?"

She nodded. "Yeah. It's just vodka, champagne and pineapple juice served in a martini glass."

"We didn't use martini glasses last night," Willow chimed in.

"Well, we had them, but Jen forgot them at home. We had no choice but to make do with wine glasses."

"I think that's why I got so drunk," Jen said. "You have crazy big wine glasses, Willow."

"I got them at the dollar store," she replied with a shrug. "And you didn't have to keep filling them up so much."

Jen shrugged, and Levi figured it was a good time to break out the champagne. Leaning down, he whispered in Willow's ear, "Do they know about your good news yet?"

"Not yet."

"Not yet what?" Donna asked. "Are you trying to find an excuse to leave already so you can go and have sex?"

"What?! No! Oh, my God! Why would you even think that?"

"Because you were whispering and being all secretive! No secret telling. Ugh...please don't be one of those couples that have to keep whispering sexy stuff in each other's ears. I hate those couples. They're the worst. Do you two want to be the worst after only dating for like ten minutes?"

"Hey! It's been longer than ten minutes," Willow argued.

"You can't count the test drive," Jen countered. "That doesn't count."

"Test drive?" Levi asked, fairly certain he was going to regret it.

"Yeah, you know, the whole fake dating thing. It was sort of like a test drive," Jen explained. "If the two of you weren't compatible, you probably wouldn't be here whispering sexy stuff to each other and plotting ways to ditch us and get out of here."

"Oh, my God," Willow groaned. "No one is trying to ditch anyone, and there were no sexy whispers!"

Figuring this was her chance to share her big news, Levi excused himself to go and get the champagne. Less than a minute later he heard the telltale squeal of good news being celebrated and was glad her friends were being so support-ive. He liked knowing she had a strong support network of friends–especially after meeting her parents.

With a little fanfare, he stepped back behind the bar with the champagne and a big smile. "We're celebrating, right?" he called out and was rewarded with another round of celebratory squeals and woos!

He never would have pegged Willow and her friends as woo-girls, but he supposed any group of girls out together and celebrating could easily turn into them.

He popped the cork and Willow flinched so hard she fell off her stool. Luckily Donna was right there to catch her before she hit the floor.

My sweet, clumsy girl...

"Here we go!" he said, handing the first glass to Willow before pouring one for each of her friends and then himself. Normally he never drank while at work, but these were special circumstances. There was no way he was going to miss out on toasting her new job.

Wait...am I supposed to toast and say something, or should her friends or...

"To Willow!" Jen called out, taking the decision away from him. "To this exciting new chapter and a career that is absolutely perfect for you! We are all so proud of you for chasing your dream!" She held up her glass, and they all cried out, "To Willow!"

Levi tapped his glass to hers first–then the girls'–and took a sip before telling her he needed to get back to work. The three of them went and found their usual table, and he knew they were going to spend a lot of time talking about her new job and then about him. And he was okay with it.

Sort of.

He only hoped she was flattering in any of the personal stuff she shared–and not so flattering that her friends were going to be ogling him or anything, but just flattering enough that they were impressed and not looking at him sympathetically.

Or with pity.

Closing time came sooner than he would have expected, and before he knew it, they were locking the doors and cleaning up. Willow had resumed her seat at the bar and he enjoyed talking with her while he and the staff cleaned up.

"Hey, Boss," Anthony said as he came out of the kitchen. "No accidents from Dex tonight. Must be some sort of record, right?"

Levi chuckled. "We should put up a chart and give him a gold star for every night he doesn't break something."

"It might work. Give him a little motivation for being careful!" Anthony walked away and a few of the wait staff walked around wiping down tables and vacuuming the floor. Within thirty minutes, they were all ready to go.

Levi took Willow with him to the office after everyone left so he could take care of the receipts for the night and closing down the system. She sat in the lone chair opposite the desk and watched him.

"I have to say, I would think your boss would be here on a Friday night."

Shit...

"Weekends seem to be so busy. You'd think he'd want to be here to help out."

"Um, yeah...about that..."

"But I guess since you were gone for over a week, he figured you wanted the hours," she said, smiling at him. "And clearly he trusts you because he puts you in charge, and even the staff calls you boss!" Then she giggled. "I don't think I've ever dated someone who was the boss before. It was kind of cool hearing them all call you that."

This girl...

She stood and walked over to him. "So, uh...everyone's gone, right?"

Looking up, he saw the look on her face. Knew that tone of voice. Nodding, he said, "Yeah. We're all alone."

"Hmm..." She looked around nervously. "And...no one's going to come back?"

"Well, I can't guarantee that." He stood and walked around the desk and over to the door, closing it. "But I can guarantee that no one's coming in here."

Her nervous laughter was immediately followed by a giddier one. "Do you think...I mean...can we...?"

Turning the lock, Levi pushed away from the door. "Oh, yeah. We totally can."

And for the first time ever, Levi found a whole other perk to being the boss.

16

Two WEEKS after coming home from their road trip and Willow was still floating on a cloud of pure bliss. She loved being a full-time nanny, and even though juggling Josh and the dogs was a little more challenging than she thought it would be–and she had the skinned knees to prove it–she wouldn't change a thing.

Well...okay, there was one thing she would change, but it had nothing to do with her job.

It had to do with Levi's.

Good grief, did he work a lot! Before their trip, when they had those two weeks together to get to know one another, she thought his schedule was flexible, but now that they were dating and trying to spend more time together, she realized it really wasn't. He worked all the time, and it was like his boss didn't even care about the pub! Levi was doing all the work! And with her working all day and him working most nights, it didn't leave a whole lot of time for them to be together.

Willow wasn't a big late-night person to begin with, but

if she wanted to see Levi, she had to get used to their dates starting at one in the morning.

That only worked on the weekends.

During the week, she was busy with Josh and the dogs and didn't think it was right to take a toddler to the pub. Although it was pretty family-friendly, she just didn't think the Moores were paying her to go on lunch dates with her boyfriend.

Something had to give. She knew she could be patient, and eventually Levi's schedule would have to lighten up. Maybe his boss was giving him the extra hours to make up for the time off he took while taking her to Florida, but...that should have been done by now, right?

It was Thursday night, and she was getting ready to make herself something to eat when her phone rang. Her heart skipped a beat at the thought of Levi calling to say he took the night off, but when she ran over to grab her phone, she saw her mother's name and number on the screen.

Talk about a buzzkill...

"Hey, Mom," she said, forcing herself to smile even though her mother couldn't see her. "How are you?"

"Fine, sweetheart. Just fine. Listen, I wanted to run something by you."

"Oh, okay." Sitting down on the couch, Willow braced herself for whatever this was going to be.

"You remember Dr. Barrett, don't you? She's been with our practice for the last three years."

"Yeah, I remember her. Is she okay?"

"Yes, yes, she's fine, but her mother isn't. The poor woman fell when she was getting out of the tub and broke her hip. Now Carol needs to take a leave of absence so she can go and take care of her mother."

"O-kay..."

"Your father and I were talking, and we thought this might be the perfect way for you to test the waters."

"Test the waters for...what?" And now her heart was racing for a completely different reason.

"Willow, you can't keep avoiding this subject forever. You have a degree, and you need to be using it. Carol said she would be more than willing to let you take on half of her patients while your father and I help with the other half. It would only be a month; a trial run."

"Mom..."

"But you'd need to be here on Monday so you can look over the case files and then start with your first patient on Wednesday. We'd like for you to be prepared."

"Mom..." she said with a little more assertion.

"We'll pay your airfare, of course. We know you probably can't afford to fly across the country on such short notice. You'll stay with us and we'll cover your rent on your apartment there in New York to help you out. This is really a wonderful opportunity, Willow. Not many people get the opportunity to join a prestigious practice right out of the gate."

Pinching the bridge of her nose, Willow willed herself to stay calm. "May I speak now?"

"Of course, dear. I'm sure you have a ton of questions."

"Actually, I don't."

Silence.

"There's nothing to ask because there's nothing I need to know. I'm not accepting the invitation," she stated, hating the slight tremble in her voice. "I appreciate the offer, and please tell Dr. Barrett that I hope her mother's recovery goes well, but I will not be coming to Seattle to cover her patients."

"Why must you be so difficult?" The exasperation in

her mother's tone was blatant and obvious. "This is a once in a lifetime kind of opportunity."

"I have a job, Mom."

"Oh, please, you babysit and walk dogs, Willow. Those two things combined barely constitute a part-time job. You're not making enough money to survive on your own. It's not possible."

"The Moores hired me as a full-time nanny for Josh," she stated. "I'm making a great hourly wage, working thirty-five hours a week, and I'm still walking the dogs. So really, I'm doing just fine! This is exactly the kind of job I was hoping to find."

"Since when?" her mother demanded. "This is the first I'm hearing of this."

"That's because you never ask, Mom. You never want to hear what it is that I want, you're only interested in telling me what you want me to do and how I need to be listening to you and dad and coming to work for you. Well, maybe now you'll listen. Maybe now you'll hear me."

"This is ridiculous. Maybe your father can talk some sense into you."

"No, Mom! Don't..."

But she already heard the muffled voices and knew any minute her father would be...

"What in the world is this your mother is telling me about you being a nanny!"

"Oh, hey, Dad. How are you?"

"Don't how are you to me, missy! I asked you a question!"

"And I asked you one," she challenged, picturing him going a little purple and the vein in his neck bulging a big at her insolent tone.

"I will not have you talking to me this way! I knew

dating that bartender was going to cause this! I just knew it!"

"This isn't about Levi, Dad. This is about you showing me some respect."

"Respect? Respect?! Young lady, maybe you've forgotten who is the parent here and who is the child!"

Go big or go home, Willow...

Wait. I am home. Does that still apply?

"Well?" he demanded.

"Can we please focus on the fact that I am no longer a child?" she said loudly. "I am a grown woman and I fully believe that respect is *earned*! You do not get it just for being my father and especially when you certainly don't respect me!"

"I have had just about enough of this tone from you. You need to apologize!"

"Um...no. I believe you do."

"Willow..."

"No, I'm serious, Dad. I am an adult and I am perfectly capable of finding my own job and knowing what it is that I want to do with my life! It may have taken me a while, but I have always known what it was that I *didn't* want to do! You never listen! No one ever listens!"

"And I'm done listening now!"

"Why? Because you're not getting your way? Because I'm not falling in line with what you want? Well, newsflash, Dad, that's not how grownups act! You don't get to run away because you're not getting what you want!"

Silence.

"Now, I'm sorry that you don't agree with my career choice, but it was never your choice to make. It's mine. I never should have agreed to study psychology. It was never something I wanted to do. Maybe someday I'll go back to school and get my degree in early childhood education, but for right now, I'm good. And as my parents, you should be proud of me for following my dreams and for finding a job that excites me!"

He let out a low, almost sinister laugh that she did not take as a good sign.

"I get it," he said quietly, almost menacingly. "I finally figured it out."

"What are you talking about?"

"You and this nanny thing. Now that you're dating a guy who owns his own business, he's taking care of you. Encouraging you to take on a low-demand job you so you're available whenever he wants to see you."

"What in the world are you talking about? Are you drunk right now?"

"Don't you dare talk to me like that! I am still your father!"

"Um..."

"I guess dating a rich guy who owns a pub so you don't have to pay your own way works for you. And that makes me ashamed of you. You're a smart woman, far too smart to be working in such a menial job. But...since your boyfriend owns his own business..."

"Why do you keep saying that?"

And then it hit her.

Levi's talk with her father back at Gammy's.

No doubt he just told her father that to get him off his back. Poor baby. Wait until she told him about this crazy conversation.

"Uh, yeah, Dad. That's what it is. Levi owns the pub and makes great money and it was all part of my evil plan to get out of working with you and Mom. You're a genius."

"Willow!"

"You know what? I think we both need some time to calm down. I'll talk to you next week. Bye!"

She hung up and immediately turned the phone off to avoid any immediate callbacks.

But it also meant Levi couldn't get through, so...

She still left it off for a little while.

Her heart was back to racing again–and hopefully it was just because of nerves and not because she suddenly developed some sort of heart condition or was having a heart attack–but Willow forced herself to go into the kitchen and make herself something for dinner.

Her appetite wasn't the best, and she was borderline nauseous, but she knew by the time she was done cooking that she'd feel better.

Or will have thrown up and need food to fill her empty stomach.

Either way, she was going to make the shrimp tacos she had planned on making.

Thirty minutes later, she was sitting at her kitchen table and scrolling through her Instagram feed for entertainment. There wasn't much going on, but it was always fun to see if Doug the Pug shared anything new or where Popeye the Foodie Dog was eating today. It was a brainless way to pass the time and provided enough smiles to get her through her dinner–which was delicious.

Once she was done, she thought about going to McGee's and seeing Levi, but she had a feeling he'd be busy and she was honestly too tired to go and then wait for the pub to close. Instead, she sent him a text to let him know she was thinking about him and would see him tomorrow.

Although, she couldn't wait to see the look on his face when she told him how her father carried on about him owning the bar. Just thinking about it made her chuckle. No wonder her father had changed his tune that day at Gammy's.

Yeah, there would be plenty of time to laugh about it tomorrow.

"Hey, there's my beautiful girl! This is a surprise!" Levi came around the bar late Friday afternoon. It was only four o'clock and Willow didn't normally come in until some time after seven. Kissing her, he said, "To what do I owe the pleasure?"

She took her seat on her favorite stool at the end of the bar and smiled. "Mr. Moore came home early today, and I figured I'd take advantage of the time to come in and see if maybe we could grab an early dinner together." Reaching out, she squeezed his hand. "I missed you."

"I missed you too," he admitted, resting his forehead against hers. "I think I can handle an early dinner. What are you in the mood for?"

She gave him a sexy smile and hoped they were on the same wavelength. Maybe if they went back to his place—even for a quickie—she could convince him not to come back here tonight and call in sick or something.

"Food," he murmured, kissing her.

So much for being a seductress...

"In that case, how about some..."

The sound of a loud crash in the kitchen made them both jump, and Levi immediately turned and excused himself.

With a sigh, Willow rested her arms on the bar and looked around. There were just a handful of people here to eat and she was the only one sitting at the bar.

"Hey, Willow! How's it going?"

"Hey, Anthony!" She sat up and smiled. "What happened back there?"

Groaning, he explained, "Dex. Dex is what happened back there. I swear, that guy is a damn mess. I don't know why Levi keeps him. I mean, I'm all for giving people second chances, but this is like his eighteenth. Levi's losing money hand over fist because of this. He's had to restock most of the dishes and glasses. It's crazy."

Levi was losing money?

"So...uh...Levi's in charge of hiring and firing?"

Anthony looked at her funny. "Well, yeah. He's in charge of everything."

She had a sinking feeling in her stomach.

Swallowing hard, she said, "Because he's the...manager?"

"Willow, Levi owns the place. He's literally in charge of it all. And he's a really kick-ass boss–seriously the best guy I've ever worked for–but he's got a soft heart. I know it will kill him to fire Dex. But hopefully, he'll just rip it off like a band-aid and move on. We need help in the kitchen that aren't total klutzes." He chuckled. "Levi's really a softie when it comes to them. Just like his grandfather was."

It was like she could feel the color draining from her face.

"Hey, Willow? You okay?" he asked, concerned.

"I...uh...I'm fine."

There was yelling coming from the kitchen and Anthony excused himself, leaving Willow beyond hurt and confused.

Not that Anthony walked away, but because of the revelations.

Holy crap...the revelations.

Why would he tell my father the truth and not me?

It took all of three seconds for Anthony's words to come back to her.

Because Levi's a softie when it comes to klutzes.

And I am their queen.

Muttering a curse, Willow slid off the stool and walked out of the pub. There was still a lot of commotion going on in the kitchen and she really didn't think she could handle talking to Levi right now.

And definitely not for a while.

Running out to her car, she pulled up the group text on her phone with Jen and Donna.

Willow: 9-1-1. Change of plans. Meet me at my place. And someone bring pizza.

Getting the mess in the kitchen straightened out took far longer than Levi had planned, and when he walked back out to the bar, Willow was gone. He didn't think anything of it; figured she realized he had some stuff to deal with and he wouldn't be able to do an early dinner. However, he firmly believed she'd be back at her usual time with the girls.

But...she didn't.

And when he tried calling her, it went right to voicemail.

It wasn't like her to get upset over something so trivial or without trying to talk it out with him, but obviously she was more pissed off than he realized.

Unfortunately, there was no way he could leave the pub

tonight. They were shorthanded, the kitchen was a disaster, and Friday nights were notoriously busy.

Never before had he watched the clock with so much frustration, and once it hit midnight, he was shooing people out the door.

"You okay, Boss?" Anthony asked. "I mean, I get that you're still pissed about the whole kitchen incident, but you've been a little short with everyone tonight."

Raking a hand through his hair, breathe sighed. "Yeah, uh...sorry. I guess I'm distracted. Willow left and I can't get her on the phone, so I'm worried that something's up."

"She seemed a little confused by what happened earlier."

Levi immediately stopped wiping down the bar. "What do you mean?"

"It was a little weird. She couldn't understand why you were in charge of so much around here or why you were going to have to fire Dex."

"What? At that point, I didn't know I was firing Dex."

Anthony leveled him a stern look. "Dude, really? We both knew that was coming."

"Yeah, yeah, yeah, whatever. Why would you mention that to Willow?"

He shrugged. "She asked what happened, and we started talking, and it was like she had no idea you owned the place."

"You told her I owned the place?" he shouted and knew how crazy he sounded.

"Well...yeah. I thought she knew. You guys have been hanging out a lot and you're dating now, so I thought it was common knowledge."

The string of curses was out of his mouth before he could stop them. "I need to go. Can you lock up?"

"Yeah, no problem."

Running back to his office, Levi grabbed his keys and was sprinting past the bar when Anthony called out to him. "What?"

"I'm sorry, man. Really. I had no idea she didn't know."

But all Levi could do was wave him off because he had more important matters to attend to.

The drive to Willow's apartment took less than fifteen minutes and it wasn't until he had parked the car that he realized he should have thought a little harder about this plan. He parked in front of her door and wondered just what the hell he was supposed to say. He could apologize, he could swear he'd never lie to her again, but was the damage already done? From everything he knew about her, she was a very forgiving person, but that was with her family. How was she going to be with him?

He looked toward the door and saw Jen and Donna walking out.

Shit.

Maybe it was just a coincidence, but he had a feeling their exiting the apartment at the same time he pulled up was fully planned.

Okay, do I sit here in the car and wait them out or...

The two of them came to stand at the hood of his car, arms crossed, and looking all kinds of pissed off.

Waiting them out? Not an option.

With a weary sigh, he climbed from the car and forced a smile on his face. "Ladies."

"Please, don't try to be all charming with us," Donna said loudly. "Because it won't work!"

He didn't think that one word came across as being charming, but...okay.

"How dare you come here in the middle of the night

after what you did!" Jen said, equally loud, and Levi had to wonder if all the neighbors were going to come out and join the discussion.

And knowing how much everyone in the complex loved Willow, no doubt it would turn into an angry mob instantly.

Taking a step forward, he decided to keep his voice softer in hopes of them following suit. "Okay, I get it. I screwed up. But I really need to talk to Willow."

"Oh, *now* you want to talk to Willow?" Donna demanded, still loud. "Are you sure you don't want to wait another seven or eight hours? Maybe another day? Or hey, maybe even another month?" She took a menacing step toward him.

At least, he imagined she thought she was menacing.

"Yeah, you had months–lots of months to tell her the truth," Jen chimed in. "And you thought coming here at this hour was the perfect time? Well...screw you!"

"Hey, shut up down there!"

They all turned to see where the voice was coming from, and while Jen yelled back, Levi did his best to get everyone to quiet down. When he reached out and touched Donna's arm, she smacked him away.

"You don't get to come here to our best friend's home and tell us what to do!" This time she wasn't quite yelling, but she wasn't being particularly quiet either.

"And screw you too, buddy!" Jen shouted to the anonymous voice. "We'll quiet down when we're done putting Mr. Lying Liarson in his place!"

"Um..."

"In case you didn't get the reference, she was talking about you."

"Uh, yeah. I got that."

"Oh, so you *know* you're a liar, and yet here we are arguing about it," Jen said, rejoining the conversation.

"I didn't think that was exactly what we were fighting about," he argued carefully.

"Don't try to get us on a technicality, Levi. We're arguing about you being a liar and everything that goes with it."

This was getting him nowhere.

"If I could just talk to Willow for five minutes...just to apologize..."

"She doesn't want to talk to you," Jen stated firmly, arms crossed again. "And even if she did, she wouldn't believe anything you had to say anymore."

"I'd really like to hear that from Willow..."

"Aren't you listening?" This coming from Donna. Honestly, it was like watching a tennis match trying to keep up with these two. "You're not going to get to talk to her tonight. Or any other night until she decides to. Which she won't. We won't let her."

"Hey, wait..."

"We can't totally stop her from talking to him," Jen said, looking at Donna. "It's not like we can babysit her twenty-four hours a day."

Donna glanced at him and then back to Jen before whispering, "Yeah, I know that, but he doesn't." She huffed. "Why would you bring that up with him standing right here?"

"What? I just think it was a pretty bold statement for you to make and not even a little bit believable."

"Oh, *I'm* not believable? What would you have said then? Go ahead. Tell me what great words of wisdom you would have said to get him to go away."

It would be wrong of him to point out that not only could he hear them, but he wasn't going anywhere.

At least, not yet.

He stood by patiently for another minute before he decided to go to the source. Casually, Levi made his move to walk around them only to stop in his tracks.

Willow had opened her door and was coming toward him.

"Willow," he said urgently, going to her. "I'm so sorry. Really. Can we just..."

She held up a hand to stop him. "I appreciate you stopping by, Levi, but..."

"No," he interrupted quickly. "No buts. Please. Just give me five minutes."

But she shook her head. "No," she said sadly. "Not tonight. I just...I can't."

He heard the sadness, the disappointment in her voice, and it gutted him. His first instinct was to go and hold her, hug her, and never let her go, but he had a feeling that wouldn't get him far and then there'd definitely be an angry mob on him.

"Just go, Levi," she whispered. "This is all just too much."

"You have to know...I never meant to hurt you. It wasn't supposed to..."

"It wasn't real," she said, her voice trembling slightly. "None of it. And that makes me an idiot."

"No! It was real! All of it! I made a mistake. Please, just listen to me," he begged.

"I've been listening to you for weeks. Months, actually," she added with a mirthless laugh. "And in all our getting to know you talks, you never thought to tell me the truth. Now I don't know if anything you said was true or not."

"Willow, please..."

She took one step back and then another. "It's late and I'm just so tired, Levi. Go." Then she turned and walked back toward her apartment with Jen and Donna quickly flanking her.

He stood there in the dark long after the door was closed and realized he had no one to blame but himself. He'd ruined what could have been the greatest relationship of his life. And for a guy who was a master at solving problems and fixing things, he realized he had no idea how to fix this.

17

TEN DAYS.

She'd been sticking to her guns for ten whole days but she was starting to weaken. Levi had called and texted her every single day, apologizing.

And she had ignored them both.

Then he sent flowers.

Her apartment could now double as a florist.

Next came every kind of cake, cookie, and candy she had ever mentioned liking while they had been getting to know each other.

And thanks to her scale this morning, she knew eating so many of them was a mistake.

Now she was staring down at a giant box of assorted dog toys, treats, and accessories. There were leashes that were meant for multiple dogs, some harnesses, and a few sweaters for the little dogs.

It was getting harder and harder to stay mad.

Lying was a big no-no in her book. And although it wasn't a terrible lie, it was still a lie.

Maybe I should have talked to him...

Yeah, it wasn't the first time she'd thought it and probably wasn't the last either. Every time Willow thought she was ready to answer his call or text, uncertainty grabbed her by the throat.

Am I too gullible? Too trusting? How will I ever know when he's telling me the truth?

The list was endless.

Her phone dinged with an incoming text and all she saw was his name and she chose to ignore it. When it rang a minute later, she was certain it was him, but then Gammy's face was on the screen and relief washed over her.

"Hey, Gams! How are you?"

"Hello, my little Willow bell! What's new with you?"

"Well, not a whole lot."

Liar.

"It's my day off, so I am getting caught up on laundry and cleaning. Fun, right?"

"Yes, you lead a very exciting life," Gammy deadpanned. "What's next? Washing your hair on a Saturday night instead of going out with Levi?"

Yeah...that.

As much as she didn't want to, Willow decided to just rip off the band-aid and tell her grandmother what was going on. "Um...Levi and I broke up."

Silence.

"So...yeah. We're not dating anymore."

More silence.

"Gams? Can you hear me?"

"Oh, I hear you just fine. The question is, do you hear yourself?"

"Uh...what?"

"That's what I'm saying!"

"I don't even know what that means!" she cried.

"Willow, why are you afraid to be happy?"

"I'm not!"

"Oh, really? Then tell me, why did it take you so long to stand up for yourself and admit that you enjoy being a nanny?"

"That's different. I was already babysitting for Josh. That isn't anything new."

"No, but you never told any of us how much you enjoyed it or how it was something you wanted to do full-time!"

"Okay, fine. You got me there, but...that's not being afraid to be happy. That was me not wanting to deal with my parents being all judgy."

"Well, you know what? Now I'm being judgy!"

"What? Why?"

"Because you're afraid to be..."

"Okay, okay, okay! Saying that over and over isn't getting us anywhere. I just don't understand why you think that."

"Because you're no longer with Levi!" Gammy cried with exasperation. "Sheesh! It's like talking with a dolphin."

"Hey!"

"Oh, stop it."

"Take it back," Willow demanded, feeling beyond hurt. "I am not like a dolphin."

"You're right. A dolphin would have understood what I was saying the first time."

"Gammy!"

"Okay, that one was uncalled for, but I still believe..." She cut herself off and let out a long, weary sigh. "What happened?"

Willow explained about the day when she showed up at the pub and Dex and then Anthony telling her how Levi owned the place. "He showed up that night to try to explain, but...I didn't want to hear it."

"So, what happened when you saw him the next day?"

"I didn't see him the next day."

"Fine, what happened when you did see him?"

"I haven't."

Silence.

And then another really long, dramatic sigh.

"Willow, you're like a granddaughter to me..."

"Oh, no, you don't! You are not going to use that line on me!"

"I believe I just did."

Growling, Willow forced herself to calm down. "I don't know what to say to him!" she cried. "I believed everything he ever said to me and now..."

"Now you don't know if you can."

"Exactly."

"So, what are you going to do?"

"Honestly? I don't know," she admitted miserably. "I miss him so much, but...I'm afraid, Gams. We all know I make a fool out of myself on a daily basis just by being a klutz. I don't need anyone else doing it for me."

"Oh, Willow..."

Unable to help herself, tears began to roll down her cheeks. It wasn't anything new; she'd been doing it for a week now. Wiping them away was almost pointless, but she still tried. "What do I do, Gams?"

"And you haven't talked to him at all?"

"No."

"Have you answered any of his texts?"

"No."

"Willow...sweetie," she said sympathetically. "Levi

doesn't strike me as someone who's going to chase after you forever. He's a good man..."

"Who lied!"

"Yes, but...it wasn't exactly a terrible lie. It's not like he killed his family or had them chained in the basement somewhere," she reasoned. "You met two of his sisters, and they were nice, right?"

"Technically, I only met one, but...yeah. She was very nice."

"And the people who work for him at the pub? Do they like him?"

"Well...yeah. Anthony said he was the best boss he ever had."

"Then maybe you should hear him out. Give him another chance."

"But what if...what if I'm wrong? What if he lies again and breaks my heart?"

"What if he doesn't, and he's the greatest love of your life and you let him go because you were afraid to let yourself be happy?"

"Ugh...you did *not* just bring that around full circle."

"Actually, I believe I did."

"Gams..." Her phone vibrated in her hand with an incoming text. "Can you hold on one sec?"

"Of course."

"Thanks." Looking at the phone, she saw the text was from Levi and it was a picture. Putting the phone back to her ear, she said, "He sent a picture. If I lose you while I'm trying to see what it is, I apologize."

"Oooh...do you think it's a sexy text? Like one of those..." She cleared her throat. "You know, those pictures of his privates?"

"Oh, my God! Stop it!" she cried, horrified. "And hold

on!" Pulling the phone away from her ear, Willow swiped at the screen to try to pull up the text. When she finally got to it, she stared at the photo for a solid minute before she realized what she was looking at.

"Willow?" she heard Gammy ask.

"Oh, my God," she whispered.

"Willow? Are you all right?"

"Oh, my God," she said a little louder and with a small laugh. "Gammy, I have to go! I'll call you tomorrow! I promise! I love you!"

"Love you too!"

Tossing the phone down on the sofa, Willow jumped up and ran to take a shower.

It was time to go and see Levi.

Staring down at the receipt in his hand, Levi had to wonder if it would have been cheaper to go and see a shrink.

How was that for irony?

Still, he had to hope this was going to work. If it didn't, he was out of options.

He'd tried every romantic gesture in the book and never got a response. Maybe he should've just taken the hint, but...he wasn't ready to give up.

At least, he hadn't been.

Right now? He wasn't so sure.

"You sure about this, boss?"

Levi turned his head and gave Anthony a small smile. "Yeah. I'm sure."

"For what it's worth, I think it's great. Way better than all those cliched things you've been doing."

Eyes wide and jaw on the ground, he said, "What? Why?"

"Dude, anyone can send flowers and candy. The cupcakes were a nice touch, but..." He shrugged. "They're kind of empty gestures. Easy. But this? This is going to speak volumes."

"I don't know. She hasn't responded yet."

"Maybe she's busy and hasn't seen the text," Anthony countered. "Not everyone sits around with their phone in their hands all day."

"I don't..."

"You have, and you do, and you need to stop. If it wasn't the newest iPhone, I would totally smack it out of your hand right now." Then he laughed. "But I like my job and can't afford to replace it, so..."

"Good to know that's the only reason you're not doing it," he murmured before walking away.

He walked around the pub, straightening chairs, making sure every table had what it needed. The lunch crowd was thinning out and Saturdays were a little slower, so he was a little at odds with himself on finding something to do to keep him from obsessing about Willow. As soon as he had sent the picture, he was certain she would respond. Everything in him screamed that he had finally gotten it right. But it had been an hour and...nothing.

Raking hands through his hair, Levi called out he'd be in his office if anyone needed him.

And then immediately prayed that someone would need him.

Specifically, Willow.

Closing the door behind him, he walked around and sat behind his desk and immediately started up his computer. There were bills he could pay, new products he could look at, or…play solitaire or Words with Friends. Gammy had gotten him into it while they were down in Florida, and he had to admit, it was kind of fun.

Looking at his phone and seeing no response from Willow yet, he opted to open the Words With Friends app and abandoned the idea of getting any work done. He had a game request from someone named IreGemGal and figured he might as well accept and play.

Their first word was moron.

Shrugging, he looked at his tiles and made the word muse. He was about to put his phone down and give them a few minutes, but it immediately dinged with another word.

Nitwit.

"Hmm…someone is obviously mad about something if this was the way their minds worked."

Levi followed up with the word win.

Yeah, because I'm such a wordsmith…

Turd.

Okay, it was hard not to start taking offense to some of these now, even though it was ridiculous. There was no way this person even knew who he was, so it was all just a coincidence, but still…they all felt like cheap shots at him.

He played the word down, and they immediately played the word idiot.

"That's it," he huffed, turning the phone off. "I'm done!" Leaning back in his chair, there was nothing left to do but work. After fifteen minutes of staring at the same page, however, Levi knew that wasn't going to happen either.

There was a knock on the office door, and it made him jump.

"Hey, Levi," Maxi said, peeking her head into the room. "We have a bit of a situation out here."

He stood. "What's up?"

"Irate customer. Claims we overcharged her for her lunch, but...we just served her what she ordered and charged her accordingly."

"Well, if it's that cut and dry..."

"Anthony's getting a little heated and I think you need to come out and smooth things over. Please?"

It was the last thing he wanted to be doing but reluctantly agreed. They certainly weren't supposed to argue with the customers, so Levi did his best to relax, put a smile on, and followed Maxi out to the bar. He looked around and didn't see Anthony or...anyone, really. "Uh...Max?"

"Over in the corner," she said, pointing to the front corner of the pub and...Willow.

His knees almost gave out with relief at just seeing her there at her usual table. Fighting a smile and afraid to be hopeful, he made his way over to her. "Hi," he said softly.

She was perched on one of the chairs at the bistro set, looking prim and serious, and so damn beautiful that he wanted to reach out and touch her.

But he didn't.

He couldn't.

Yet.

"Hey," she said with a small smile. "So, um..." Holding up her phone with the picture he'd sent, she continued, "I got this earlier and wanted to come and see things for myself."

Then she looked up.

And around.

And then at him.

Her smile grew. "You've made some changes."

Shrugging, he said, "Yeah, well...someone mentioned to

me how it might be time to fix the place up a bit. Lighting seemed to be a huge issue, so I thought I'd start there."

And he had. In the last three days he had changed all of the lights over the tables to the ones Willow had mentioned a time or two–the trio of mason jars–and he had to admit, they were pretty damn perfect for the space.

"It's only the beginning though," he explained. "We're going to change out some of these tables and chairs, freshen up the outside a bit, get some new signage, and...fix the sidewalk."

Nodding, she said, "About time on that last one. Look what kinds of trouble it's already caused."

"Trouble?"

She nodded again. "If it had been fixed months ago, I never would have fallen, you never would have come out to help me, and never had to deal with my crazy family."

Feeling slightly bold, he took a step closer. "You may not believe this, but...I never saw any of those things as trouble. If anything, I'd say that sidewalk was the biggest blessing of my life."

"Levi..."

And then he did touch her. Reaching up, he caressed her cheek. "Meeting you was one of the greatest moments of my life, Willow. I don't regret it for a minute."

"Hmm..."

That was it? That was all she had to say?

Swallowing hard, he tried not to take it personally and immediately pulled his hand back. "So, uh...what do you think of the lights? Is this how you imagined it would look?"

She looked around again and nodded enthusiastically. "Definitely. And I know the sun's still out so I can't really tell, but I bet when it's darker out and you really need these, they'll offer much better views of the place." Then she met his gaze. "I may even come back later and see for myself." Then she hopped off the stool.

"Oh, uh...you're leaving?"

Shrugging, she said, "Well, I came to see what I needed to see, and it all looks amazing." She grinned. "Like I knew it would."

When she went to walk past him, Levi placed his hand on her arm to stop her. "Don't go."

She froze and slowly turned her head to look at him. "Why should I stay?" But there was no heat behind her words, just a softly spoken question.

"Because I miss you so damn much that I can barely stand myself, Willow." She turned fully to face him and he knew he had this one chance to say what he had to say–to make things right.

And it scared the shit out of him.

"At first, when we first met, it didn't seem like there was ever a reason to mention that I owned the place," he began gruffly. "It never really came up. And then once we started getting to know each other, you always sounded so insecure about what you were doing for a living and putting yourself down for not doing something more, and I didn't want to be someone who made you feel bad about yourself." He paused. "But in the end, that's exactly what I did and I hate myself for it, Willow. It kills me to think that I hurt you."

Her expression turned sad as her eyes welled with tears. "You should have told me sooner. I shouldn't have had to learn about this major part of your life from Anthony and my father."

"Your father?" Okay, that was new information.

She told him about the phone conversation she'd had with her father right before coming to the pub that fateful day and it made him hurt for her all over again.

Slowly, cautiously, he pulled her into his arms and held her. "I swore I wasn't going to tell anyone else before I told you; you have to believe me. But," he let out a long breath. "That man just pushed all of my buttons and it was out before I could stop it."

"I'd like to say I'm mad about it, but...I know it was necessary at the time and it really did help to put him in his place." She pulled back and looked up at him. "But I'm not like him, Levi. I don't judge a person by what they do for a living. It doesn't matter to me. And I would have fallen for you whether you were a bartender, the boss, or the guy who washes the dishes."

"I know that," he admitted, caressing her cheek again. "You've got a good heart and you're an amazing woman, and I've missed you so damn much." He leaned in, resting his forehead against hers. "Tell me I didn't ruin this. Tell me you'll give me another chance. Tell me we can start over. Tell me..."

She silenced him by pressing her lips to his and then kissing him senseless.

Levi's arms banded around her, and for the first time in almost two weeks, he felt like he could breathe again.

"Geez, get a room, you two," Maxi said as she breezed by.

"Yeah," Anthony said, walking by on their other side. "Take the night off, for crying out loud. This is a family place."

Lifting his head, Levi smiled down at Willow. "What do you say? Can I take you out on a proper date tonight and finish groveling?"

"Hmm...define...proper." And with a sassy wink, she stepped from his arms, taking one of his hands in hers. "Because I had other plans for us."

This girl...

Grinning at his employees, Levi gave them a quick wave. "It looks like I'm taking the night off."

"Please, don't show your face in here until Monday," Anthony called out. "Do us all a favor, okay?"

"Done!" Willow replied happily, dragging him from the pub.

"I really did want to take you out tonight."

"And I really wanted you to take me to bed. It's called a compromise, Levi."

They were sprawled out in his bed and he felt like everything was right with his world. He hadn't had to grovel too much before Willow jumped him.

He really liked it when she did that.

"Well, hopefully tomorrow, you'll allow me to take you out for breakfast then. I know a place that serves the best waffles."

"Oooh...I do love waffles. As a matter of fact, I love..." She stopped talking as her phone chimed. With a muttered curse, she rolled over and reached for her purse, which was on the floor next to the bed.

"Everything okay?"

"Yeah, I think it's Gammy. It was the Words With Friends notification. I want to silence it until tomorrow."

He chuckled softly. "I should reach out to her for a game. She's the one who introduced me to it. What's her screen name on there?"

"Oh, it's IreGemGal."

Why does that sound so familiar?

Then it hit him and he laughed out loud.

"What?" she asked. "What's so funny?"

Rolling off the bed, he found his phone and sat down beside her, pulling the game app up on his phone and showed it to her. "Look at the words she played!"

Then Willow was laughing hysterically. "Oh, my goodness! That is so Gammy! I love it!"

"Hey! I think it was a little insulting."

"Aww...poor baby," she cooed, cupping his cheek. "Did my sweet little old grandma make you sad?"

With a slight pout, he said, "I wouldn't say sad, but she certainly didn't make me feel good..."

"Well, tomorrow you can call her out on it. But for the rest of the night, the phones are off, and you have my full attention."

"Hmm...I like the sound of that."

"Mmm...that's good because...I like you. A lot."

"Oh, yeah?"

"Yeah."

Leaning in, he placed a soft kiss on her lips. "And I like you too, Willow. A lot. Actually, I think I'm in..."

Her hand instantly covered his lips. "Don't," she whispered. "Not yet."

Disappointment washed over him.

"It's too soon, Levi, and we have some things to work through." Slowly, she removed her hand. "But just know, it means a lot to me that you wanted to say it."

It would have meant more if he had actually had the chance to say it, but...he knew he would.

Soon.

"Do you believe in love at first sight or do you think it takes time to grow?"

It was a little after midnight and they were lying in Willow's bed, naked and exhausted, but she couldn't help but want to talk. It was one of her favorite things to do with him.

"We never did finish those questions, did we?" he asked before yawning loudly.

"We are right now...if you answer the question," she teased, placing a soft kiss on his chest before snuggling closer.

"I kind of remember you asking me that one in the car."

She shrugged. "I may have, but...refresh my memory."

"I don't know if I have enough brain cells left to think and answer questions. I'm not even sure I know what day it is or my own name."

Crawling on top of him, she cupped his face in her hands and kissed him soundly. "You're Levi Sullivan, pub owner extraordinaire, boyfriend extraordinaire, and..."

Dare I say it...

"And...?" he prompted.

"The man that I love."

There. I said it.

And it felt like a giant weight had been lifted from her shoulders.

Levi's arms banded around her as he kissed her softly on the lips. "I kind of like all those descriptions."

"Oh, yeah?"

He nodded. "Definitely. Especially that last one."

She could seriously feel herself blushing from head to toe. They had been back together for a month now and things had been going really well. Levi was taking a little more time off from the pub so they could see each other at a decent hour a few times a week, and Willow was helping him with some of the decorating at the pub.

And loving every second of it.

Levi had teased her that maybe she should forget about going to school to get her early childhood education degree and instead go into interior decorating. It was something she actually considered, but realized it was more like a hobby for her. Working with kids in a loving and educational environment was always going to be her first love.

Well, that and Levi because...yeah, he was definitely her first real and true love and she was so happy she could finally say it out loud.

"I love you, Levi."

His hand anchored up in her hair as he said, "I love you too. I have for a long time, but...I didn't want to say it too soon and spook you. I already messed things up once between us. There was no way I wanted to do that again."

"It's never a bad thing to tell someone you love them. At least, I don't think so." Leaning down, she kissed him and kept on kissing him until they were both breathless. "Say it again."

Luckily, he knew exactly what she meant.

"I love you, Willow. So damn much." Then he kissed her and kept on kissing her as he rolled them over so he was the one on top. "Do I believe in love at first sight? Absolutely. It happened to me several months ago."

And yeah, she was totally blushing now.

"A beautiful girl tripped right outside my window. And the first moment her eyes met mine, I was lost."

It wasn't the first time he'd mentioned having feelings for her before their fateful road trip, but it was the first time he admitted how deep those feelings ran.

"That makes two of us."

"Yeah?"

She nodded. "Yeah." Ducking her head, she explained, "When I told my family I was dating someone? It was you."

"Well, yeah. That's why I went with you to be your fake boyfriend."

"No," she said with a small laugh. "Before that. When I first made up a boyfriend, I told them his name was Levi and...and...totally described you to them."

"Willow, I...you never told me that."

"It was a little embarrassing."

"You never need to be embarrassed with me. Ever. You can tell me anything."

"Anything?"

He nodded. "Anything."

That got her thinking. "Can I...tell you that I'm really thirsty right now and wish I had something to drink?"

And before she knew it, he jumped up and ran to the kitchen and came back with a bottle of water for her.

"Wow. Thank you." She took a long sip and then

studied him as he got comfortable under the blankets again. "Can I tell you...that I really didn't like that movie we watched earlier?"

His eyes went wide. "Seriously? What was wrong with it?"

"I don't know. I'm just not a *Star Wars* fan, I guess."

"Hmph...I wish I had known that before the whole I love you thing," he teased and then immediately laughed and wrapped her in his arms. "But I guess it's okay to have some flaws...I mean, not everyone likes those kinds of movies, right?"

"Sure, just like not everyone knows all the songs in *Aladdin*."

"I don't sing!" he argued, still hugging her tight. "And I'm a grown man! Why would I know that?"

"Because you were a child once! And the cartoon version was popular when we were kids!"

"Are we seriously naked and discussing a Disney movie because...that just seems wrong."

She sighed dramatically. "You're right, you're right. So tell me...what *should* we do while we're naked?"

Slowly, he rolled her under him. "How about I show you instead?"

And as he began to kiss his way down her body, she thought no suggestion had ever sounded better.

AND NOW FOR A PREVIEW OF

Looking for more RoadTripping antics?
Check out an excerpt from

DRIVE ME
Crazy

DRIVE ME CRAZY

As FAR AS wedding days went, Grace Mackie could say with great certainty that this one completely sucked.

And considering she was the bride, that was saying something.

Sitting alone in the bride's dressing room in the exclusive Lake Tahoe resort where her fiancé had *insisted* they have their destination wedding, she felt bored and oddly disappointed. This wasn't the wedding she had always dreamed of. As a matter of fact, it wasn't even the wedding she had planned.

Two weeks ago, Jared suggested the idea of eloping and no matter how much Grace resisted, he steamrolled ahead and now...here they were. Granted, the resort was the most luxurious she'd ever stayed at; her gown was amazing, and... even though California isn't exactly the destination that came to mind when she thought of destination weddings, it certainly didn't suck.

The downside was that they went from a big, family-filled wedding to a small and intimate event that most of her family and friends couldn't afford to attend. She had argued that point–among others–with Jared, but he had promised they'd have a big party when they got back to North Carolina. Getting married in Tahoe was a dream of his so she figured it wouldn't be so bad.

Except it was.

She was alone in this gorgeous dressing room and wished her best friend Lori or even her parents were here with her. A light knock at the door had her turning.

"Hey, Gracie! Thirty minutes until showtime! Are you ready?" The super-perky and extremely annoying wedding planner, Tilly, said with a smile as she walked through the door.

Smiling serenely, Grace replied, "Yes, thank you." Smoothing her hand down the white satin gown she was wearing, she tried to present the perfect image of the calm and serene bride-to-be.

Even though internally, she was like a squirrel in traffic.

"Great! In about twenty minutes, I'll come back and..."

"Tilly," Grace quickly interrupted before she could go any further. "If it's all right with you, we've gone over the schedule dozens of times and I'd really appreciate a few minutes to myself."

Tilly, with her severe bun and power suit, nodded. "Of course, Gracie. Anything you need," she smiled broadly and made her way back out the door, gently closing it behind her. At the sound of the soft click, Grace sagged with relief.

She hated being called Gracie. No one she knew *ever* called her Gracie. And yet for some reason, Tilly insisted on calling her that.

Catching a glimpse of herself in the full-length mirror, she should have been a happy and smiling bride. But was she? No. Instead, she was a neurotic mess who was dealing with more than your run-of-the-mill wedding jitters. She was angry, disappointed, and she knew if she didn't speak up for herself one last time, this was the way her entire marriage was going to go—with Jared making decisions she hated and then being resentful forever.

Knowing she wasn't going to breathe easy until she talked to him, Grace decided to go find him and hash this out. If it meant calling off the wedding, then so be it. It wasn't like she had any real investment in it. None of her family were here, Jared had made all the arrangements, and she had very little input into any of it.

Suddenly all the signs she should have seen were right there in front of her.

She was going to find Jared, tell him how she felt, and maybe they could look into couples counseling or something. It would be a good thing. It would help them grow closer. Looking back now, she realized this was a pattern that had gotten completely out of control. Why hadn't she noticed it sooner?

"Hindsight and all," she muttered, opening the door and stepping out into the hallway. They had toured the resort yesterday and she knew where the groom's dressing room was, so there was no need to ask for assistance from perky Tilly. At the end of the hall, she turned to the left and saw the door to Jared's room was ajar. The closer she got, Grace could hear him talking. Was Tilly giving him the thirty-minute speech too?

"You have to trust me, baby. It's all going to be okay. This is only temporary," she heard Jared saying.

Temporary? What was temporary?

"How could you do this, Jared? You said you loved me! You said we were going to be a family!"

What?!

Slowly, Grace moved closer to the door and tried to figure out who Jared was speaking to.

"We will, baby. We will," he promised. "You have to trust me, Steph. Marrying Grace will help me secure this promotion, and then six months from now, I'll divorce her and we'll be together. Just in time for the baby to be born."

Steph? *Steph?* Wait...the only Steph she knew was Jared's assistant, and he wouldn't...

"How am I supposed to come into work every day knowing you're sleeping with her every night?" Steph cried.

Grace heard Jared's soft laugh. "Baby, you need to relax. Grace and I haven't slept together for almost two months. What's a few more?"

Grace was about to barge through the door and put a stop to this, but...

"Just because she was stupid enough to fall for that whole 'wanting to make the wedding night sex better' excuse before doesn't mean she'll keep falling for it, Jared. And besides, tonight is your wedding night!"

"Don't worry," he cooed. "I'll come up with an excuse. The only woman I plan on sleeping with from now on is you."

Rage filled her, followed by a wave of nausea. How could she have been so blind? When Jared had mentioned not having sex to enhance their wedding night, it sounded kind of sexy. Hell, she had been horny all this time, and for what?

Taking several deep breaths, she told herself to calm down. Everything would be all right. She'd get through this. And then, something weird happened. She was suddenly calm—like eerily calm. It was true that Jared needed her to secure his promotion—Grace had been grooming him for the position of junior vice president of operations practically since they met! Her job as a career coach meant it was her specialty and Jared had begged her to help him move up in the company. She'd helped him change his image and his wardrobe and gave him lessons in manners and how to present himself in social situations. He was a complete doofus when she met him! And now that she transformed him, someone *else* was going to reap all the benefits of her hard work?

Well, she had news for him...he was *never* going to pull it off without her. He had definitely made great strides and his bosses were impressed, but without her there beside him, there was no way he was going to secure that promotion. His bosses weren't completely wowed by him yet and she had no intention of sticking around and helping him any longer. True, she could marry him and when he asked for a divorce, take him for everything he was worth, but that wasn't her style.

Wait, do I even have a style? She wondered.

Turning around, she made her way back toward her room and calmly walked inside and closed the door. In the corner was the small satchel that had her makeup bag, her wallet, her iPod and earbuds, her phone, and...

Before she knew it, the bag was in her hand and she was walking back out the door. The hallway was still deserted as she made her way to the rear exit and stepped outside. The sun was going down–Jared had said a sunset wedding would be romantic–and as she looked out at the lake, she had to admit the view would have been stunning.

"No time for that, dummy," she muttered, pulling her phone out of her bag and quickly pulling up the Uber app to request a ride. Saying a silent prayer that she wouldn't have to wait too long and risk someone finding her, she sagged with relief when the app showed a car was only five minutes away. Doing her best to stay out of sight, Grace hid behind some tall shrubs and prayed no one would come out and find her. Of course, a woman in a blindingly white gown didn't exactly blend into the greenery.

If they weren't so close to the ceremony time, she would have run up to their room and grabbed her luggage. Unfortunately, she didn't want to draw any attention to herself and would just have to deal with making her escape in her gown.

Staring at her phone, she willed the damn car to hurry up. The ride to the airport would take an hour, and she was hoping to get enough of a head start that should Jared try to come find her, she'd be on a plane before he could reach her.

Wishful thinking, but still...

Behind her, someone came out the back door but luckily, it was a janitor and he didn't even look in her direction. Her heart was beating a million miles an hour and when she glanced down at her phone again, she saw the car was two minutes out.

In any other circumstances, she would be pacing. Unfortunately, that wasn't an option right now and she suddenly wished she had packed a change of clothes in her satchel. If she were in jeans and sneakers, she would be trekking toward the road to meet up with the car and burning off some of this nervous energy. But no, she was stuck in this stupid, bulky gown hiding behind a shrub.

"Worst wedding day ever."

Seriously, in the history of wedding days, this one had to set some kind of new record in awfulness.

Off in the distance, Grace saw a car pulling into the resort driveway and was relieved when she realized it was her ride. Sprinting as well as she could from the bushes, she rushed to meet it and quickly jumped in.

"Are you Grace?" the driver asked.

"I am, I am," she said quickly. "Just drive. Please!" He looked at her like she was crazy but fortunately didn't hesitate to get moving. It wasn't until they were off the resort property and a few miles away that she finally felt like she could breathe. Sagging against the back seat, she immediately began searching for flights back to North Carolina. It didn't take long for her to realize she might not be leaving California or even the Lake Tahoe area tonight. Muttering a curse, she continued to search.

"Are you okay?"

She wanted to roll her eyes at that one. Did she *look* like she was okay? She was sitting in the back of a Toyota Corolla in a wedding gown and heading to the airport alone. However, she didn't think the poor guy would appreciate her sarcasm and opted to bite her tongue.

"Um...yeah," she said with a small smile. "Just...I'm not having any luck finding a flight out tonight." She scrolled the screen some more. "Where's the next closest airport?"

"That would be Sacramento. But it's two hours away in the opposite direction," he explained. He looked like he was close to her age, maybe a few years younger, and Grace remembered the app saying his name was Mark.

"Thanks, Mark. If I happen to find a flight out of Sacramento, would you be willing to drive me there?"

"Uh...I'd have to adjust the route and it's not that easy to do," he said with some hesitation. "I mean, we'd have to pull over somewhere so I could do it and..."

He prattled on a bit about all the steps it would take for him to change the route, but Grace wasn't fully paying attention. Her main priority was finding the first flight she could to get out of here. Unfortunately, it didn't take long for her to realize it wasn't going to happen. She was stuck. Her only hope was to book a flight for first thing in the morning and find a hotel as close to the airport as possible.

And pray it was next to a mall so she could buy a change of clothes.

Her phone began to ring, and Grace was surprised it had taken this long for it to start. Jared's name and picture came up and she felt sick at the sight of him. She immediately rejected the call and did a quick swipe of her screen to block his number. Not that it would stop him. All he'd have to do was grab someone else's phone and try again. Still, it was a start. Next, she turned on the do not disturb feature on her phone so she wouldn't be bothered for a little while.

"Do I need to turn around?" he asked, interrupting her thoughts.

With a weary sigh, she put the phone down. "No. We can keep going. There are no available flights tonight. I'll have to find one for the morning."

"I don't know where you're trying to go, but you could always rent a car and drive."

Again, she suppressed the urge to roll her eyes but...the idea had merit. Sure, a cross-country drive wasn't ideal, but it would give her plenty of time to clear her head. There would be no distractions and no chance of Jared–or anyone else for that matter–coming to talk her out of what she was doing.

"Mark," she said excitedly, leaning forward, "you're a genius!"

He smiled at her in the rearview mirror. "Wow. Thanks!"

"Okay, so where is the closest rental car place? I mean,

we don't have to go all the way to the airport for that, do we?"

"It might be easier, and considering it's a Saturday night, I would imagine the smaller places might be closed already. The airport car rental offices have to stay open later." He shrugged. "At least, I think they do."

Maybe he had a point, but reaching for her phone, Grace figured she could find that out for herself without any problem. "Aha! There is a car rental place just outside of Carson City and it doesn't close until eight!" She leaned forward in her seat again. "Can you get me there by eight, Mark?"

It had just started to rain, so he flipped on the windshield wipers and grinned at her. "As long as this rain stays light, we shouldn't have a problem."

Relaxing back in the seat, she felt like things might finally start going her way.

"Dude, are you all right?"

Finn Kavanagh was so busy muttering curses that he almost didn't hear the guy. Pacing back and forth in the crowded parking lot, he wasn't expecting anyone to come up and talk to him. "Yeah. Peachy, except my car is gone."

The guy looked at him in shock. He was glassy-eyed and looked no older than twenty; there was no doubt he'd used a fake ID to get into the casino, and right now was of completely no use to Finn.

"You gonna call the cops?"

Under normal circumstances he would have, but considering he knew *exactly* who had taken his car and why, it was pointless.

But he wanted to. Boy, oh boy, did he want to. Cursing again, he paced and turned and...oh, right. He still had an audience. "Uh, no. No, I'm just gonna call...a cab or something." With a forced smile, Finn walked back toward the casino as he pulled out his phone. With the help of an app, he knew he could have a ride here in less than five minutes, but he had a call to make first.

Pulling up the number, he hit send and–surprise, surprise–it went right to voicemail.

"Hey, Dave," he said through clenched teeth. "Classy move taking the car. Where the hell are you? In case you've forgotten, I'm eight hundred miles from home, and I got here in the car you currently hijacked, you son of a bitch! You need to get back here and..."

Beep!

If he didn't need the phone so damn much right now, he would have tossed it in frustration. Not that he expected his brother to answer the phone, but he also didn't expect the bastard to leave him stranded in Carson City over a petty fight.

Okay, so *maybe* pointing out how irresponsible his brother was wasn't the smartest thing to do, but who knew he'd be so willing to prove Finn right immediately?

They had decided to take this road trip together as a way of bonding. Honestly, they had never gotten along, and after trying again and again, to find Dave jobs and keep him from mooching off their parents, Finn thought the time away together would help. The idea of them being in neutral territory and away from prying eyes seemed perfect.

Clearly, he was wrong.

Now he was stranded. Dave had his car and Finn needed to get home to Atlanta so he could get back to work. Granted, he was his own boss, but the garage could only run for so long without him. Actually, it probably would be fine without him for a while, but he was responsible and the garage was his baby. He hated being away from it any longer than he had to be.

And that just filled him with rage again because thanks to his brother, he had no choice but to delay his return. Chasing Dave across the country wasn't going to be a quick and easy task, no matter how much he wished it could be.

Looking at his phone, he did a quick search for car rental places in the area. There weren't many, and the smarter thing to do would be to just go to the Tahoe airport, but that was wasting time he didn't have. The sooner he got on the road, the better chance he had of catching up with his wayward brother. Once he made a mental note of the closest place, Finn pulled up the app for Uber and ordered a car to take him there. There was no way he was flying home, even if it was the fastest way to get there. Finn had a fear of flying and just the thought of getting near an airplane was enough to make him feel a little sick. Hell, even walking back to Atlanta was more appealing to him than flying.

It started to rain and he groaned. It was the icing on the cake of the crappiest day ever. He'd already lost all the money he'd brought to gamble with and now he was going to have to pay to rent a car to get home. His luggage was in his car because he and Dave had planned on leaving tonight after dinner. As soon as they had finished eating, his brother excused himself to use the men's room and never returned.

Just thinking about it pissed Finn off more than he thought possible.

His ride pulled up just as the rain really started to come down, and he'd never been more thankful for anything in his life. Climbing into the car, he thanked the driver and immediately tried calling his brother again.

"Come on, man," he all but growled into the phone as the call went to voicemail again. "This is bullshit, Dave. It's my damn car and I can have the cops on your ass for this!" His driver eyed him suspiciously, but Finn didn't care. "Just...call me back." Again, the urge to throw his phone was great, but it would hinder more than help him.

Throwing his head back against the seat cushion, he started thinking his plan through. Maybe he should have just stayed at the casino and waited Dave out. His brother was many things, but he wasn't despicable enough that he'd strand Finn and steal his car.

Or was he?

The phone rang, and he nearly jumped out of his skin. "Dammit, Dave, where are you?"

A low chuckle was the first response. "Just drove through Fallon, but I'm considering heading south and going back to Vegas," Dave said. "Remember how cool the strip was?"

Finn mentally counted to ten before speaking. "Fallon's what...an hour from Carson City? How the hell fast are you driving?"

Laughter was the only response.

"Can you please just stay put and I'll meet you there so we can head home like we planned, okay?"

"No can do, bro. You see, you wanted to lecture me on how irresponsible I am, so you shouldn't be surprised by all of this. I mean, we all know Perfect Finn is never wrong."

If his brother were standing in front of him, Finn would strangle him. There wasn't a doubt in his mind that he'd do it. Dave could test the patience of a saint.

"Shouldn't you be trying to prove me wrong?" he asked

through clenched teeth. "I mean, that is what you normally do! Why do you feel the need to prove me right *now* of all times?"

"Ha-ha!" Dave said, laughing heartily. "I don't really care what I'm proving. All I want to do is piss you off just like you pissed me off. Doesn't feel so good, does it?"

"Dave..."

"Dammit, Finn, where do you get off passing judgment on me?"

"Right now, I think I have every right! You stole my car!"

"Technically, I'm borrowing it."

"No, you're not. You're stealing it. Borrowing it implies I gave you permission, which I did not. And how the hell did you get my keys?"

"When you went to the men's room while we were waiting for our food, I swiped them," Dave said flippantly. "So really, you have no one to blame but yourself for leaving them lying around like that."

Pinching the bridge of his nose, Finn had to wonder how he was going to get through this–or better yet, how he was going to keep himself from beating the crap out of his brother when they were both back in Atlanta.

"Dave," he began, trying to be reasonable, "you know I need to get home. Let's just agree that things got out of hand and move on, okay? Now, where are you? I'm in an Uber and can meet up with you."

The low laugh Dave gave as a response did not fill Finn with hope.

Letting out a long breath, he willed himself–again–to stay in control. "It's getting late and we're wasting time here."

"You got that right."

"It's already an almost forty-hour drive back to Atlanta, Dave. Four grueling days of driving," he added. "We weren't going to get too far tonight, but we can make up time if you just tell me where you are so I can meet you."

"Vegas."

"You're not in Vegas!" Finn yelled. "It is physically impossible for you to be in Vegas already! Now enough is enough! Do not make me call the cops! I'm serious!"

"Sorry...bad...breaking...up...later..."

"Don't hang up! Don't hang up!"

Dave hung up.

The things that flew out of Finn's mouth would make most people blush, but he didn't care. When he kicked the seat in front of him, the driver yelled, "Hey!" and that instantly snapped him out of his tantrum. He was screwed; there were no two ways about it. His brother had his car and he wasn't getting it back any time soon. The sooner he resigned himself to that fact, the better off he'd be.

So, he had to rent a car, so what? And so what if he was going to have to stop and buy himself clothes and supplies to get him through the trip? Worse things could happen. But the worst of it all was how it was going to take him longer than the planned four days. Finn believed in being smart and not overdoing things and knew driving for ten hours a day alone wouldn't be smart or safe.

Something Dave had mocked him about on their original trip.

There was a flash of lightning, and the rain was really coming down. At this point, Finn knew he would be smart to grab a car and then find a hotel and start driving first thing in the morning. With a sigh, he sat back and stared out the window until they pulled into the rental car parking lot.

"Holy crap! Did you see that?"

Finn looked out the front window toward the building and saw...wait...what was he seeing? "What the hell is that?"

The driver laughed awkwardly. "Looks like a bride–or at least, someone in a wedding gown."

And sure enough, that *was* what they were seeing. Whoever they were, they fell getting out of the car and were now in a heap of white satin on the pavement. Finn quickly climbed from the car–thanked his driver–and immediately ran over to help her.

At her side, he held out a hand to her and noticed the guy who was with her coming around to do the same. "Hey, are you okay?" Finn asked, noting the dirty gown and the curses flying out of the woman's mouth. He pulled her to her feet and held on until she was steady. The rain was pouring down on them and he did his best to guide them up onto the sidewalk and through the doors of the rental office.

She was a little breathless and pointed toward the car she'd just vacated. "My bag," she said, shaking her hand. "My bag is still in the back seat!"

"No problem," he said, hoping to calm her. "I'm sure your husband will bring it in."

Pushing him aside, she walked back out the door and slapped a hand on the trunk of the car as it was about to pull away. Finn watched with mild curiosity as she opened the back door and grabbed her bag before slamming the door shut again.

Okay, not her husband, he thought.

Because he had manners, he moved to open the door for her. "Thanks," she muttered, shaking the rain off herself– and onto him. He wanted to be mad, he seriously did, but what would be the point?

With a shrug, he walked over to the agent at the counter

and did his best to smile. "Hey...Carl," he began, reading the agent's name tag. "I would like to rent a car."

The agent smiled but it didn't quite meet his eyes. "Then you've come to the right place!" he said in a semi-flat tone. Finn would bet good money this was a repeated exchange at a car rental office.

Beside him, the bride stepped up and said the same thing to her agent–an older woman named Tammy. He looked over and gave her a small smile and wasn't surprised when she didn't give him one back. Any bride trying to rent a car while still in her wedding gown couldn't possibly be having a good day.

Finn handed over his license and credit card and waited. The only sound in the place was the typing coming from Carl and Tammy's computers. Finn looked around and saw the office was a little run-down and there weren't any cars in the parking lot.

That's when he started to worry.

The cars could be around the back, couldn't they?

"Um..."

"Oh, uh..."

Both agents spoke at the same time as they glanced nervously at each other. "Is there a problem?" he and the angry bride asked at the same time.

"Well, it looks like," Carl began.

"There seems to be," Tammy started.

"Oh, for the love of it!" angry bride snapped. "What's the problem?"

Finn had to hand it to her, she was pretty fierce. Even he stiffened up at her tone. Deciding that one of them should be respectful, he looked at the agents and smiled. "Is there a problem?" he asked.

"We only have one vehicle available," Carl said.

"Oh, well...okay." This didn't seem to be a problem for him since he got here first. "I'll take it."

"Wait, wait, wait," angry bride said, moving closer to him. "Why do you get it? We got here at the same time."

"Actually...we didn't," he corrected. "I got to the counter first, and that was after I held the door for you to come back in."

If looks could kill, he'd be a dead man for sure.

"Look, um...I know this is a bad situation," he reasoned, "but it can't be helped. It's been a really bad day and I need this car."

"Oh, really?" she asked sarcastically, motioning to her ruined gown. "And do I look like someone whose day has gone well?"

"Uh..."

"Because it hasn't!" she cried. "If we're going to get into some sort of contest over whose day was worse, believe me, buddy, I'd win!"

He was beginning to see that.

Unfortunately, he needed this car too. Maybe if he reasoned with her...

Holding out his hand, he said, "I'm Finn. Finn Kavanagh. And you are...?"

Swiping her dripping blonde hair away from her face, she eyed him cautiously. "Grace. Grace Mackie."

She didn't shake his hand.

"Look, Grace, it seems like we're both in a bad way right now. But you have to believe me when I say I *have* to have this car. You see, my brother stole my car, and I've got to get back to Atlanta and..."

"Today was supposed to be my wedding day and I found out my fiancé has been cheating on me with his assistant..."

"Okay, that does sound bad, but you see, I've got a business and..."

"And she's pregnant with his baby," she continued. "Oh, and he was planning on divorcing me in six months, so he and his baby mama could be together. He was just using me to get a promotion."

Finn's shoulders sagged even as he bowed his head.

Yeah. She had him beat.

Without a word, he motioned toward the desk and simply gave up. There had to be other rental places in town, right? And if not, he'd call for another Uber and do...something. There was a row of chairs against the wall and he walked over and sat down. He found this place by searching on his phone, so he'd just have to do it again and hope he'd find another one.

Scrolling...scrolling...scrolling...

The rustling of wet satin had him looking up. Grace was two feet away and still staring at him hostilely. "Problem?" he asked, letting his own annoyance come through.

"Listen, it seems to me we've both had a crappy day and...well...I'm heading across country too. So, if you want to share the car..."

He was instantly on his feet. "Seriously?" Then he got suspicious. "Why? Why would you even offer? You know nothing about me, and for that matter, I know nothing about you."

She rolled her eyes. "Both Carl and Tammy mentioned there not being another rental place nearby. The closest one is about twenty miles from here and is closed for the day. Your only other option is the airport and..."

"I'm not flying!" he snapped and immediately regretted his reaction. "I mean...I don't really like flying so..."

"No, I mean there are car rental places there you can

try, but it's still a bit of a drive to get there too." She paused and fidgeted, and Finn figured her dress had to be a bit of a pain to move around in—even more so now that it was wet. "Nothing today has gone as planned and I'm not looking forward to driving across the country alone."

"I get that, but still...how do you know you can trust me?"

"Honestly? I don't. But Carl and Tammy have your license and would know I was leaving with you, so if anything happened to me, you'd be the guy everyone would go after." Then she paused, and her gaze narrowed. "Is there a reason I shouldn't trust you?"

"What? I mean, no! There's no reason," he stammered.

"Tell me about yourself," she said before turning to the curious agents. "You guys listen in on this too. You're witnesses."

"Witnesses? That's just..."

"I'm just trying to be practical, Quinn," she said.

"It's Finn," he corrected and then cleared his throat. "I'm Finn Kavanagh and I'm from Atlanta, Georgia. I was born and raised in East Islip, New York, and moved to Atlanta when I was eighteen. I'm thirty years old and I own my own auto repair shop, Kavanagh's. You can look it up online. We have a website and a Facebook page," he added.

"Tammy, can you check on that please?" Grace called over her shoulder, not breaking eye contact with Finn.

Finn glanced toward the counter and saw both agents typing and nodding, and when Grace looked over at them, they both gave her a thumbs up.

It was ridiculous for him to sag with relief, but he almost did.

"Anything else?" she asked. "What about your family? You married?"

"No."

"Girlfriend?"

"No."

"Boyfriend?"

"No!" he shouted a little too defensively.

"Any siblings other than the car-stealing brother?"

He shook his head. "Nope. Just Dave."

"Why'd he steal your car?"

"It's a long story..."

And for the first time since he'd met her, Grace gave a small smile. "Good thing we've got a long drive ahead of us and you can tell me all about it."

This is crazy, he thought. There was no way he was going to drive cross-country with a complete stranger. He didn't do things like this! He was fairly practical and cautious, and this had disaster written all over it.

Grace walked back over to the counter and Finn followed. "My turn," he said.

"For what?"

"Tell me about yourself."

She leaned against the counter and looked at him with mild annoyance. "Why? It seems to me I'm the one at greater risk here."

He gave her a bland look, crossed his arms over his chest, and waited.

With a sigh, she said, "Fine. Grace Mackie, career coach, age twenty-eight. Recently ran out on my wedding. I was engaged to the cheating jackass for six months and we dated for a year before that. I have two brothers and one sister, who are all happily married to non-cheating jackasses."

"A career coach?"

She nodded. "I too have a website and Facebook page,"

she turned to Tammy. "Executive Career Services by Grace out of Raleigh, North Carolina. You can Google it." They waited all of two minutes before Carl and Tammy gave another thumbs up.

"Looks like we're both who we say we are," Grace said, her smile growing a little.

"Looks that way," he agreed. "The only problem is you're going to North Carolina and I'm going to Atlanta. How's that going to work?"

She considered him for a moment. "I'd be more than willing to go to Atlanta with you and fly home from there. Unlike you, I'm not in a rush. The longer this trip takes, the better."

Finn didn't take that as a particularly good sign, but he wasn't going to question it right now. Hell, if she wanted to camp out in Atlanta once they got there, who was he to argue?

Still, he wasn't so sure this was going to work.

"Are you willing to split the driving?" he asked.

Grace let out a mirthless laugh. "Dude, I was planning on doing *all* the driving a few minutes ago. If there were more than one car here, I *would* be doing all the driving. So the fact that now I don't have to? Um...yeah. I'd say I'd be willing to split it."

Okay, so she was snarky, but he was going to blame it on the fact that she'd had a bad day.

For now.

"We each pay our own way, right? We'll split the cost of gas, but other than that, you're on your own for the things you need."

She rolled her eyes before shaking her head. "Do you even hear yourself? We just met, for crying out loud! Why would I expect you to pay for anything for me?" Then she took a menacing step toward him. "Are you always this uptight and ridiculous?"

"Ridiculous?" he cried, mildly annoyed. "How am I being ridiculous?"

"Um...excuse me," Tammy called out, interrupting them. "But we're getting ready to close so...are you going to take the vehicle? We can put both names on the rental agreement if you'd like, or we can leave it in Miss Mackie's name."

For a moment, neither spoke. Then Grace seemed to relax a bit. She studied him for a long moment before speaking. "So what do you say, Finn Kavanagh? Are we taking this road trip together?" She held out her hand to him, and for a moment, Finn questioned his own sanity for even considering this. Unfortunately, she was his only hope right now.

And before he could question himself any further, Finn met her hand and shook it. "Looks like it, Grace Mackie."

DRIVE ME CRAZY is available everywhere now!
https://www.chasing-romance.com/drive-me-crazy

ABOUT SAMANTHA CHASE

Samantha Chase is a *New York Times* and *USA Today*
bestseller of contemporary romance that's hotter than
sweet, sweeter than hot. She released her debut novel in
2011 and currently has more than sixty titles under her belt
– including *THE CHRISTMAS COTTAGE* which was a
Hallmark Christmas movie in 2017! When she's not
working on a new story, she spends her time reading
romances, playing way too many games of Solitaire on
Facebook, wearing a tiara while playing with her sassy pug
Maylene...oh, and spending time with her husband of 29
years and their two sons in Wake Forest, North Carolina.

Where to Find Me:

Website:
www.chasing-romance.com
Facebook:
www.facebook.com/SamanthaChaseFanClub
Instagram:
https://www.instagram.com/samanthachaseromance/
Twitter:
https://twitter.com/SamanthaChase3
Reader Group:
https://www.facebook.com/groups/1034673493228089/

Sign up for my mailing list and get exclusive content and chances to win members-only prizes!
https://www.chasing-romance.com/newsletter

ALSO BY SAMANTHA CHASE

More of Me

Return to You

Meant for You

I'll Be There

Until There Was Us

Suddenly Mine

A Dash of Christmas

The Shaughnessy Brothers Series:

Made for Us

Love Walks In

Always My Girl

This is Our Song

Sky Full of Stars

Holiday Spice

Tangled Up in You

Band on the Run Series:

One More Kiss

One More Promise

One More Moment

The Christmas Cottage Series:

The Christmas Cottage

Ever After

Silver Bell Falls Series:

Christmas in Silver Bell Falls

Christmas On Pointe

A Very Married Christmas

A Christmas Rescue

Christmas Inn Love

Life, Love & Babies Series:

The Baby Arrangement

Baby, Be Mine

Baby, I'm Yours

Preston's Mill Series:

Roommating

Speed Dating

Complicating

The Protectors Series:

Protecting His Best Friend's Sister

Protecting the Enemy

Protecting the Girl Next Door

Protecting the Movie Star

7 Brides for 7 Soldiers

Ford

7 Brides for 7 Blackthornes

Logan

Standalone Novels

Jordan's Return

Catering to the CEO

In the Eye of the Storm

A Touch of Heaven

Moonlight in Winter Park

Waiting for Midnight

Mistletoe Between Friends

Snowflake Inn

Wildest Dreams (currently unavailable)

Going My Way (currently unavailable)

Going to Be Yours (currently unavailable)

Seeking Forever (currently unavailable)

CPSIA information can be obtained
at www.ICGtesting.com
Printed in the USA
LVHW091703280720
661754LV00002B/178

9 798647 164582